FALSE
MISTRESS

The Marwood Family Saga
Book Three

Amy Licence

SAPERE
BOOKS

FALSE
MISTRESS

Published by Sapere Books.

24 Trafalgar Road, Ilkley, LS29 8HH

saperebooks.com

ISBN: 978 0-85495-083-6

To Rufus and Robin

For, as I have read in volumes olde,
A false lying tongue is harde to withholde;
A slaunderous tongue, a tongue of a scolde,
Worketh more mischiefe than can be tolde;
That, if I wish not to be controlde,
Yet somewhat to say I dare well be bolde,
How some delighte for to lie, thycke and threfolde.

Against Venomous Tongues, John Skelton

ONE

Autumn had taken England in its hold. In every lane and every village, leaves kindled into a blaze of red and yellow. The early morning saw soft mist linger, clinging to the hedgerows, and to sheep chewing blandly in the fields. Before long, gentle sunshine had burned the mist away. It lit the spires of churches, the ripe apples being picked in orchards, the hay bales stacked ready for the barn. It shone on the side of a carriage, drawn along by four grey horses, with the sign of a star and crescent moon painted on the side.

At the carriage window, an elegantly dressed lady in her late forties peered outside at the changing scenery.

"Well, I am very much looking forward to seeing Raycroft Court, even if it is such a long drive. I have heard it is the finest building in Sussex, well situated, with beautiful grounds."

Lady Elizabeth Marwood was growing restless after almost five hours on the road. Often, illness kept her confined to her house, sitting in her chamber or taking slow walks about the garden. This long coach journey, during which she had been squashed knee to knee with her family, was taking its toll.

She wore the best London fashions to compliment her pale colouring: a gown with hanging sleeves in sea-green, embroidered with Venetian silver and decorated with pearls. Her once-golden hair, now streaked white at the temples, was drawn back under a white coif, on top of which was placed a half-moon French hood, after she had grudgingly accepted the

7

new style was here to stay. The best clothes, though, for all their beauty, had a habit of being stiff and uncomfortable.

"And I will be grateful for a chance to rest. Anyone who says that travel is nothing more than sitting still has never journeyed any distance in a carriage. All this bumping and jostling around is quite exhausting. I shall be covered in bruises, I am sure!"

Illness showed itself in her face. Her delicate features were now pinched, and the taut skin over her cheekbones was paper-thin. In recent years, she had seen the best London doctors, including those recommended by the queen herself, who had prescribed dietary changes and the letting of her blood, but her malady came and went, sometimes as a faintness, or an ache in her breast and side. Only rest made a difference. Sometimes she was as weak as a babe, whilst at other times, the life seemed to return to her.

"Does no one else feel thrown about like rocks in a sack?" she asked the rest of the carriage. "Or is it just me?"

Seated opposite, her eighteen-year-old daughter Thomasin was a little more patient.

"Here, Mother, take another of these cushions for your back. It won't be much longer now, then you will be able to rest. The worst of the journey is over."

Thomasin passed across one of the tasselled silver cushions. Her mother wriggled, elbowing Thomasin's elder sister Cecilia in the process.

"Mother, be careful, would you?"

"Well, you might move over a little. You have all that space beside you, whilst I am squashed up against the side here."

Cecilia sighed and made a fuss about inching along the padded seat. At least there were only two of them on that side, thought Thomasin, whilst she had to share the opposite seat with both her father and cousin Ellen.

Having been in the service of Queen Catherine, travelling about the country from Windsor, to Hampton, to Greenwich, Thomasin Marwood was accustomed to the long hours of waiting. If she'd had the choice, she would have preferred to be riding on horseback alongside them, with her long dark hair flying in the wind, rather than trapped inside the Marwood carriage.

Her mother would never have allowed it, of course, if only to preserve Thomasin's new dress: a deep forest-green velvet, inlaid with an embroidered stomacher in white and yellow, and a string of pearls. She had to look the part, Elizabeth said. There was no point serving the queen if you looked like a kitchen maid, and she had to always be alert, as you never knew who you might meet. Her mother was referring to a husband, of course. She was always on the lookout for potential husbands for both her elder daughters, who were now, at eighteen and twenty, well past the usual age of marriage. There was plenty of time for that, though. Thomasin had had her heart bruised already, and was in no hurry to become any man's wife.

She followed her mother's gaze through the window, seeking the brief glimpses of countryside visible from the road. Flashes of green and yellow, blocks of brown. They were driving through a spectacular holloway, a sunken road typical of this part of southern England. Overhead, the trees met in a canopy, sending long shadows snaking across the track. They had left their Suffolk home, Eastwell Hall, first thing that morning and the roads were clear and dry, so they were making good speed. Another hour should bring them within sight of Raycroft, Sir Hugh Truegood's country seat. Perhaps not even that much.

"I am looking forward to it, as well," said Cecilia, readjusting her skirts. "It's so thrilling to be invited to such a distinguished house. I do hope we will make a good impression."

"Of course we shall," said Lady Elizabeth, surprised. "How could we not? We chose our clothing with care, we have new shoes, and thankfully our manners are always impeccable."

Thomasin turned her head aside to conceal her smile.

The startling likeness between the two women opposite was even more apparent due to their proximity, with their icy blonde colouring, their straight noses and their clear, water-like eyes. They had even co-ordinated their clothing; Cecilia's cream-coloured dress had pale green sleeves and silver details like that of her mother, with the addition of miniver fur on her lower arms. Despite having spent most of her years in the Suffolk countryside, she had perfected a regal manner and, even in the coach, carried herself with elegance. At first glance, the eldest Marwood daughter appeared as aloof and haughty as her mother could be. Yet twenty-year-old Cecilia had learned some harsh lessons, and was no longer the romantic country girl chasing an ideal that she had been this time last year.

"It's so long since I have been anywhere at all," Cecilia continued. "Another year in the country, when I should have been married. I want to see new places and new people."

No one flinched when she spoke of marriage, but they were all thinking the same thing. Cecilia's wedding would have gone ahead last autumn, had she not been wooed secretly by the frivolous William Hatton, who had then deserted her and brought shame upon them all. They had all tried to blot out the memory of turning up at the king's chapel, only to discover that the secret was all over court and the bridegroom had left. Only time had lessened the sting.

Cecilia carried on, her thoughts racing ahead. "And I am so excited to return to London."

Sitting there now, in her delicate gown, Cecilia looked as innocent as the spring. But she had always looked that way, Thomasin remembered. At eight, she could pull the cat's tail and lock Thomasin in the barn, or she could tell a barefaced lie, and still have the face of an angel.

"Well, we shall see," said their mother, patting Cecilia's arm.

Thomasin looked outside again. She was excited about the visit, as they all were. A few days as a guest on a country estate would be very pleasant. Sir Hugh Truegood was a friend they had met in the spring, a real gentleman — handsome, accomplished, and intelligent. But staying with him at Raycroft wasn't what was really stirring her blood. Her mind was already skipping ahead to what would come afterwards.

After their stay with Truegood, the Marwood family were to part ways. Thomasin and her cousin Ellen were returning to Queen Catherine's household at Westminster. The glorious, glittering, troubled court, like a diamond with all its brittle edges and brightness. The queen had written to them only last week, summoning them back to her side, and both were keen to go. Thomasin's parents and Cecilia would stay with Sir Matthew Russell, Thomasin's uncle, in his London residence, the ancient Monk's Place. If all turned out well, they might also pay a visit to the court, and their paths would cross again. It would be good to see her uncle Matthew, Thomasin thought, as he had always been so kind. Cecilia's broken engagement may not have been forgotten, though. William Hatton had proved that he could blithely carry on with the courtly game, but it was not so easy for a woman to bounce back from scandal.

Thomasin shifted slightly in her seat. She was elbow to elbow with her father in the centre, and her cousin Ellen Russell sat on the far side. Sir Richard Marwood had slept much of the way, waking only to insist they stop for refreshments, before falling asleep again, while Ellen sat quietly, lost in contemplation.

"I am surprised that Lady Truegood extended her kind invitation to all of us," Lady Elizabeth continued, wrinkling her nose. "Especially given that she has never met me, only you, Thomasin. And even you, Ellen, were included in the invitation, much to my surprise."

Again, Thomasin turned her head to hide her amusement. Her mother had no idea of the romance that had blossomed between Hugh Truegood and Ellen at Greenwich Palace that summer, which was the sole reason for the family's invitation to Raycroft. But she was not about to correct her mother. The secret was still hidden in Ellen's heart.

"And the son," continued Lady Elizabeth. "You met him at Greenwich?"

"At Hampton Court," replied Thomasin. "Actually, no, it was in the hunting lodge at Windsor, just before we had to flee from the sweat, but he came with the king to Greenwich afterwards, didn't he, Ellen?"

Ellen's round face lit up with the smile that could transform her simple features. She was not a traditionally attractive woman, but there was something pleasing about the symmetry of her large eyes and small, rounded nose. Her colouring was warm, a mid-brown that was best described as mousy, but she shone with a healthy openness, incapable of deceit.

"And what is the son like?"

Thomasin met Ellen's eyes, offering her the question, but her cousin was content to let her answer.

"Very personable. He is a merchant to the Low Countries, and he has seen the emperor, so you can imagine he was approved of by his aunt, Queen Catherine."

"Oh," said Lady Elizabeth. "A merchant?"

"A little more than that. He runs an entire trade network. Someone has to, or else how would you wear such fine cloth or hang tapestries in your chamber?"

"But his mother is a lady. I wonder why she permits it."

Thomasin frowned. "Even ladies can fall upon hard times."

"He is the most kind and thoughtful gentleman you could meet," piped up Ellen. "His manners are far better than many of the lords supposed to be above him."

Lady Elizabeth and Cecilia exchanged raised eyebrows. "Of course, we forget you are accustomed to observing such distinctions, Ellen, being raised among merchants in the north," Lady Elizabeth replied.

"I am accustomed to gentlemen," Ellen replied simply, refusing to take offense at their slur upon her humble origins, "from my time serving with the queen."

The horses drew to a halt at a crossroads. In the fields opposite, an army of men were scything down the hay and gathering it into golden bundles. Women and children walked behind them, gleaning the strands left behind and carrying them in their aprons. Some stopped and held up their hands to shade their eyes as they looked at the Marwood coach, with its four grey horses and aristocratic crest.

The sweet smell of their harvest reached the occupants inside.

Sir Richard snorted and jolted awake. "Are we here?"

"Not yet," replied Lady Elizabeth, looking outside.

"What have I missed?" He straightened his shoulders.

"Trees, fields, trees, more trees," said Cecilia in a bored tone.

One of the farmers had come up to speak with the coachman, wiping his brow in the sun as he held off his carved scythe. He had an open, friendly face, tanned by outdoor work. As Thomasin watched, he nodded and pointed down the road to the left. The horses started up again and the coach rumbled on.

A village flashed past, with beamed houses built close to the road, a pretty church and busy forge. Barely were they out the other side, when the trees rose up again and the road became narrower, rising and falling. One side of the road fell away steeply, into a tree-lined valley, making Thomasin a little uneasy about the carriage wheels going too close to the edge. The trunks were thick and ancient, the silence complete.

"This must be the Ashdown Forest," said Ellen. "Hugh wrote that it comes up to the edge of the park and the hunting is excellent."

"Did he?" asked Lady Elizabeth, in an arch tone.

"I am sure we are near."

Ellen was right. Presently, the trees on one side gave way to a walled park, running the length of the road. After another mile, they turned in through a pair of tall cast-iron gates, and in the distance they saw the dignified, red-brick splendour of Raycroft Court.

TWO

The Marwood carriage drew up outside a wide-fronted house with mullioned windows and a central tower. It faced east, capturing the afternoon sun, which was that distinctive September shade of yellow. The bricks were interlocked in the fashionable Flemish style, laid in a black diamond pattern. Stacks of twisted chimneys stood out against the blue sky.

A number of servants were already lining up outside, in livery of green and black, embroidered on the breast with an oak leaf in brown silk.

Thomasin's father, having now fully recovered his senses, was the first to step outside, before reaching in to assist his wife. They still made a handsome couple, Thomasin thought, married for over two decades despite the differences in their characters. It had been a love match, overcoming their parents' disapproval, and six healthy children attested to its success. The little ones had been left behind in the family's Suffolk home: Lettice, who was blossoming into a beauty at thirteen, jolly Alice aged six, young master Digby, the family's only son of nine years old, and toddling Susanna.

Cecilia, Thomasin and Ellen climbed out in turn, gazing up in awe at their surroundings.

"It's twice the size of Eastwell," whispered Sir Richard. "I should have become a merchant."

A large man in a formal robe and hat bowed before them.

"My Lord, ladies. Welcome to Raycroft. I am Peter Southey, Sir Hugh's steward. Please, come this way."

The entrance was cool and smelled of old stone and ash. Thomasin's first impressions were of dark wood and high, beamed ceilings. Ahead of them, a magnificent carved staircase occupied the centre of the house, twisting up once, twice, with an ornately decorated rail and bannisters, where carved fruit and leaves had been polished to a shine by the hands of many generations. It was truly magnificent; she felt slightly overawed.

Southey paused for a moment while they stood in admiration.

"The original house was built over two hundred years ago as a hospital, endowed by the local monastery of St Luke, but this wing was added by Sir Hugh's grandfather."

He led them through a carved screen into the great hall, with heavy beams meeting overhead and coats of arms hanging around the walls. The hearth was lit at the far end, despite the warm weather, and fresh flowers had been placed in jars in the window alcoves, adding a sweet, heady scent above the woodsmoke.

A central table was laden with wine and small beer, grapes and cheese, white bread and wafers. Heavy wooden settles along the wall welcomed them with cushions.

"If you would like to take some refreshment, I will inform my Lady that you have arrived. Sir Hugh is overseeing some emergency repairs in the park at present but will be here shortly."

Thomasin took the opportunity to look around. She was reluctant to sit down again after being cooped up in the coach, so she stretched her legs by pacing down the length of the hall, noticing the little details: the linenfold carved panels, the smooth polished floor, the pristine hangings on the wall with the colours still bright, the gleaming silver candlesticks and brackets. Wandering to one of the windows, she looked out over a chapel and a neatly kept garden, full of thriving plants and stone statues. Beyond them, she caught a glimpse of a grey-blue lake.

"It's so fine," said Ellen, sidling up to her. "Almost too fine."

"It is overwhelming," Thomasin agreed. "Just try to remain calm. You know how Hugh feels about you. Trust that."

"I was not born to this."

"Many are not, but they rise above their station. Think of Wolsey, or Cromwell. Luck can bring about transformations. You deserve this."

And yet, surrounded by such beauty and abundance, Thomasin felt a flash of envy rising within her. Last summer, Hugh Truegood had been attracted to her first, before he'd noticed Ellen. Had things played out differently, all this might have been hers. But no, she told herself, laughing at the memory, she could not marry a man who couldn't hold a conversation or dance, not for all the fine houses in Sussex.

The family regrouped as Southey returned, followed by an old lady walking with a stick. She was no more than sixty, but her progress was slow as she dragged one leg a little behind her. Her clothing appeared to belong to an earlier age, her headdress plain, with a thick folded wimple so her face was barely visible. Diamonds sparkled on her fingers.

"Lady Truegood," announced Southey, although the old woman at once waved him away with her stick.

Sir Richard bowed, Lady Elizabeth dropped a curtsey, and the others followed their example. The old woman looked at them long and hard before speaking. Thomasin felt like a creature pinned by the gaze of a hawk.

"You are Hugh's friends?"

She spoke abruptly. They were all taken aback by the coldness of her tone.

"I am Sir Richard Marwood. This is my wife, Elizabeth, my daughters Cecilia and Thomasin and my niece Ellen."

"Too many names." Lady Truegood stared from one face to another, pausing briefly before Cecilia. "Hmm. You're a pretty one. Married?"

Cecilia blushed and shook her head.

"Good for Hugh."

Thomasin felt mortified, but Lady Truegood was not finished yet. She looked at each of them in turn, stepping closer and squinting, until it became apparent that her eyesight was weak. She dismissed Ellen with a grunt, then ran her eyes over Thomasin's dark eyes, tanned skin, and small nose sprinkled with freckles.

"What are you, another daughter?"

"I'm Thomasin Marwood, my Lady, and this is my cousin Ellen Russell."

Lady Truegood's head snapped up, as if she had not expected a reply. "I suppose you both are unwed, too?"

"I am. We are…" Thomasin replied, taken by surprise.

The stick tapped upon the floor with impatience, although the old lady did not move.

"How long are you here?"

Even Thomasin's diplomatic father was thrown by her directness. As he sought an answer, she repeated her question.

"How long? Speak up."

"Your son invited us for three days. I apologise for any inconvenience this may cause to your Ladyship."

Lady Elizabeth was less prepared to pander to the old woman. "We have come all the way from Suffolk."

Lady Truegood whipped round her head with surprising speed. "A strange choice."

But Lady Elizabeth was not easily deterred. "My Lady, when I heard your name, I had hoped that you might be the Lady Truegood who had served the late Queen Elizabeth, as I did years ago."

"She's dead. Did you know she's dead?"

They exchanged glances, a realisation dawning about their hostess. The late queen had been dead for twenty-five years now.

Sir Richard stepped in. "Is your son here? We can wait for him."

Lady Truegood did not answer. She simply turned and shuffled away, dragging her foot as she went.

"Remarkable!" protested Lady Elizabeth. "Most remarkable. I have never had such a welcome, or lack of it. I am sure it is not the woman I once knew."

"She has clearly lost her mind," replied Sir Richard. "All will be well when Hugh appears, I am certain."

Thomasin sat beside Ellen on one of the settles. "What do you make of her?"

Ellen shrugged. "It is as your father says. She is old and her mind has gone. She is to be pitied."

"You are always the kindest person I know."

Ellen smiled gently. "We might all be like Lady Truegood one day."

It was a quarter of an hour before Sir Hugh Truegood came striding into the hall on his long legs. He was dressed for the country, in a simple russet doublet, a white shirt, and outdoor boots. His head was bare to the elements. The simplicity of his attire was quite in contrast with their surroundings, putting them more at ease. Thomasin was struck again by his colouring: the coppery red hair, the tanned skin, the amber eyes. He had a big frame, wide shoulders, and broad cheekbones. There was no doubt he was a handsome man.

"Sir Richard, Lady Elizabeth, ladies, my sincere apologies."

He bowed low before shaking hands with each of them in turn. Thomasin noticed him linger with Ellen, who was struggling to conceal the pleasure she felt at seeing him again.

"You are all most welcome. I had hoped to be here to meet you in person, but we had an old tree come down last night, blocking one of the roads in the park that my tenants use for market."

"It is good to meet you, Sir, and thank you for your kind invitation," said Sir Richard.

"It was the acquaintance of these charming ladies that convinced me to open my home." Hugh beamed at Thomasin and Ellen. "I hear that you already met my mother. Please excuse her; age has affected her mind. I am away so much, she is often alone and unused to visitors. I hope your journey was not too arduous."

"Not at all, and the weather was kind."

"Come, let me show you your rooms. You can rest and refresh yourselves before dinner."

"Thank you, that would be most acceptable," said Lady Elizabeth, beaming and offering Hugh her arm.

Just like the house, dinner did not disappoint. A long table covered with fresh white cloths and crystal glasses had been set up in the hall, topped by the huge silver centrepiece of a ship. Its carved sails and bow caught the candlelight, after which Thomasin could make out the delicate filigree work on the rigging and the little crow's nest on the mast. No doubt it had been fashioned in some workshop in Burgundy or Antwerp.

As they approached the table, musicians were already playing on the pipes and lute. Hugh Truegood had directed Peter Southey to arrange the seating, so that he had Ellen and Lady Elizabeth placed on either side of him, then Thomasin and Cecilia in the centre, while Sir Richard, to his consternation, was placed at the end, beside the seat reserved for Lady Truegood. She came shuffling in, upon the arm of Peter Southey, looking up in surprise, as if she had forgotten that they had guests. The presence of her son, though, appeared to make her more subdued.

"It truly is a most magnificent house," piped up Lady Elizabeth, as soon as they were seated and the servants were pouring out wine. "How long has it been in your family?"

"I am the fifth generation," replied Hugh. "The original wing was given to my great-great-grandfather by Henry V after the battle of Agincourt."

The table was impressed.

"And your father?" Lady Elizabeth continued, returning to her memories. "Might our paths ever have crossed? Richard and I were at court in the early years of the king's reign, and I was there occasionally before, although it was after the days of the old queen."

"My father was a diplomat to the Low Countries. He founded our company in Antwerp and supplied the king with tapestries and manuscripts. It is him I have to thank for our current prosperity. But Mother was at court during that time; she did serve the queen."

Thomasin shot a look at Lady Truegood, to see if she minded herself and her late husband being spoken of, but she appeared to be absorbed in her wine glass.

"I don't think I recall him," confessed Lady Elizabeth. "It is so long ago, although I had thought I recognised your name."

"Father spent much time out of the country, sending his merchants to London. He disliked court."

"And he is no longer with us?"

"He died when I was eight, but he had not set foot in England for two years by that point."

"Do you have any brothers or sisters?" asked Cecilia.

"One sister, who died in infancy. No more. It is just myself and Mother."

"You have never married?" asked Lady Elizabeth, rapidly calculating.

"I have not yet had the good fortune. I have been away too much."

The question hung in the air. Hugh's words "not yet" implied a future intention, but not even Thomasin's mother was bold enough to ask outright if that was now his plan.

Servants brought in the plates, laden with rich country fare: venison with prunes, chickens baked in herbs, coneys in wine sauce. A rich ripe cheese and a creamy slab of freshly churned butter sat beside the warm, white bread. Thomasin needed no encouragement, reaching to assist her mother from the portion they shared. Hugh served Ellen first, saying a few soft words for her ears alone.

The food was simple, fresh and delicious. The venison was particularly tender, falling apart in the mouth. When she tasted the wine, Thomasin found it to be mellow and smooth, far more so than the usual English wines.

"This is excellent," said her father. "The meat is most wonderful, quite rare, even at the king's table."

"Killed this week in the park," explained Hugh. "I am fortunate in my huntsman. I should send up a haunch to the king."

"The wine is especially good," Thomasin added.

"From a chateau in Burgundy I discovered a few years back. I struggle to drink anything else now."

"I can see why."

Thomasin noted that Lady Truegood was only served with one dish, a bowl of bread pieces, or sops, dipped in thickened wine. She selected one piece at a time and delicately waved it through the sauce, before placing it carefully on her tongue and sucking. She made no effort to interact with the guests now her son was present, but seemed happily absorbed in her own world.

"So," said Hugh, when their plates were full, "you plan to go from here to London?"

"Yes," replied Sir Richard, "we are to stay with my wife's cousin, Matthew Russell."

"*Sir* Matthew Russell," Lady Elizabeth interrupted. "He lives at Monk's Place, in Thames Street, formerly owned by the Bishop of Rochester. A most splendid house, if you ever get to see it."

Thomasin winced at her mother's tone.

"But he has invited me to assist him with a delicate matter of business," continued Sir Richard. "It's quite curious. I suppose there's no harm in me sharing it."

He paused to take more wine. Thomasin knew what was coming. She had been present when her father had received the letter at Eastwell Hall that summer.

"Matthew wrote to me last month, having learned of the death of a distant cousin. He was asking for some legal advice. This man was a recluse, living alone in the Essex countryside, and Matthew was thought to be his only heir, set to inherit after the old man died in the spring. At first it seemed to be a straightforward case. But now it seems that he had fathered two children with a local woman — unmarried, of course —

and a counter claim has been launched for the money. Not a word about them in his will, though."

"An interesting case," said Hugh. "Which side do you think it will favour?"

"There are precedents both ways. I will need to examine all the paperwork and see whether the children have anything in writing to prove their identity or their claim. Well, I say children, but they must be in their twenties."

"I hope it is resolved to the satisfaction of all. Is your brother-in-law inclined to be generous?"

"He is a generous man," acknowledged Sir Richard. "He is often kind to…"

"But it is not about generosity!" interrupted Lady Elizabeth. "If the money is legally his, it must remain in the family, protected."

It struck Thomasin that should her uncle Matthew succeed in retaining his inheritance, the beneficiary would be his reprehensible son, Barnaby, Ellen's estranged husband. But would Ellen see any of it? They had been married for five years, and although their current separation was permanent, Barnaby was dragging his heels over a divorce. If only that impediment was removed, Thomasin did not doubt that Hugh would propose to Ellen. The softness in his looks at dinner, their regular letters, this family invitation to Raycroft — all seemed to suggest his enchantment with her. But still, Ellen was legally married. This money could bring her freedom.

"I suppose the inheritance must be a considerable sum of money, to make it worth disputing?" asked Cecilia.

"Enough, in that case, that a solution might be found to satisfy both sides? Surely?" Hugh smiled at the table. "Can the children be provided for, as the other claimant already has a most splendid house?"

Thomasin looked at Hugh, to see whether he was being arch in repeating her mother's words, but his face appeared as genuine as his simple solution. She should have known; he was always straightforward, one of the few men she knew who was without guile. It was one of the reasons he and Ellen were a perfect match.

"That is a unique way of looking at it," said Lady Elizabeth, with a hint of tartness. His use of her words had clearly struck her differently.

"But one that allows for fair distribution, to provide for all."

"It sounds very much like you have been reading Sir Thomas More," smiled Thomasin, liking Hugh a little more. "In his book *Utopia*, he advocates the spreading of resources, to allow for all to be fed and sheltered. It is a most forward-thinking solution."

But for all his kindness, Hugh was not a man to pursue an abstract theory, or spend his days absorbed in literature. He shrugged his huge shoulders. "No, I don't get much time to read books."

"Well, you are a Utopian in spirit," Thomasin replied graciously.

"Who are these two adult children?" asked Cecilia. "I suppose they are our cousins in a way."

"Ursula and Gilbert Aston, both unwed, from Prittlewell in Essex," her father answered. "Their mother owned a tavern near the Priory there. That is all I know."

"A tavern?" asked Lady Truegood, lifting her head as if she had only just come to life. "A tavern? Who lives in a tavern?"

"Some distant relations, Mother," Hugh tried to appease her.

"Of ours?"

"No, of our guests."

"From a tavern? Heavens, what have we come to?"

"I apologise," said Hugh softly. "Please take no account of it."

"Fear not. None has been taken," said Thomasin.

The old woman slurped on her sops.

Lady Elizabeth turned away from the noise. "And do you have plans to return to court, Sir Hugh? Or are you bound to more travel?"

"I am bound to visit Bruges and Antwerp at the end of the year, but the king requires my presence shortly, for a tournament he is planning."

"How gratifying," replied Lady Elizabeth. "We are likely to meet at court then."

After dinner, Hugh rose and addressed his guests. "Shall we walk in the gardens, as there is an hour of daylight still left?" He offered his arm to Ellen.

"That would be most pleasant." She smiled, her cheeks dimpling in pleasure as she accepted.

Southey came to assist Lady Truegood to bed as the servants began to clear away the plates.

Following their host, the guests made their way out through a small courtyard where a fountain played, along a colonnaded walk. The gates at the end spread wide to reveal the park, emphasising the open space, all bathed in shades of green. A long central lawn stretched ahead, flanked on one side by an orchard and on the other, by the statue garden that Thomasin had glimpsed from the window. It was in that direction that Hugh led them, his head bent towards Ellen's, her face turned up smilingly to his.

"I did not know that Ellen knew our host so well," observed Lady Elizabeth. "They seem to have an intimacy."

"We made a good acquaintance at Greenwich," replied Thomasin. "I suppose they're speaking of those days."

"He seems a very pleasant young man."

"Yes, he has a good heart."

"And a beautiful home," added Lady Elizabeth, "although some of his notions are very strange. You should not encourage him when it comes to reading, especially not More's outlandish notions."

"Well, as you saw, he took no encouragement from me. He has no time to read; he's too busy chasing up new weaves of cloth overseas."

"Yes, I suppose that is one blessing."

Thomasin looked at her mother, thinking she was joking, but she was in earnest.

Cecilia paused at the threshold of the garden, by the stone carving of a lion rampant. "It really is a wonder that he has not married. All this and no wife. He must be thirty years old. I can see no good reason for it."

"Many people are unmarried," replied Thomasin, "for perfectly good reasons, some of which are apparent and some of which are not."

"Oh, hush!" snapped her mother. "You have an answer for everything. Being in the queen's service has made you impertinent."

"I shall reprimand her on your behalf when I return," said Thomasin, smiling and skipping ahead to catch up with Ellen and Hugh.

A circular pond was set in the centre of the garden, ringed by a low stone wall. Rising from the centre was a statue of a woman in Greek robes with lily pads clustered about her feet. Through the clearer waters, orange, white and black shapes moved sinuously, darting from one side to the other.

As Thomasin drew near them, Hugh was pointing into the water, and Ellen stared down, transfixed.

"This is my favourite place so far," Ellen was saying. "See that one, the big white one? His back broke the surface."

"You can be the one to feed them tomorrow, if you like," promised Hugh. "They are fed every morning."

"The gardens, your home, it is all idyllic."

"Even Mother?"

Ellen smiled gently. "Is this not her home too?"

Thomasin stepped up to the edge of the pool, following the fishes' motion with her eyes. "Please don't think badly of us, Sir Hugh, for my mother's insistent questions or our connections with taverns."

He laughed. "Nothing could induce me to. Oh, look, there." They followed where he pointed. "The moon has appeared."

It was true. Against the darkening sky, still a mid-blue, the bulbous harvest moon was visible above the forest trees, yellow and full. It was strange to see sun and moon together in the sky: day and night signified at the same time, a reminder of the coldness amid the light. Thomasin closed her eyes, turned her face away from the moon, and bathed it in the dying rays of the sun.

THREE

The air was heavy with the scent of incense. Thick and spicy, it took Thomasin straight back to the chapel at Windsor, and memories of Queen Catherine prostate upon the stone floor in prayer. Soon enough, she and Ellen would be back following her devout routines.

The day following their arrival at Raycroft Court was a Sunday. Not long after waking, the occupants had been summoned by bells to attend the little chapel by the garden. Built entirely of ancient stone, with solid grey walls and carvings, it was a primitive place, barely able to hold twenty people. A simple altar stood at the far end, over which a plain white cloth was draped, topped with gold candlesticks and a wooden cross.

"Good morning," said Hugh, standing in the doorway to welcome his guests.

It was a fresher day. Thomasin had changed into her lighter, pale grey dress, with the velvet trim and furred oversleeves. The usual French hood sat over her thick, dark hair, which she caught in a jewelled net behind.

"I hope you slept well?"

"Thank you, very well indeed. I was most comfortable."

Raycroft had so many rooms that Thomasin had been spoiled with a bedchamber all to herself, sleeping deeply and waking to the sound of birds. However, it had meant she'd been unable to speak with Ellen in private, as she'd hoped.

"I have been meaning to tell you," she said, placing a hand on Hugh's arm, "how very sorry I was to hear of the death of

Charles Collins. He was a good man, in a world where many are unscrupulous. I am truly sorry for his loss."

Charles and Hugh had been close, both hunting and riding with the king, but the poor man had become an unexpected victim of the sweating sickness that June.

"Thank you. It's comforting to hear how many people regarded him highly. He's with God now, but he's not the only one. Many good men, and women, were lost to the terrible disease. Thank the Lord, it now appears to be abating."

Thomasin nodded. She'd not spoken to anyone but Ellen about William Carey. Gradually, through the late spring, she had grown close to Mary Boleyn's estranged husband, appreciating his humour, warmth, intelligence and gentleness. It had been an unexpected friendship. He had taken her by surprise with his declaration of love, and many obstacles would have stood in their way, not the least his marriage. But this had not impeded his feelings. Then, almost as quickly as it appeared, that possible future had been snatched away.

She still thought about Will, remembering him in her prayers. Wrapped among her possessions was a round miniature portrait that he had bequeathed to her before succumbing to the illness. It showed an open, smiling face painted by Holbein, the visiting Dutch artist he'd spoken of with such enthusiasm. His death had left her deeply saddened, but not utterly bereft; she had not felt as strongly for him as he had for her, but perhaps that was only because she had not had time to let love grow. It was the utter waste and senselessness of his death that moved her. It left a void in her life, for she had lost a beloved friend, the one man she had truly trusted. The only man she could have imagined as a constant in her life.

"There have been no cases locally?" she asked.

"Thankfully not. The village has been clear for a month. You will have passed through it on the way here. Hartfield?"

"Oh yes, briefly, I think."

"And you have also recovered fully?" he asked, with a flash of concern. "I heard that you also had the sweat at Greenwich?"

"Fortunately, it was a mild case, and I am quite recovered now, thanks to the kindness of my cousin. You know Ellen nursed me throughout it, quite alone, risking her life for mine?"

A broad smile split his face. "She is a remarkable woman."

A clergyman in brown robes appeared in the chapel doorway before them.

"Friar Antony, this is Thomasin Marwood, a gentlewoman in the household of Queen Catherine."

"It is a pleasure to welcome you, my Lady, especially given that you dedicate your service to our true and Christian queen. Will you come inside? The service is about to begin."

"He comes over from the monastery every Sunday," Hugh whispered to Thomasin. "And he is always most punctual, in order to return in time for his dinner. Come, let us join the others."

Inside, the chapel was lit only by flickering candles. As her eyes grew accustomed to the gloom, Thomasin spotted her parents, with Cecilia and Ellen on one side. On the other sat Lady Truegood in splendid isolation, with Peter Southey and five or six figures behind them, mostly staff from the kitchen, laundry and stables.

Thomasin slipped into a seat beside Ellen, just as the friar began to murmur the Catholic rites.

After the service, the sun had lit up the sky with a golden, autumnal warmth. Hugh suggested that they ride in the park and assured them that his stables had horses suitable for all. Lady Truegood shuffled away on the arm of a maid, and Thomasin's mother announced that she needed to rest, having overtired herself after yesterday's journey, and no doubt by her many vocal exertions. Thomasin and Cecilia assisted her back to her chamber, and saw that she had all she required, before rejoining the others.

They were quickly settled in the saddle and admired the pale sky. Thomasin took to her mount at once, a placid white mare who obediently followed those in front. As they passed along the stable path, she breathed the air in deeply, moved by the expanse of peaceful greenness, anticipating much pleasure from exploring. There was much to see in the grounds, as Hugh led the horses around the lawns, beyond the formal gardens with the fishpond and on to circle the lake that Thomasin had spotted previously. Upon closer inspection, it proved to be a good-sized spread of water in a kidney shape, with a central island where geese and a pair of swans had their nests. A little wooden boathouse on the far edge promised the opportunity for rowing.

After the lake, they took the track along the edge of the woods, passing through the park gate and into a field of wildflowers. The heads of the flowers, white, yellow and red, rippled alongside them in the breeze, scattered between tall grasses. Beyond the field lay a track, which led them on to the little village of Hartfield.

Thomasin spotted the church spire first, then the tall redbrick chimneys rising above the hedgerows. They turned into the central street, busy with activity, as it was market day. Horses were tethered outside the forge where flames leapt high, and the shop fronts along the way were displaying fresh bread, apples and pears, cheese, eggs, leather goods and shoes. Most villagers turned and bowed their heads out of respect to Hugh and his party as they walked through at a slow pace. More than once he paused to greet people and ask after their welfare.

When they broke out onto the other side of the street, the horses picked up a gentle trot along the leafy road back. Thomasin was between her father and sister, while Ellen and Hugh paced a little ahead, out of earshot.

"It is a most pleasant house and grounds, everything you would wish for, almost as good as Eastwell," judged Sir Richard. "I could move here quite comfortably tomorrow."

Thomasin smiled. "You would never leave Suffolk. Only Wolsey, or the king himself could command you to."

"Or my brother-in-law Matthew, on this occasion."

"I didn't know we had these other cousins," interjected Cecilia. "I wonder what they will be like."

"We are unlikely to meet, unless they desire to come to London for some reason. All should be settled without a need for their presence."

"I should like to meet them at least one, if we are related."

"It is through marriage, rather than blood. They are on the side of Matthew's late wife, the Astons."

"And they are not legitimate?" Cecilia asked bluntly, shrugging at Thomasin's frown. "It's a fact; it's the law. They weren't born within wedlock, and that matters, doesn't it, Father?"

"Unfortunately you are right, in the eyes of the law," her father confirmed, "but it is more complicated. They are direct blood descendants of the old man, whereas Matthew is a descendant by marriage only, and they may already have possession of the contested property."

"And there is a will in which they are not mentioned?" Cecelia pressed. "It seems fairly straightforward to me."

"Matthew doesn't really need a house in Essex, though, does he?" asked Thomasin. "And it sounds as if this disputed home is the Aston children's home. Barnaby Russell will inherit Monk's Place, so he is already provided for."

"That is true," Cecilia admitted, "but it's a question of what is right legally, not morally."

"That seems a shame."

"I cannot disagree with you," said Sir Richard. "And after all, when have men ever been content to be merely provided for?"

Ahead, Hugh and Ellen had reached a ford. The road dipped down and on one side a stream bubbled up, spilling across the road prettily before pooling away on the other. The horses picked their way through, allowing Thomasin to catch up with Ellen, while her father brought his horse up alongside Hugh.

"All is well?" asked Thomasin softly. "I haven't had the chance to ask you yet."

Ellen smiled coyly. "As I'd hoped. We've had a good talk this morning."

"I am pleased. He seems as fond of you as ever."

"I believe so."

Hugh had drawn to a halt and was shading his eyes as he looked at the sky ahead.

"It's darkening," he said, as the other riders drew up. "We should make our return with a little more speed, as I fear a storm is coming."

Above the forest, they could see that a bank of clouds had rolled in, its edge a flinty shade of grey.

"Come," agreed Sir Richard, "no need to worry; we should have plenty of time to make it back to the house before the rain arrives if we are prompt."

The way back felt shorter. At a trot, they soon passed along the side of the forest, back into the park and in sight of the lake. Facing in that direction, they could see the full splendour of the house, raised slightly as the gardens sloped upwards. Smoke was pouring from its chimneys against the rapidly darkening sky.

"Here we are, almost back," Hugh called.

They were riding into the courtyard as the first drops spattered the cobbles. Thomasin rapidly dismounted and turned to help Ellen, but Hugh had already assisted her cousin himself.

"Go," he urged, "get indoors and warm yourself before the fire."

Thomasin needed no more encouragement and followed her father and sister through the entrance hall. Bright, welcoming flames roared in the hearth and Southey was already pouring glasses of spiced wine.

Thomasin's mother was seated by the fire, with a blanket over her knees and a smile on her face. It was the figure opposite, though, who rose to his feet and drew their attention.

"Look," Lady Elizabeth called to her husband, "see who is here unexpectedly, our good old friend."

Standing before them, beaming in greeting, stood the impressive form of Sir Charles Brandon, Duke of Suffolk, swathed in furs.

As they took their seats at the dining table, the rain began to lash the windows and the light inside darkened. Charles Brandon laughed and raised his glass.

"A toast to good fortune. We have all narrowly avoided a soaking today."

Thomasin drank, along with the others. She was pleased to see the Duke of Suffolk again, having become better acquainted with him during her time in the queen's household. He was a tall, handsome man, now in his early forties but still the best jouster in the field. Married to the king's sister Mary, he had been a fixture at court since the start of Henry's reign and had proved himself to be a tactful, sympathetic friend to Catherine.

"So you are on your way back to court?" asked Hugh.

"Yes, I have been down in Portsmouth, checking the king's ships. I'd hoped to make it back to London tonight, but the storm clouds were chasing me up from the west, and I thought it best to stop. Some of the roads around here are dreadful, and I am humbly grateful for your hospitality, Sir Hugh. You are most conveniently situated."

"You are most welcome, and fortunate to find a bed spare, when the place is already full."

"Yes, it is delightful to find friends unexpectedly."

"Southey," called Hugh, "send word to the kitchen to begin service as soon as possible. I am sure Suffolk is ravenous."

"Ravenous indeed after that ride. I must fill up, sleep and be on my way. The king expects me."

"How fares the king?" asked Sir Richard tentatively.

"Well enough, but impatient. Have you heard his latest scheme?" Charles Brandon turned his eyes upon Thomasin, but she shook her head.

"We have been absent from court since early June, when they left Greenwich."

"Ah, I see. Of course. You saw Bishop Foxe return from Rome?"

Thomasin nodded at Ellen. "Yes, that was on one of our last days."

Charles Brandon sat back in his seat. "It is a sorry tale. Truth be told, I wish it was over, as this business of the king's marriage drags on and on to the detriment of everyone's health."

"Is the king still chasing after that woman?" Cecilia snapped, mindful of the cruelty she had experienced at court last autumn. Although she had erred, and paid the price for it, the king's vivacious paramour, Anne Boleyn, had encouraged her to conduct a secret love affair, then mocked and blamed her for it once she was exposed.

"Yes," said Brandon, raising his eyebrows. "You are direct, Mistress Marwood, and I recall the reasons why. Yes, Anne is back at court; she returned in late August, to the great woe of Queen Catherine and all those who love her."

"She had the sweat, did she not?" asked Thomasin.

"And she recovered, yes, as did her father, and they are now at Durham House, as there is no space for them at Westminster. She seems bolder than ever, as if her survival has confirmed her position, as if she is destined to become queen."

"Poor Catherine," said Ellen.

"But the main news is the progress of the cardinal." Brandon addressed himself to the room. "The Pope has granted Henry the right to hold a court in England, to rule on the validity of his marriage. Two cardinals are to preside over it; the king's own favourite Thomas Wolsey, who will say whatever his master wishes, and Lorenzo Campeggio, who has departed from Rome but makes very slow progress due to his ailments."

"Does Henry have hopes of him?" asked Sir Richard.

"High hopes, but he is also realistic. Campeggio has received his instructions from the Pope, and since the sack of Rome, the Pope is controlled by the emperor."

Thomasin thought of the many times she had seen Catherine broken by grief, collapsed in private tears, then admirably pulling herself through it, with the conviction of her faith and her anointed queenship.

"The queen will fight this all the way."

"As she should," Brandon nodded, sadly, "but it will not get Henry an heir."

"He already has an heir," replied Thomasin, thinking of Catherine's only surviving child, the twelve-year-old Princess Mary.

Brandon shook his head. "He will never accept a woman on the throne, nor a daughter of his married to some foreign prince. Mary is charming, and she is approaching marriageable age, but any husband she takes will end up ruling England. It would restart a civil war."

"She was betrothed to the emperor once, was she not?"

"Indeed, but that was mere diplomacy. Without a son, the king fears the influence of whomever Mary might wed."

"But what of his illegitimate son?" Sir Richard asked. "The boy Henry, Duke of Richmond and Somerset, is he not? Surely those titles signify some future intent?"

"There was a rumour last summer," added Thomasin, "that the boy was to be wed to Mary."

Cecilia gasped. "A half-brother and sister? Surely not?"

"That was the rumour."

"Henry would not allow it," Brandon said. "He fears a misshapen child more than a female heir. But the boy is young and strong. He has been hidden away in the countryside with his tutors this past year or so, but there is some talk of bringing him back to court, setting him up permanently in Eltham Palace or even sending him to Calais. It all depends upon the rulings of these cardinals. Anne has promised Henry a son."

He nodded in response to the shock in the room. "Yes, apparently she has, and Henry is determined to make her his wife. She plays perfectly upon his fears."

"She must have some secrets that I am unaware of," said Lady Elizabeth pertly, "for I am a mother six times over and each time I convinced myself I was bearing a son."

"And how many sons do you have?" Brandon asked.

"Just the one."

It was growing late. They had eaten well, the fire in the hall was fading and the shadows were lengthening. Peter Southey was lurking in anticipation of putting the house to bed. Thomasin's parents and Cecilia were making their excuses, yawning and disappearing while Lady Truegood had already been abed for the past hour. Thomasin was almost the last, but as she headed for the great staircase, she paused, remembering that Hugh and Ellen were still up, wandering the corridors on the premise of him showing her the portraits.

Charles Brandon accompanied her out of the hall.

"Queen Catherine will be grateful for your return," he said in a fatherly tone. "She misses your good sense and wit."

"I will be pleased to return. Ellen, too."

"I am sure, but it is your service in particular that I know the queen values. She spoke to me of it just last week."

"Oh." Thomasin blushed, silenced by modesty.

Through the dark corridor, they heard a giggle.

Brandon turned and peered into the gloom. "Servants should be abed now, not lurking and listening."

He was about to take a step towards the sound when Thomasin stopped him.

"I think it may not be servants."

"Oh?" Brandon raised his busy eyebrows. "Then who?"

"I believe our host is giving a private tour."

"A private tour?"

"Ssh. Do not say I told you. Ellen will never forgive me."

"Ellen? Ellen and Sir Hugh?"

"It is about time she had some happiness in her life. I hope to hear the match announced before long."

Brandon frowned. "But is she not already wed?"

Thomasin blushed. "To my cousin, who treated her most dishonourably. We expect to hear of their divorce proceedings any day. He is dragging his heels."

"No children?"

She shook her head.

"It may be tricky. There is wrong on his side, but she must be careful to remain above censure and caution her behaviour until it is all resolved, or else it may prejudice her case. Warn her about it."

"I will."

"Now, I must retire. I plan to leave early in the morning, so long as the rain has stopped. I will bid you a safe journey, and no doubt we shall meet again soon at court."

"I do hope so. Good night."

If Thomasin was a little surprised at the abruptness of his departure, she soon forgot it as she heard more muffled laughter in the darkness. She would give the lovers a little privacy. Climbing up the staircase, she ran her hand over the carved surfaces. There might not be time to speak in private with Ellen tonight and discover if Hugh had proposed ahead of their departure in the morning.

FOUR

The rain had ceased in the early hours. When Thomasin stepped out through the main doors at Raycroft Court, the air was fresh and the sky was clear. She filled her lungs with the scent rising up from the ground. Birds sang in the dripping trees and puddles lined the road.

"The ground may be a little wet," said her father, appearing beside her, "but it appears that the storm has passed."

He looked tired, Thomasin thought, as if he had not slept well, or his mind was preoccupied.

"Not too wet, I hope," she replied. "Will you be able to sleep in the carriage again?"

He looked at her, reading into her words. "You are right, I am tired. Your mother was keen to explain all her plans for us at court to me last night, and you can imagine it took a long time. This visit has given her new confidence in Cecilia's reception."

"I hope it will be as she wishes. Time has passed. There are fresher scandals, and the sweating sickness has erased many memories. With any luck no one will remember what happened last year, or else they will not care."

"I think so long as we remain quietly in the background, no big speeches, no masques, no dramas, all will be well." But then Sir Richard saw his daughter's smile. "I know, you think me too optimistic? Your mother will push her forward regardless of what I advise."

"Perhaps there may be limited opportunities to attend court? If there is plenty to keep them busy at Monk's Place?"

He caught her meaning at once. "I think you might be right. Visits to dressmakers and confectioners can take a long time."

They stared out together across the park. A pair of birds were swooping low, dipping down over the trees.

"And you? How are you, Thomasin? Are you looking forward to returning to court?"

Thomasin watched the birds settle on the branch of an old oak. "I am. I like being in the queen's service."

"That is good. I am pleased it is working out well for you. Is there anything else?" His voice faltered.

"What do you mean?"

"Well, I hope I do not speak out of turn, but it is my duty as a father to raise this matter."

"What is it, Father?"

"You are the same age now as when we arranged Cecilia's marriage. Yes, the doomed one. But do you ever think of it? Is marriage something that appeals to you?"

Thomasin was taken aback. "I ... I ... no, it's not something I have thought of. I am content as I am, serving the queen."

Her father nodded. "But at some point, perhaps, you will consider it?"

"I am not averse to it, certainly, if the right man were to present himself."

Sir Richard laughed. "The right man. How like you, Thomasin. I wonder who the right man could be?"

She smiled, with the events of the past year crowding in upon her. Who indeed? She thought of the likely candidates. Not the first man to touch her heart. Rafe Danvers was dark, seductive and compelling, yet he'd proved himself to be a creature of the Boleyns, always serving them first, no matter whom he hurt.

Then there had been Giles Waterson, a distant cousin on her mother's side, who made her laugh, his smile concealing private sorrow, and had stood by them so stoically during Cecilia's disgrace. He had ridden with her to Windsor, when she entered Queen Catherine's service, but now she heard he was in the north, and rumour added that he had acquired a fiancée. She missed his friendship. And that of gentle Will Carey, whom she must pass over with regrets, God rest his soul.

Then her mind turned to the dazzling Nico Amato, one of the Venetian ambassadors, who had such charm, such suave good looks and elegance, with his golden dancing eyes. He had distanced himself from his countrymen and, with her assistance, gained a position as clerk within Cardinal Wolsey's household. Perhaps their paths would cross again at court.

"The right man," she repeated softly. "Does such a thing exist?"

"It is something I could look into for you."

"Thank you, but I am quite content, for now."

"For now."

Out of the entrance behind them came Thomasin's mother and Hugh Truegood, followed by Cecilia and Ellen.

"It has been wonderful," Lady Elizabeth was gushing, her arm linked through her host's, "but far too short a time to form a proper acquaintance. I do hope we shall see you soon at court."

"I plan to attend, yes," he replied, his chestnut eyes warm with kindness, "as the king depends upon me for a tournament he plans to hold at the end of this month. I must complete my affairs here, and be certain that Mother can be left again."

"Is she quite well in body?"

"She suffered from apoplexy whilst I was last away; as you may have seen, it affected her left side. Her leg does not function so well, and her eyesight is poor. I may need to engage help for Southey."

"Of course. But still, I hope it is speedily done."

Thomasin cringed at the insensitivity of the remark.

"Tell me, Sir Hugh," interrupted Cecilia, "do you dance?"

"Well," he laughed, surprised at the change in topic, "I do, when I must, but it is not the sport at which I excel."

"Hugh is an excellent archer," beamed Ellen, unable to contain herself.

"Is that so?" Cecilia raised her brows.

"We witnessed his skill at Hampton Court," Thomasin added. "The queen was most impressed."

The Marwood carriage rumbled round the side of the house, pulled by the four familiar grey horses.

"Here we are," announced Thomasin's father, "all set and ready to go."

"I regret that you must leave so soon," said Hugh. "I cannot persuade you to remain a day or two longer?"

The women looked at Sir Richard expectantly.

"Nothing would give me greater pleasure, Sir Hugh, I assure you, but I am bound to the service of my brother-in-law, with whom I have promised to meet in two days' time."

"Then you must come again and stay longer," said Hugh, smiling at Ellen.

"Thank you, we certainly shall," said Lady Elizabeth quickly.

"Your journey should not be too arduous now that the rain has ceased. I have spoken with your coachman regarding the best possible route, suggesting that you avoid the road through the ford, as it will likely be wet and rutted."

"You are most thoughtful," smiled Lady Elizabeth, advancing towards the door. "The perfect host. Thank you again for your wonderful hospitality."

Ellen was the last to climb into the carriage. Thomasin noticed Hugh walk her round the back to the other side, in order to gain a few extra minutes alone.

"Where is Ellen?" demanded Lady Elizabeth, wedged into her corner. "What is taking her so long?"

"Have a little patience," said her husband, gently. "She is coming, and London is not going anywhere."

The pair appeared on the other side, and Hugh handed Ellen into the carriage, both full of smiles.

"There, at last!" Lady Elizabeth pronounced. "Are we ready?"

Hugh stood back as the driver cracked his whip, pulling the coach away from Raycroft Court. An unexpected hope arose in Thomasin that it would not be for the last time.

The carriage bore them away down the leafy Sussex lanes, back through the village and now north again in the direction of London. Thomasin's mother closed her eyes, trying to sleep, and Ellen retreated into her mind, to prolong her happiness for a little longer. Thomasin looked out of the window as much as she could, keen to see the passing world in all its variety.

They had not been travelling for a half hour when the first drops of rain began to patter on the carriage roof.

"Not again," grumbled Sir Richard. "Let's hope it's just a passing shower."

But as the horses proceeded, the skies darkened and threatened to drive the drops down harder.

"Pull up the window shutters, quickly," he insisted, plunging them into darkness inside.

"Oh no, Father, that's intolerable," Thomasin objected at once. "We cannot travel like that, in complete darkness."

"It is either this or we get soaked. Which would you prefer?"

"Can we not leave them open just a little, to allow some light in? I doubt we would get very wet."

"Well, your mother would, sitting by the window," he replied, nodding at Lady Elizabeth, "and Ellen on the other side."

"Oh, I don't think it would be so very much," said Ellen at once. "I'd really rather have the air and the view."

"Very well. But do not come complaining to me when you both take a chill and can't go to court. Illness is an expensive business, you know."

Lady Elizabeth perked up at once. "Illness is expensive? I am sorry to have given you such great expense; it was most inconsiderate of me to fall so ill, so often."

"Now, that is not what I meant at all," Sir Richard hastily corrected. "I meant to impress upon the girls the needlessness of expense in their case, if they brought illness upon themselves."

"Brought illness upon themselves? Needlessness of expense? I can hardly believe my ears; I had no idea that you begrudged the care of our health."

"You know full well that is not what I meant, and being trapped inside a coach in the rain is not a good place to pick a quarrel."

But Lady Elizabeth seemed determined to do just that. "We would not be trapped in this coach if you had not rushed us away from Rycroft so soon."

"I did so to honour my agreement with your own brother."

"Would he truly have minded, had it been a few days later?"

"Enough," Sir Richard urged, "enough of this now. We have left, we are here, cease your quarrelling, woman."

Thomasin shifted uncomfortably in her seat. Her parents rarely argued. However, in the last year, since the revelations that had come out in the wake of Cecilia's failed marriage, the harsh words had been more frequent. She looked at her mother, who had turned her face away. It was hard for her to forget what she had learned: that Lady Elizabeth had shared the king's bed in her youth. Once, Thomasin had feared that King Henry might even have been her own father, but her likeness to Sir Richard had made her put that idea from her mind. Yet it was a difficult fact to bear, and she was in no doubt that it had redefined her family.

Suddenly, the carriage began to rumble and bounce then plunged downwards on one side. Thomasin was thrown forward in her seat, against her mother's knees. A loud crack sounded from outside; they lurched to the left and came to a halt.

"God in Heaven!" cried Sir Richard. "What now?"

The door sprung open, flapping on its hinges at a strange angle. The coachman stood outside in the rain.

"My Lord, Ladies, are you hurt? My apologies. A wheel has come off the axel; the pin has snapped."

"Can it be fixed?"

"Not at the moment, not here. It will take a farrier. I'm afraid you cannot remain within, my Lord."

"We must leave the carriage?" Lady Elizabeth clasped the side to steady herself.

"I am afraid so, my Lady."

"How hard is the rain?"

"Still light, but persistent."

"Well, there is nothing for it. It will not be safe to remain inside," said Sir Richard, climbing out carefully, as the steps were at an angle.

He turned and offered his hand to Ellen, then to Thomasin. Climbing out, she felt the instability of the carriage, balanced on its three remaining wheels. The fourth had come clean off and lay in the road. They had come to a stop in a narrow lane between tall trees. There was no verge beside them, with the land sloping down on one side and up on the other.

"We are in the middle of nowhere!" declared Ellen.

"Do you have any idea of where we are?" Sir Richard asked the coachman.

"We have crossed into Kent," the man said, "and passed the village of Markbeech a way back. But I saw no signs of a forge there."

"And ahead?"

"I am not certain, my Lord."

At that moment, they heard horse hooves heading towards them along the road. A rider on a black horse bore down upon them, rearing up suddenly as he spotted the carriage.

"My good sir," called Sir Richard, waving his arms, "might you be of assistance to us?"

He was an unlikely looking fellow, dressed in a dark cloak with livery underneath, appearing to be in some haste.

Drawing in his reins, he eyed the carriage. "That's gone, that wheel. You'll need a farrier for that."

"Yes, indeed. We will! Do you know where the nearest one might be found?"

"That'll be the next village on, Hever."

"Hever?" said Lady Elizabeth, appearing in the doorway.

"Smith there will fix you up, good as new. Man called Fisher."

"Thank you," said Sir Richard. "Is it far?"

"Not a mile, but getting there will be a problem."

"The horses can pull the carriage so long as it's empty," said the coachman, "but it does mean you'll all have to make your way."

"What a nuisance." Lady Elizabeth finally climbed out, with Cecilia behind her. "My good man, we are people of quality, and cannot stand by the road in the rain for hours. Is there somewhere you would recommend where we might pass the time?"

"Only one inn at Hever," he said, "but you'll prefer the welcome at the castle, I don't doubt. That's where I'm headed now."

"Hever Castle?"

"Home of the Boleyns."

A sinking feeling struck Thomasin, heavy and unsettling.

Lady Elizabeth must have been feeling the same. Her voice quietened. "Nowhere else?"

"Not near here, not for miles. It is only a short walk through the fields. Look, you can almost see the roof from here."

Sir Richard followed his gaze. "Then so be it. Hours might pass before the wheel is fixed."

"I will ride ahead and let them know. Most of the family are in London, anyway. Who shall I say is coming?"

"Sir Richard and Lady Elizabeth Marwood, with three guests."

"Very good, Sir. Follow the road until you see the path to the left, then it is straight on to the castle. You can't miss it. I will ride ahead and warn them of your arrival."

"We are most grateful."

Thomasin's mother waited to speak until the man was out of sight. The rain was growing heavier, driving through the trees.

"We absolutely cannot go to Hever. Not with that awful family there. Do you forget how cruelly Sir Thomas treated us? How he scorned me and our daughter? How his Anne laughed in our faces whilst she flirted with the king under his wife's nose?"

"You would rather stay here? You heard what the man said. Most of the family are in London."

"Most? Most is not all. Which are they? He did not give names. I do not wish to see any of them."

"I do not see, unfortunately, that we have a choice. It is either that or stand here in this downpour. They will be gracious, I am sure."

"I am less sure about that," replied Lady Elizabeth, "and I am not inclined to be gracious to them. We will be beholden to a family that helped cause our ruin."

"We are not so ruined, and we do not have a choice. Look at those dark clouds approaching. We should not waste time. It is a matter of our safety and health, especially yours." Sir Richard looked pointedly at his wife.

Lady Elizabeth raised her chin in annoyance, but when her husband started walking up the road towards the field path, she had little choice but to follow. With a sinking heart, Thomasin picked up her skirts and trailed after them.

FIVE

The rain hastened their progress through the field. Although it appeared to be a well-used path, the grass at the side had grown unruly, and the trees along the boundary were too tall to offer any real shelter. Forced to proceed in single file, they stepped cautiously over puddles gathering in the ruts of the plough, and the large stones cast aside by the farmer. The ground was waterlogged after the previous day's downpour, but at least the clog of autumn leaves made the occasional steppingstone.

Thomasin was grateful that she was wearing her sturdy leather travelling shoes. Cecilia had insisted upon rejecting hers in favour of her soft, velvet ones, to make a better impression upon arriving in London. Her leather shoes were still packed up in one of the trunks strapped on the back of the carriage.

"Oh, this is intolerable, intolerable!" she complained, slipping upon an island of wet grass. "The velvet will be utterly ruined!" Pausing to wipe her brow, she looked down at Thomasin's feet. "You don't want to swap, do you? You seem so sure-footed, and then at least we will both arrive looking a mess."

Thomasin concealed a smile at her sister's audacity. "No, thank you for your kind offer, but I do not want to swap."

"Oh, well. So long as you're all right, then."

Refusing to be irritated by Cecilia's attitude, Thomasin strode ahead. Ellen was walking alone, lost in her thoughts, no doubt back at Raycroft in her mind. Sir Richard had offered his wife his arm, and Lady Elizabeth was leaning upon him, keen to reach civilisation again.

"How are you?" Thomasin asked, drawing alongside her cousin.

Ellen smiled, revealing her dimples. "I am well, thank you, in spite of these circumstances."

"We have not yet had the chance to speak privately. Any news?"

She shook her head. "All was the same. He was sweet and attentive, as I had hoped."

"But he has not made a definite offer?"

"Not yet, although he hinted at it, in his talk of me being again at the house."

"That is frustrating."

"Perhaps. He is the cautious type, I think, despite wherever his heart is engaged."

"But he is honest, and true as his name. I am sure the proposal will come, in time. So long as you wish for it?"

Ellen's cheeks dimpled in pleasure. "I do, very much. It is only this business with Barnaby that concerns me. If only it could be speeded up."

"Why don't you speak with Father about it, get his advice?"

Ellen shrugged. "It would not seem fair, as he is Barnaby's family."

"He is as much your family, too. Think about it. Father would be keen to help as best he can. He has always been your advocate in this matter."

"Now we just need to get this awkward visit over with."

"I think I would rather sleep in a ditch!"

It was delivered with spirit, and Ellen looked at her cousin, knowing she was only half joking.

As they neared the house, the knot of unease began to grow in Thomasin's stomach. Hever Castle. She had heard it spoken of once or twice, as the seat of the Boleyns. They had been resident here as recently as the summer, when Anne was struck down with the sweat. As such, it was one place Thomasin had thought she would never be welcome, nor desired to visit.

Her history with Anne had not been a warm one, although it had started out positively enough. A year ago, when the Marwoods were newly arrived at court, both she and Cecilia had been dazzled by Anne's vivacity and wit. The gifts, the dancing, the favour — all had been exhilarating, and she had allowed herself to be swept up in Anne's glamour, like a moth fluttering round a bright flame. Thomasin remembered the first time she had laid eyes upon her, as Anne stalked down the great hall in her red dress, to dance seductively before the king. She would not have thought then that such a beauty could be so cruel. Henry was ready to lay the world at her feet, but Thomasin had found her to be sharp-tongued and careless of the lives of others.

Worse, though, Thomasin feared to see Anne's father, Sir Thomas. From their first meeting he had impressed upon her his limitless ambition, his criticism of those he deemed less than himself, his ruthless determination. There was also his son George, a hot-head, quickly roused to temper, although Thomasin felt a little more sympathy for him and his wife Jane now, after they had lost their longed-for child in the summer. The young couple had been unable to grieve properly, because the loss had to be kept secret from King Henry. It was feared that he might question Anne's childbearing abilities if he heard of her sister-in-law's miscarriage.

And finally, there was Rafe Danvers. The man who had stolen Thomasin's heart, almost suffocated her with his beauty, so that she was unable to forget him. How she had desired him, this time last year. How she had longed for his touch, hung upon his every word. Those dark, dancing eyes, the blue-black hair, the firm roundness of his shoulders, the curve of his back, the way he stood. The way he had kissed her with those brooding lips, held her close against him. He had awakened a flame in her that she had not known existed. And then he had broken her heart.

Too late she had learned her lesson. For all their passion, Rafe remained an instrument of the Boleyns, dependent upon Sir Thomas for his livelihood, bound to fulfil his will. And part of that will had been to turn the Marwood family to the Boleyn cause. Desire could not conquer duty, and Thomasin could not forget his behaviour at Greenwich that summer. The beautiful mask had slipped, revealing an ugliness blotted by cruel words and drink. Could it be that everyone was corrupted by life at court? That kindness and good intentions rapidly gave way to the cruel fight for survival? She tried to blot him out again.

"Look, there!" Her father was pointing through the trees. A stream of smoke was rising from a chimney stack set behind battlements. "Not much longer now."

The field ended in a line of trees. Breaking through, they found themselves looking down at a road, which sloped past them into a shallow valley. Light caught the glint of water, the line of a stable roof. Sitting in the centre of it all was the seat of the Boleyns. A solid, squat, pretty little castle made from yellow-grey stone, far smaller than she had imagined, although her points of comparison were Windsor and Greenwich. It was even smaller, though, than Raycroft, but far more neatly made. Almost like a child's drawing of a perfect castle.

"Well," said Lady Elizabeth, alongside her daughter. "It's not even as big as Eastwell. I wonder at the Boleyns' pretensions."

Her voice was cut off by the rain, which chose that moment to renew its efforts. They hurried forwards, down the road towards the entrance. For all her apprehension, Thomasin was grateful to have somewhere warm and dry to shelter.

A steward was waiting on the bridge to welcome them.

"Sir Richard and Lady Elizabeth Marwood? My Lady is honoured to offer you her hospitality."

Thomasin and Ellen exchanged a cautious glance.

"Please forgive me, but I must ask first whether you are all in good health. No symptoms of illness or infection? You understand why I must ask, as this house was quarantined in the summer."

"We are all in good health and have had no contact with the sweat these past two months."

"I thank you. Apologies again for our caution. Please, come this way."

They followed him over the little bridge and passed through a solid stone entryway, where wooden gates stood folded aside. A few stone steps led them down into a charming little courtyard, cobbled underfoot. Thomasin looked up to see they were surrounded on three sides by timbered buildings with lead-paned windows. It felt homelike and intimate.

From an open door ahead, a middle-aged woman appeared in a grey and silver gown, her hair hidden under a hood lined with pearls. Thomasin recognised Anne's mother, Lady Boleyn, at once, after seeing her at Greenwich. Born into the Howard family, she was still beautiful, with her aristocratic bearing and noble features. It was from her that Anne had her claim to status. Lady Boleyn had initially been the one who was favoured at court, and she had elevated her husband from trade, when Thomas was merely a diplomat.

But Thomasin's guts twisted at the sight of her. Their last meeting had been in Queen Catherine's rooms. Lady Boleyn had chaperoned her daughter in what became a very uncomfortable game of cards. Thomasin would never forget the queen's brave comment as Anne won a hand, observing that she would not stop until she had won a king.

Now, Lady Boleyn gave no sign of any former unease between them, but smiled gently at their approach.

"Sir Richard, Lady Elizabeth, it is an honour to welcome you to Hever."

"We are so very sorry to impose upon you," Sir Richard began, awkwardly. "If our carriage had not broken, we would not have dreamed of interrupting your peace. Necessity alone forces our hand."

Her father had overdone it a little, Thomasin felt. His words made it sound as if otherwise they would have avoided the Boleyns at all costs, which was true, but it wasn't the message he intended to convey to their hostess.

To her credit, Lady Boleyn merely smiled. "Not at all. It is no interruption. I am here quite alone and my page, whom you met on the road, informed me of your circumstances. You are welcome to shelter here, whilst your carriage is fixed, for as long as you need."

"That is most generous of you."

"Yes," added Lady Elizabeth, with a shallow curtsey, "such kindness, my Lady."

"The village farrier is a good man, and has served us here for years. He will do his best for you, then send the carriage down to the house."

"Thank you, my Lady, most kind."

"I am sure it is no less than you would do, if our situations were reversed. Please, come in out of the rain."

Thomasin blushed to think how little she would wish to have Anne and her family stay at Eastwell.

Lady Boleyn stepped aside to allow them into the timbered entrance hall. It was a long, narrow room, bright and inviting, such a relief after the rain and long tramp through the field. A fire was blazing in the hearth and chairs had been brought up close to it, set with cushions. Servants were waiting to take their outer garments and pour wine from silver decanters.

Thomasin received her glass gratefully, as she and Ellen moved closer to stand by the fire. Thomasin's mother and sister placed themselves on two of the carved wooden chairs, Cecilia trying to hide her muddy shoes under the hem of her skirts while she stared around in wonder.

"This isn't so bad," Ellen whispered, leaning in.

"At least she's alone," Thomasin replied.

"I am so grateful that Anne is away from home. It would make this a very difficult visit otherwise."

Thomasin tried not to think about that. She took one of the little spiced pastries offered by a servant, suddenly realising how hungry she was.

"We were travelling up from Raycroft House, in Sussex," her father was explaining to their hostess, "the country seat of Sir Hugh Truegood. It should only be a two-hour ride to London, and we are expected by my brother-in-law, but this misfortune befell us."

"I abhor travel," said Lady Boleyn. "My husband thinks nothing of jumping on a boat for France or the Low Countries, but I would much rather stay at home, away from the stresses of the road. I do not doubt it was most unsettling for you all."

"We were most fortunate that it occurred close to a house such as this, and kindness like yours. Had we been a few miles ahead, I do not know what we should have done. And good fortune again that your page happened to be passing on that road, and stopped to assist us."

"And the rain!" complained Lady Elizabeth. "The skies were quite clear when we left Sir Hugh this morning. Such a charming gentleman and a beautiful house and estate. Not that there is any comparison with Hever," she hastily added. "I have no idea why he is not already married with a family."

"He is a merchant," explained Sir Richard patiently, "and frequently travels abroad. He has had little time to put down roots."

"It is hard for the wife of a man who must travel," nodded Lady Boleyn. "You spend a lot of time alone, waiting."

There was a sweet, floral scent in the air. Thomasin struggled to identify it. It was not the usual rose or lavender, but perhaps a flower grown in the Hever grounds. Her eyes were drawn off to the dark passageways and doorways, imagining Anne sailing through them in her bright finery. Or perhaps a younger Anne, a girl of ten or twelve, dreaming of visiting the court and seeing the king and queen.

"Your family are currently at court?" Lady Elizabeth asked.

"My husband and children are presently in London," Lady Boleyn confirmed, "at Durham House, so they have easy access to court."

"You did not wish to go with them?" asked Lady Elizabeth.

"Court has become —" their hostess paused, her dark eyes flickering — "a very busy place. I may go up and join them presently, but it is not a prospect I relish. Lately, I have found it to be so full of noise and activity, far more suited to my children, to the young, with so many changes. Their lives are speeding ahead. I find myself unable to keep up sometimes."

Thomasin wondered whether her parents would dare allude outright to Anne's position as favourite at court. Her mother could not resist.

"I am sure now that Anne has the king's ear, things must be going more smoothly for your family."

Their hostess turned her dark eyes on her guest. "Smoothly?"

"I suppose, I mean, the situation is developing well for Anne, is it not? Now she is close to the king?"

Lady Elizabeth looked to her family for support, but they all held back, unwilling to commit to a delicate situation. Thomasin had not forgotten how appalled her mother had been when she first heard about the king and Anne.

Their hostess set herself down in one of the empty chairs. "You may be surprised to learn that I almost wish we had never found ourselves in this position. Of course, I wish the best for dear Anne. I always hoped she would find the highest match she could. And the king; I wish for his happiness too, and it may be that Anne will bear him the son he desires, if God is willing." She looked at Lady Elizabeth. "You will recall, Lady Marwood, many years ago, when we served Queen Catherine together, as a new bride. She was so excited, so happy in those early days, and she and the king were so much in love. The whole world lay at her feet."

"I do remember," replied Lady Elizabeth.

"And now it has come to this. As a mother, it is difficult to witness the pain Catherine has been through. The losses of all those children that God saw fit to take from her."

"It is indeed a tragic situation," echoed Sir Richard, hoping to steer them away from dangerous ground. "But it all must be part of God's plan. There is little we can do but submit to his wishes."

Both women ignored his unhelpful comment.

"It may be that Anne will one day be queen," Lady Boleyn continued, speaking as if she was thinking aloud. "If the Pope will allow it. And now this new court is to be held, it seems to come closer. King Henry really might put Queen Catherine aside and marry my Anne. Yet I cannot quite turn my mind to it. She was always a spirited girl, intelligent, witty, with something about her; I knew from early on that she would be unusual, that she would do something. This was why we sent her to the Low Countries, to the court of the Archduchess. I thought she would make a great marriage, perhaps to some duke, but I never imagined this. With Mary, it was different. She was more easily content, more pragmatic. Anne has ideas, radical ideas she picked up in Europe."

The room was silent. No one knew how to respond. It was a surprise to hear Lady Boleyn speaking so openly about her daughter.

A thought seized Thomasin. "I was most sorry to hear of the loss of your son-in-law, William Carey. Please accept my deepest sympathies."

Lady Boleyn bowed her head. "I thank you. The sweat does not discriminate. My own husband escaped from it lightly, but Anne took it worse. She came here to recover, thank the Lord for his mercy. Several times I feared it to be all over, but in his goodness, he saved her. I cannot help thinking it is for some higher purpose."

Thomasin could not prevent the unbidden thought that Anne's death from the sweat would have been considered a blessing in some quarters.

Rain lashed against the window panes, seeming to stir Lady Boleyn out of her mood. "You must forgive me for speaking so plainly. I am alone here with my thoughts."

Thomasin's mother nodded. "I understand how that feels. It is hard to be in the countryside, alone, without company. Our minds dwell overmuch on our children."

"That is it. That is it entirely. I think I was happiest when they were little, all three of them here with me."

"Time moves so swiftly, I have always felt."

And it seemed that an understanding had been established, mother to mother.

SIX

Later, they dined in the great hall. Lady Boleyn led them proudly through to a room open to the rafters, with long windows on either side of a carved stone fireplace. The Boleyn arms sat prominently in the centre, overlooking the table.

"I am afraid there are no minstrels to play for us today," she apologised, indicating the empty gallery above them. "My husband took them all with him to London."

"It's a splendid gallery," observed Sir Richard, peering up at the intricate panels and carved archways.

"We had that built," she said, smiling, "the year after we inherited the place. We made so many changes, the entrance hall too, the gallery above it, and later I will show you the long gallery, with its views. It makes the title of castle feel a little misleading. Please, be seated."

Thomasin and Ellen took their seats together. It was a strange feeling, sitting at the Boleyns' table, wondering which place was usually Anne's, and which Mary's. Thomasin thought of William Carey, too, who must have been a guest here. He would have heard the minstrels play in the gallery, once, as he waited to eat.

Thomasin was rapidly revising her first impressions of the place. Hever was compact, but the opulence and style displayed inside proved that size was not always the measure of magnificence. There was a pleasing beauty to the rooms, an attention to detail and proportion, that made each of them into a welcoming, intimate space, as well as being imposing. More than the vast elegant scale of Raycroft, this felt like a family home.

"I suppose Sir Thomas was influenced by his travels, when it came to furnishing the house?" asked Lady Elizabeth.

"He was fortunate enough to see the most splendid new architecture in the Low Countries and France, in some of the new chateaux at the courts of King Louis and Francis. He was ambassador there, of course," Lady Boleyn explained to the girls.

"I would love to travel to France," replied Cecilia, her mind racing with possibilities, "and see the court there."

Thomasin had not really considered travel before, as the English court had all been so new, with so much to learn. However, she had often heard Queen Catherine talk of her native Spain, and even her ambassador friend Nico Amato had spoken warmly of Venice, making her wonder what those places looked like.

"It is eight years since I was last there," mused their hostess. "You were not present, I think?"

"No," replied Sir Richard. "We were still living entirely in the country, then, with no court position."

"I do not need to tell you that you missed a rare spectacle. The Field of Cloth of Gold, they called it. The tents filled the entire field as far as the eye could see. There was a palace built just for that summer, painted to look like brick and marble, filled with gold plate and decorated inside with the sun, moon and stars, glowing with wax branches. And a chapel, a dining hall, lists for jousting. The two kings dressed entirely in gold, shining in the sun, laughing as if they had been friends since birth. I never saw anything like it, before or since."

"What it is to be a king," muttered Lady Elizabeth.

Servants offered wine, and the dishes were elegant and subtle, flavoured with spices and a good deal of expensive saffron.

"This is so strange," whispered Ellen at her side. "I cannot quite feel at ease."

"It is not what I had expected," Thomasin replied, "but the welcome has been warm."

"And the two young ladies are returning to court?" asked Lady Boleyn, speaking to them directly.

"Yes," Thomasin replied. "We're rejoining the household of Queen Catherine at Westminster."

Across the table, her mother caught her eye, frowning.

"Do not be uneasy," said Lady Boleyn. "The situation is a difficult one. Of course Catherine is Queen, and must be called so, especially by those who serve her, until the court finds otherwise."

Thomasin reddened and turned her attention to her food.

"The time passes," continued their hostess. "If we have not heard from the farrier shortly, I shall order the beds to be prepared for you. At this rate, you would be travelling after dark, which is no safe way to proceed amid these narrow country lanes."

"Oh, that is too kind of you, although we should not wish to impose," said Sir Richard.

"I cannot turn you out into the night. It is two hours at least from here to London, and the evenings are drawing in."

Thomasin drew in her breath at the thought of spending the night in Anne's home. Dining here was one thing, but sleeping in one of the beds was so intimate. Yet the idea filled her with a strange excitement. To sleep in Anne's old room, in her old bed, would be something she had never anticipated.

At that moment the Boleyns' steward entered the hall and approached his mistress, bending to deliver a message in a low tone.

Lady Boleyn nodded. "Show him in. He may eat with us. Letters from court," she explained to the table.

The door opened to admit a man in a riding habit, fresh from the road. His cloak was thrown back, and in one gloved hand he held a packet of papers, striding to deliver them in his wide-topped boots. His dark eyes flashed across the room. He took in the visitors with a little start. Thomasin flushed uncomfortably as she struggled to conceal her shock at the sudden appearance of Rafe Danvers.

Rafe's confident stride came to a halt as he registered their faces. "Forgive me, my Lady. I was unaware that you had guests."

That voice, that deep, soft voice again.

"Rafe, you know Sir Richard Marwood and Lady Elizabeth, their daughters Cecilia and Thomasin, and their cousin Ellen Russell."

He gave a short bow, clearly uncertain as to whether he would be well received by them. Although his relationship with Thomasin had been secret, the Marwoods all knew he had sided against them when it came to Cecilia's affair. But then, so had the Boleyns, their current hosts.

"Our carriage wheel broke on the journey to London," said Sir Richard. "It was good fortune that it occurred close by."

Rafe looked wildly across at Thomasin, before reaching into his saddlebag.

"Your letters, my Lady." He placed the packet on the table beside Lady Boleyn, as her hands were occupied with the meal.

"Very good," Lady Boleyn replied, putting down her knife and dabbing at her mouth with a white napkin. "Tell me, do they contain anything pressing? Is all well?"

"As I left, all was well."

"Then I shall defer the pleasure of reading them for a short while. Come, Rafe, take a seat. There is still food aplenty, and you must be tired and hungry from the road."

He obeyed, taking the nearest place at the end of the table, closest to Thomasin's father.

Suddenly, Thomasin found herself unable to eat. Her hands became clumsy, her throat unable to swallow.

Ellen leaned in. "What's the matter?"

"Nothing, I am well," Thomasin managed to say. She put down her meat and reached for her glass. Sipping the wine slowly helped to steady her. Being forced to stop at Hever was one thing, but nothing had prepared her for the physical, visceral surprise of Rafe appearing unexpectedly.

"Tell us all the news from court," urged Lady Boleyn, after Rafe had loaded his plate.

"The king is well," he began. "He has been hunting, and meeting with his council, but he and Anne have been most merry, taking pleasure in hawking and dancing. She visits most days, or else he visits her at Durham Court."

"Does she have everything she needs?"

"I think there are one or two books she has requested, but nothing of significance. She has written the titles in her letter. Mary is also there, and in good health, but George and Jane have gone to Essex."

"And has my Lord written?"

"Not at this time. He has been very busy with the king and Cardinal Wolsey, ahead of the court they are holding soon."

"Very busy," Lady Boleyn echoed, not quite managing to keep the emotion from her voice. "It is a very important matter indeed, which must require much of his time. Is there any news on the Italian cardinal?"

"According to his last letter, Cardinal Campeggio has left Paris and is travelling towards the Channel, but his progress is very slow as he suffers terribly from gout in his feet. The other news is that your brother, the Duke of Norfolk, has returned to court."

"Thomas?" Their hostess sat up. "Thomas is back at court? He has not set foot there lately. So has his feud with Wolsey been forgotten?"

"You may read for yourself," said Rafe, "as he has written to you in his own hand. He has been much in conversation with your Lord and the king; he hopes that you will come to court so that you may meet again."

"Then I shall seriously consider it," Lady Boleyn said, holding up her glass for more wine. "It is a good few years since we met. I wonder how he fares, and I have an inclination to see him again. You will remember my brother, I am sure, Sir Richard?"

"The last time I saw Sir Thomas Howard, he was in mourning for his wife."

"Goodness, how long ago that was."

"She was a daughter of Edward IV, was she not?"

"You are right. She was the present king's aunt. He has remarried, of course, although this match is less harmonious. No doubt you will meet her, if she is at court."

"That she is," Rafe confirmed. "She has entered the service of Lady Catherine."

Thomasin and Ellen exchanged glances. No doubt they would soon be meeting Lady Howard, then, if they were serving in the same household. Will Carey had not been a lone voice; here was another Boleyn family connection who backed Queen Catherine over Anne.

They proceeded to eat a while more in silence. The tension was unsettling, Thomasin felt, with so much unsaid between them. She managed to steal a glance across the table in Rafe's direction. He had changed little since their last meeting in the summer at Greenwich. His hair was swept back, high off his forehead. The particular shape of his brows, the soft place where they met above his eyes, never failed to draw out tenderness in her. His dark eyes were cast down, the line of his jaw and throat so familiar. She tore her eyes away. How was it possible to have been wounded by someone so deeply, and yet to still admire their beauty?

"Mr Danvers," Lady Elizabeth began, "I well recall our acquaintance at court, last autumn. Do you?"

Thomasin curled up inside. Her mother was testing Rafe, provoking him into admitting his role in Cecilia's shame. "Mother," she whispered.

"No." Lady Elizabeth raised her hand slightly to warn her daughter. "We met at Westminster, did we not, but later you dined with us at Monk's Place?"

"I did indeed, my Lady," he replied, trying not to engage too far.

"And you were then much in the company of Sir Thomas Boleyn."

"I am his ward."

"If you recall," added Sir Richard, "Mr Danvers was of assistance to me when I injured my ankle that time."

"Of course," Lady Elizabeth nodded. "And what are your origins, Rafe, pray remind us?"

"My father was a surgeon, who served this family before his death, after which Sir Thomas kindly took me into his service."

"A surgeon? Ah, this is how you tended Sir Richard's injury."

"He was an excellent one," added Lady Boleyn. "We were grateful for his care on many occasions."

If Lady Elizabeth had been attempting to shame Rafe for his low birth, or his loyalties, she had failed. Thomasin hoped she would stop there, but she knew her mother too well.

"You will remember my elder daughter, Cecilia?"

Rafe paused in his meal and looked Lady Elizabeth straight in the eye. "I remember both your daughters, Madam."

This time, Lady Elizabeth was wise enough to remain silent.

After the meal, Thomasin and Ellen stepped outside into the courtyard. The castle gates had been closed now, making a safe, attractive space inside, where lanterns warmed the cobbles. Evening was falling and beds were being made up in the rooms around them. The autumn air was soft and filled with the same sweet scent as pervaded the house.

"I shall be glad when this day is over," Thomasin admitted, "and we are safely at court again."

"Lady Boleyn has been kind, I think."

"I am surprised. My mother, less so. Still, by morning we will be on the road again."

"And then to court. I am looking forward to being back in Queen Catherine's service. I wonder how things stand with her."

"You heard what Suffolk said last night; they are awaiting the arrival of this Cardinal Campeggio, but his connection to the emperor suggests he will be sympathetic to Catherine's cause."

Ellen nodded. "He may take her part. But honestly, even though it is what she wants, and it might seem to solve the matter, I don't know if that would be for the best. Even if the Pope rules against Henry, would it make him give up Anne and return to Catherine? I fear he is too far down his path to turn back."

Thomasin nodded at the wisdom of this. "You may well be right. Unless a way can be found to reconcile him to her; if Anne failed him somehow."

"She has him convinced that she is the answer to all his prayers. Perhaps it would be better for Catherine to retire to a convent. She is past childbearing now; she could live out her final years and devote herself to God, and to her daughter. Wouldn't that be kinder?"

"It might be kinder to herself, yes. But she never will. It is not in her character. She believes God chose her to be Queen of England, so to give up would be to fail Him."

"But isn't it God who took all her children?"

Thomasin shrugged. "I can't answer that. But there is also Princess Mary, don't forget. Any child the king has by Anne might replace Mary, and Catherine would never see that happen."

"Poor Catherine," said Ellen. "I will pray that her suffering is eased and that God finds some way through this for her; it must be that He is testing her."

"Has she not been tested enough?"

A noise in the doorway startled them and they fell silent at once. The broad-shouldered figure of Rafe Danvers stepped into the courtyard. Thomasin stiffened, hoping he had not overheard their talk.

"Please," he said, outlined by the light from behind, "don't be alarmed. I'm glad I caught you. I wished to speak a word or two with you, Mistress Marwood."

Ellen stood between them, her eyes questioning Thomasin about this development, prepared to defend her. But

Thomasin resolved to give him a moment's grace. After all, she was a newcomer on his territory.

"It's all right, cousin, I thank you. I will hear what he has to say."

"Are you sure?"

"All will be well."

"Then I shall step inside and seek out the others."

Rafe stood aside to let her pass. His demeanour was entirely humble, his eyes gentle, like the old Rafe she had known. Should that change, Thomasin realised, she need only call out and instantly be heard.

"Thank you," Rafe began, after Ellen had gone. "Thank you for allowing me this moment. I do not deserve it."

Now she was closer, Thomasin could see how little he had changed, physically. His hair was, perhaps, a little longer, but the details were all exactly like those which had wrung her heart the previous year. Her old weakness returned undimmed — her susceptibility to beauty, the pull of desire. She dragged her eyes away, annoyed at herself. How badly he had treated her before. She must not, could not forget that.

"I wanted to apologise for my presence here, Mistress Marwood, Thomasin. I hope I have not made you uncomfortable. I would not have wished to startle you in such a way, had I known you were here. I promise you, I had no idea you would be at Hever."

"Nor did we. You could not have known," Thomasin replied, stiffly, "as we had no way of anticipating it either. Our carriage accident brought us here entirely by chance, as my father explained."

"So the accident was genuine?"

"Of course it was genuine. We were travelling from Sussex to London; we have been staying with Sir Hugh Truegood.

Our wheel came off in the rain; the axle snapped. What can you mean?"

He looked abashed. "I had wondered whether, maybe, it was devised so that you might visit Hever."

"You thought we might have pretended to crash, walked through the mud and rain and imposed ourselves on Lady Boleyn's hospitality without cause?" Thomasin was tempted to walk straight back into the house. He didn't deserve any kind of explanation from her. "Why, for the love of goodness, would you imagine we would do such a thing?" But the answer was dawning in her mind and her temper responded immediately. "You thought this was some subterfuge? What, for Queen Catherine? Are we reporting back our findings to the queen? Should I go and write her a letter, to tell her that we ate beef for dinner and that the beds are comfortable but the room was a little chilly? Do you think she would be distracted from her prayers and good works for such nonsense?"

She recalled the plan that had sprung against Queen Catherine at Windsor, when Thomas Boleyn had bribed the Venetian ambassadors to get information about Catherine's intentions. This smelled of the same nonsense.

Rafe held up his hands. "Please, don't overreact. That isn't what I meant."

"Then what exactly did you mean?"

"Merely that you may have been curious, as I would have been. I'm sorry, sometimes I speak before I think. Can we start this again? I meant no harm by it."

Thomasin stood, angrily, deciding whether or not to leave.

He saw her wavering and jumped in to try and change her mind. "I'm happy to see you looking so well."

He waited but she gave him no reply.

"I don't know if you remember the last time we were together at Greenwich, in June, Thomasin, walking in the gardens. We were both there when the servant collapsed on the path, taken by the sweat. I heard later that you had fallen victim to it, although I had no idea how severe it had been. I had not heard news of you, so I hoped you had recovered. I can't tell you how pleased I was to see you earlier."

"As you see," said Thomasin, still cross, and remembering the harsh words he had given her at Greenwich, "I did recover, thanks to the kind ministrations of my cousin Ellen, who found me and cared for me."

"Then I am grateful to her. It is a matter that has occupied my mind. Many were taken from us and I was also fortunate to recover, while some of my companions were not so blessed."

"You had the sweat too?" Thomasin felt her heart jump in alarm, even though he stood there before her, and the danger had clearly passed.

"I remember little of it. I lay in my chamber for three weeks, I am told, before I was able to think and act for myself again."

This was news to Thomasin. "And I, about the same, at Greenwich."

"I was also at Greenwich, in the west wing, after the king and the Boleyns had left."

"And I was in the east wing."

They looked at each other, thinking of their parallel experiences. They had been in two wings of the same building, separated by a few bricks and mortar amid their sufferings.

For a moment, Thomasin held his gaze, then tore her eyes away.

Rafe slipped back into the formal. "I was sorry to hear of the death of your friend, Mr Carey."

Thomasin turned her head away. The last words Rafe had spoken about her friendship with Will had been harsh ones, ugly ones.

"Was there ... I mean ... did you...?" He struggled to find the right expression. "Was there an understanding between you?"

There had only been a few spoken words and a single love letter, which had arrived too late. But it was not Rafe's business. Thomasin gave her head a terse shake.

"I am sorry, still. I think you lost a dear friend. I'm also sorry for my actions in the summer, warning you away from him, and him from you. The way I spoke to you was wrong. I admit I acted out of jealousy."

"Jealousy?"

"Of course. But I should not have done so; it was not my place. I have no right to seek your good will."

"No," she repeated. "It was not your place."

A noise in the doorway halted their speech.

"Ah, here you are." Sir Richard was peering outside in search of his daughter. "Come, we are shortly to be shown to our rooms." He shot a hard look at Rafe.

"Pray excuse me," said Thomasin, heading towards the light.

"I am leaving early in the morning," Rafe said quickly, placing a hand upon her arm. "I do hope I shall see you again at court."

Words eluded Thomasin, but his touch made those conflicting feelings arise again — attraction tempered by the memories of his cruelty. With a shrug, she disappeared inside.

"Anne?"

Thomasin froze at the name.

Lady Boleyn was sitting before the hearth, her hand raised to her throat in an unguarded moment. "Anne, is that you?"

"I'm sorry, no."

"No, it is not," Lady Boleyn repeated softly. "My apologies, for a moment there, in the dim light, you looked just like my daughter. My Anne."

The comparison was surprising. No one had ever marked it before, but like Anne, Thomasin had a head of thick, dark hair, although her hazel eyes and rosy cheeks may have seemed darker in the gloom.

"The Marwood girl, aren't you?" Lady Boleyn held out her hand. "Come closer, child, stay with me a moment. My loneliness sometimes makes me have strange fancies."

Thomasin stepped into the warmth of the fire, watching her father's retreating back.

Lady Boleyn took her hand and placed her other one over the top. "It's nice to have young people here. I do miss my children. Pray, tell me. What do you make of her, my Anne? I know what I think, as a mother, but it is not a mother's love that can guide her now. So headstrong she is, so certain of her convictions since she outgrew Hever. When she was growing up, I never dreamed she would rise so high. I fear for her. She came back from France so different, so aloof. I hear the things they say about her, the things that are whispered when we walk by. I understand why, but she is truly a good person in her soul, I believe that. What do you think of her?"

Thomasin was lost for words. This sudden intimacy, the questions. The mother's love.

It was a surprise to think of things from the other perspective. Thomasin knew too well what it was like to be whispered about, to walk through a room where everyone stared and you felt the urge to hang your head in shame. She had not forgotten, though Cecilia apparently had. But to think of the effects of rumour upon Anne, who always seemed so poised?

Thomasin sought a neutral answer. "She is very beautiful."

Lady Boleyn nodded. "They say so, just as they said of me many years ago. You wouldn't think so now, not after so many children." She saw the question in Thomasin's eyes. "Yes, I lost many. Just these three survive. I was beautiful then, praised by the poets, don't you know? And I am not so old, even now. Not so old."

Her lips curled in a wry smile. Thomasin wondered how she might creep away without seeming rude.

"But Anne is not a traditional beauty, is she?" continued her hostess. "She does not have the golden-red hair and the blue eyes of the manuscripts. Not like Catherine of Aragon, or the king's sister Mary, not like that. But Anne has it in her eyes, doesn't she?"

This was impossible to deny. Thomasin recalled the way those dark stars could light up a room.

"And she has him enthralled, the king. Anyone can see it. His wife can see it. Do you really think Anne will become his queen?"

"I don't know, my Lady. It must be judged by a higher authority than myself."

"But a daughter of mine, Queen? Am I to be the grandmother of a future king? Will fate allow the Boleyns to rise so high?"

Thomasin looked back at her: the faded lines on her face; her body heavy and tired, yet almost bird-like with age. "My Lady, may I ask why you are not at court with her?"

Lady Boleyn sighed. "I can't bear to watch it, if truth be told. The uncertainty, the hope, the pain it's causing. I can't turn a blind eye to the pain. Like a long, sad dance. I wish she was married away in Ireland and a mother of children already."

"You would not see her much if she was in Ireland."

"No. But I will see her little if she becomes Queen. But now it is begun, they are set upon this path. You must take care, Thomasin, with the cards life deals you. You must take care."

And with that, she gathered up her skirts and turned away into the shadows.

SEVEN

Darkness had fallen, stealing across the misty valley and through the trees. The lights of Hever Castle flickered behind diamond-paned windows, illuminating the rooms and corridors within. Candles guttered and fires burned down in grates. Gradually, as the evening deepened, each bright speck was extinguished, plunging the building back into the pitch black of its rural surroundings.

Yet in one room, in the top corner of the castle, Thomasin lay awake, blinking into the unfamiliar shadows. Sleep would not come, partly due to the day's excitement, and partly because it was strange to be lying in this little room, under the Boleyns' own roof. She and Ellen had been placed in a smallish chamber, oddly shaped, reached by a winding flight of stone steps. The roof was domed on one side, sloping gently towards the windows. Outside, there were views over the moat, across the fields, which now lay under a blanket of stars.

The house had long since retired. Down the corridor, Thomasin's parents were sleeping in a magnificent room once occupied by the king, with a carved bed, wooden panels and a matching ceiling. Cecilia, being the eldest, had her own space elsewhere, to her great delight. Lady Boleyn had retired to her own private quarters, and the servants had cleared away all signs of the meal. The cook took his rest, the stable boy had retired to his loft, and Rafe, Thomasin realised, was sleeping somewhere under this roof. Perhaps in an anteroom somewhere, or on a truckle bed in a corridor. Somewhere she might stumble over him, if she went looking for a drink in the darkness.

She turned over and tried to banish him from her mind, but the questions kept returning. Was he asleep already, or was he lying awake like her, thinking over their conversation? He had sounded sincere in his apology, but he was so inconsistent — sometimes warm, sometimes distant, sometimes even angry towards her. He was beholden to the Boleyns, she understood that. The chains that bound him for his livelihood meant that he could not think, or feel, or speak freely. And so he always seemed an enigma, just beyond reach, even at the times when he was closest, his hand upon hers, his eyes embracing her. Would the barriers ever come down? Would the real Rafe ever be revealed to her?

"I know what you're thinking," whispered Ellen in the bed beside her, making her cousin jump.

Thomasin lay still, doubting very much that she did.

"You are wondering whether Anne ever slept in this room, in this bed. Do you think she would be angry knowing that we are here?"

Thomasin smiled in the dark, thinking of the conversation she had had with Lady Boleyn. "I expect she has a far grander bed to sleep in at Durham House."

"Unless she is staying at court?"

"I think not. I do hope they leave at night and sleep in their own home. It is difficult for the queen when they are in the same place; Catherine would be tormented to have Anne constantly present."

Ellen was reflecting. Thomasin could tell by the silence that she was building to another remark.

"You don't think…? I mean, I could be wrong, but I was wondering…"

"What?"

"Do you think that she and Henry have, you know…"

"That Anne has shared her bed with the king?"

"Do you think so?"

The thought struck Thomasin as unlikely. As an unmarried woman, she knew the dangers this could lead to. Would Anne have risked her reputation, or even chanced a pregnancy? What would be her fate then? Would it speed King Henry into action, or would she be married off, cast aside? And what would that mean for Catherine?

"It has never been rumoured," she reflected, trying to recall instances of gossip. "Surely people would have spoken of it, if they had? It is well-known that her sister Mary was intimate with King Henry, so I see no reason why it would not be spoken of."

"Maybe people would have, if they dared speak. Perhaps fear or threats keep them silent."

"Yes, I suppose that it would be treasonous to suggest such a thing. No one speaks of the illegitimate boy or his mother, or even much about Mary Boleyn once being the king's mistress. Not now that it has passed."

Or even about her own mother, Thomasin realised with a jolt. Not since Thomas Boleyn had reminded them that Elizabeth Marwood had shared the king's bed once or twice in her youth.

"You think Anne is untouched, then?" asked Ellen.

Untouched. It sounded so pure. Thomasin could hardly claim not to have been touched by a man. Yet she had stopped short, halted Rafe instead of giving in to his pleas. But in this case, the meaning was very specific.

"Well. She is unwed," Thomasin replied cautiously.

"Anne spent all those years in France, didn't she? At the Valois court. And everyone knows what King Francis is like!

He even had Mary too, didn't he? People don't mind speaking freely about him."

"Of course not, because he is French! But, Ellen, that does not mean he has corrupted every woman he has ever set eyes upon. I thought that Anne was part of the French queen's household, and Queen Claude is extremely pious."

"I have heard that, too." Ellen paused. "But Anne is cunning, is she not? Her manner is … flirtatious. I am sure she has tricks, you know, to prevent such occurrences."

Thomasin felt very small, stung by her own inexperience. "You forget, Ellen, that I am unwed. I've never known a man's bed the way you have, and I can't imagine the tricks you allude to."

Yet she had known passion, she reminded herself, physical passion that felt so overpowering that she had almost submitted to it. And only one man had made her feel that way, who now lay under this very roof.

"Your time will come, soon enough," Ellen whispered, "and believe me, there was precious little enjoyment in sharing a bed with Barnaby! What matters is that you choose the right man, then all will follow, without you needing to think about it."

"But the tricks? What tricks do you mean?"

"Well, there are things a woman can do, when she lies with a man, to prevent herself conceiving a child. Charms and herbs to start with, or by careful washing, or lying on one's side, or even by making him withdraw from the fight."

Thomasin lay silent, thinking about this world to which she did not belong, and how her cousin suddenly sounded so much wiser and older than herself.

"Any woman may lie with a man if she is careful enough," continued Ellen, "but it is not without risk. Sometimes these methods fail in spite of the most careful planning."

"So do you think Anne has lain with Henry?"

"It is difficult to say. But a man's passion can be increased by denial. If she had submitted too soon, there would be no more incentive for him to pursue her."

"And that is what she wants — for him to pursue her until the time is right. She cannot yield or fall pregnant before his divorce from Catherine is secured."

"You mean *if* his divorce is secured," Ellen corrected.

"She can't end up pregnant and unwed. Her trump card is a son born in wedlock. I don't think she would throw that away."

"Which is why she is so desperate for this new cardinal to arrive, so that the case can be tried."

"Perhaps they might even be wed by Christmas, with a child arriving next year. 1529 might end it all." Thomasin pictured the scene.

"And what of Catherine, then? She will not accept it, or retire quietly."

"No, it is not her way. But if the case goes against her, she may not have a choice."

Thomasin lay in the darkness, thinking back over their words. Perhaps a time might come when she could ask Ellen more. Perhaps she might allow herself to wonder, to experiment, to take a risk. What were these herbs and chants her cousin spoke of? Could she possibly be so bold as to lie with a man, to submit to her passion?

It would take a special man to make her abandon her caution, to forego her chastity. A man who aroused in her the deepest desires, who made her long to offer herself to him — a man with whom she might allow herself to become that vulnerable. She longed to experience that, to know that sort of satisfaction, that connection of one body to another. She shivered. There was only one man who had ever made her feel that way. But Rafe had turned out to be a man she could not trust.

And afterwards? After she had given herself to him? Reality began to sink in. Ellen was right; their relationship would forever be altered. Would he lose his desire for her, stop pursuing her, or even lose his respect for her? Or, once she had given her virtue away, would he cherish that gift, protect her from scandal, and commit to her if there was a child?

Surely she could only expect all those things from a husband. The law, the Church, and the court demanded that a husband protect his wife. And her own heart was in agreement. It was more than the joining of bodies; marriage was the union of two souls. She could not doubt that she physically desired Rafe, but what of his mind, his soul?

The more she considered it, the more she saw that her precious gift was best given to a man who had pledged in church to value it. Passion was one thing, but the consequences of yielding to it outside of marriage could be severe. Without that pledge, a man could simply walk away. And this realisation made her ache all the more for Queen Catherine, and understand the motivation behind Anne's long game.

Ellen's breathing beside her had become heavier. It was time to sleep. Thomasin wondered if Rafe was dreaming, so close as to be within reach, utterly unaware of her thoughts. She closed her eyes.

Suddenly, Thomasin was awake. The room was still. A little moonlight revealed the sleeping form of her cousin, but otherwise all was quiet. She had no idea how much time had passed, nor what had roused her. She could recall no dream, no disturbance, nothing to interrupt her peace. The sound of an owl hooting outside seemed to answer her question, and she rolled onto her side, trying to settle. But her mind was awake now, jolted back to consciousness.

Another sound reached her. Muffled voices down the corridor, trying to remain quiet, but shot through with a thread of concern. Now she was fully alert and sleep was impossible. Swinging her feet out of bed, she placed them lightly upon the wooden floorboards and moved towards the door. Ellen stirred slightly, making her freeze. Should she wake her? It might be nothing, and she would have broken another's sleep. As she watched, Ellen murmured then fell silent again. Thomasin gently opened the heavy wooden door and crept outside.

A distant glimmer of light passed along the end of the corridor. A moving candle, sheltered by someone's hand. It appeared to be travelling away from her, blotted by a shadow. There was the sound of light footsteps, then the silence of a tread reaching the softness of rushes. Thomasin crept along a little, to where the corridor was lined with windows overlooking the courtyard. The night poured in, making it all seem a ghostly grey.

At the far end, a figure stopped and turned. In the glow of the candle, Thomasin recognised the tall, lean shape of her father, a coat thrown over his nightgown.

"Father?" she whispered, although it was quiet enough for her voice to carry. She moved towards him. "What's the matter?"

"Thomasin, is that you? I am sorry to wake you. It's nothing to worry about. Your mother had a slight turn; she's restless and breathless, and there is pain in her limbs again. It's the excitement of today; she's overdone it."

"Oh dear, poor Mother. Shall I go to her?"

"No, that will just get her more worked up. She doesn't want anyone to know. I am just fetching some more wood for the fire — she feels the cold so. And I'll bring her some wine. She will not sleep without it."

"Of course, but please, let me do it. There is more than enough of each in my chamber, and it will save a trip down to the kitchen."

"Thank you, that is kind of you."

"Wait, I will be right back."

Thomasin hurried back along the passage and crept into her bedroom. Ellen was still asleep. She quickly gathered an armful of wood and picked up the decanter, still half full of wine.

As she headed back towards her father, she could see that he was no longer alone. Another figure stood at his side, glowing faintly in the candlelight. Rafe was peering towards her. His dark hair was tousled, his shirt open to reveal his wide throat.

Thomasin coloured at the sight of him, suddenly aware of her shift, her bare feet and the straggling hair about her face. As soon as she had handed over the wood, she tucked her hair back behind her ears, but she knew that his eyes were upon her.

"Now, there is nothing to fear. You should return to bed," her father tried to reassure her.

"Will she sleep now? Will she be able to travel in the morning?"

Sir Richard looked unsettled. "That is another question entirely. It may not be possible. We shall have to wait and see. When does the queen expect you?"

"Tomorrow, at the latest. She wants us all back ready for the reception of the new cardinal."

"This is difficult. The carriage will be ready in the morning, but your mother may not be. We might need to delay by a day or two; these things are unavoidable. I shall write to the queen and explain the circumstances."

"Excuse me, Sir, may I assist?" Rafe stepped forward. "I am due back in London tomorrow. I was to take the small carriage back for Lady Anne's use. I would be most willing to accompany the women on their journey."

Thomasin dared not make a sound.

"In theory, that would work," said her father. "I could bring Elizabeth and Cecilia up to my brother's place in our carriage, once she is fit and able."

"You can rely upon me. I would ride alongside and they would be safely at Westminster long before sundown."

"It is a big responsibility." Sir Richard eyed Rafe, recalling his allegiance to the Boleyns and his former role in Cecilia's disgrace. But there was no one else to undertake the commission, nor had he ever anticipated being a guest at Hever. "I shall make my final decision in the morning. What time do you leave?"

"I can depart at whatever hour suits you, as long as it is before midday."

Sir Richard nodded. "Very good."

Rafe gave a bow and turned back to his chamber.

They waited until his footsteps had receded and the click of a door shutting was heard.

"What do you make of this fellow?" Sir Richard asked Thomasin. "He works for Boleyn, whom I do not trust in the slightest. We may be under his roof, but that does not alter the fact that Sir Thomas is the most slippery and duplicitous serpent of them all."

"I can hardly disagree with that," Thomasin whispered, "and Rafe serves him."

"Son of a surgeon, isn't he? Or something similar? But can he be trusted?"

Thomasin hardly dared breathe. "It is for you to decide, Father."

"But would you be comfortable under his care? And Ellen?"

Rafe was dangerous, but not in the way her father meant. Thomasin chose her words carefully. "I am sure he would not let any harm come to us."

"I shall wait and see what the morning brings, but he might be our best option, if the queen requires you so urgently. Now, get back to bed and try to sleep."

"Good night, Father," Thomasin whispered demurely, and hurried back to her chamber.

EIGHT

"Make sure you stick to the main roads and go directly to Westminster," Sir Richard said, as he led Thomasin out to the carriage.

"Of course," said Rafe, following behind, his cloak thrown over his shoulder. "The coachman knows the route well and how to avoid any dangers."

The vehicle was smaller than the Marwoods' one, which now sat in front of Hever Castle, its axle fixed and gleaming. The Boleyn carriage was more rounded, painted black with a touch of green. Soft fittings and cushions made it comfortable inside. Two white horses were harnessed in front, their reins hung with tiny bells. The letter B was monogrammed on each side.

"The king fitted it out for Lady Anne this spring," Rafe explained, as Thomasin took her seat, "to bring her to and from court. It allows her greater independence."

Ellen followed her inside, spreading out her skirts as she sat beside her cousin. Both young women burned with excitement about this sudden change to their plans, but neither dared show it yet.

"I will ride close beside the carriage all the way," Rafe promised, "until the steps of Westminster Palace. We should arrive early in the afternoon, and the conditions look dry."

"I don't see why I can't go too," said Cecilia, who had followed them out and stood frowning at the carriage. "There's room enough, and there's no reason for me to stay in the country any longer."

"There is good reason, as you well know," replied her father. "You are not a lady of the queen's court. This carriage is going to Westminster, where there is no place for you. You will go to Monk's Place with us in a day or two."

"Will Queen Catherine not take me into her household too? I can help her dress and dance as well as Thomasin can."

"Unfortunately not." Sir Richard's tone was curt. The queen might have forgiven Cecilia's folly last autumn, but she would not have forgotten it yet. The ladies of her household were of the highest moral character. "Now, go up and see your mother."

Cecilia gave a sulky wave goodbye and disappeared back across the moat, through the castle gates.

Sir Richard closed the carriage door and stepped up to the window. "You remember what I told you. Keep the door locked, and do not get out until you are within the walls of the court itself. When you are driving through the London streets, draw the curtain and sit well back; do not answer to any cries or questions."

"We know, Father," Thomasin replied, a little impatiently. "Remember we have travelled with the queen."

"There is no harm in taking care," he urged. "Write to me at Monk's Place at once, so the letter is waiting when we arrive. Do not delay. We may be as little as a day behind you."

"And we shall all meet again at court in a few days," said Ellen.

"I shall certainly be at court," nodded Sir Richard, "although I cannot speak for the women."

Rafe climbed up into his saddle. "We should be off. My regards to Lady Elizabeth, and may your journey be a smooth one."

They turned to see Lady Boleyn crossing the bridge. She walked in a stately fashion to the coach and ran her eyes over it. "So, you are leaving already?"

"Thank you so much for your kind hospitality," Thomasin replied at once. "I shall never forget my stay here." Especially not the conversation about Anne, she thought, although Lady Boleyn gave no signs of recalling it.

"It was a pleasure to have some company. Sometimes I prefer to stay in the country while my family are at court, but it is also nice to see people from time to time. You may be sure that you will be safe with Danvers. I wish you a speedy journey."

It took Thomasin a moment to realise that she was referring to Rafe. Then, the lady stepped up close to the window and quietly put her hand on the sill, holding out a piece of paper. She lowered her voice. "Will you give this to my daughter, Anne, when you see her? You will have access to her soon enough, and I would like it to go from your hands, because of the resemblance."

Sir Richard's brows twitched in surprise.

Thomasin took the paper. It was folded into an envelope and sealed with red wax. The thought of having to seek an audience with Anne was not a pleasant one, but she could not refuse such a direct request, especially after their talk.

"I shall put it into her hands myself."

"I knew you would. Thank you. God speed you."

"And now," said Sir Richard, unwilling to dwell on a sentimental departure, "you must be away. We shall see you before the week is out. God speed."

The coachman cracked the whip and the carriage pulled away. Thomasin stared back to catch a last glimpse of Hever, thinking how strange it had been and wondering whether she would ever return there.

"I can hardly believe it!" breathed Ellen, when they were out of sight of the house. "Here we are, on our way!"

Catching each other's eye, Ellen and Thomasin burst into laughter.

"And who would have thought we'd be alone, save for the handsome Mr Danvers."

"Oh, stop it, Ellen, he will hear you." Thomasin could see the back end of Rafe's horse as he rode on her side. "But seriously, I am so glad we are bound for court again, after such an absence."

"Will you deliver your charge?" Ellen nodded down at the letter.

"Of course I will. I promised as much. I shall hand it to Anne, just as I said."

"In person?"

"Yes, in person."

"I do hope Queen Catherine does not mind."

"She can only mind if she knows about it, and neither you nor I are going to tell her."

Ellen stared down at the letter, as if she could crack the seal with her eyes. "You do not wonder what is inside it?"

"Of course I wonder, but I imagine it is the warm wishes of a mother to her daughter."

"You are not tempted to read it?"

"Yes, I am, but I won't. That would be most wrong." Thomasin tucked the letter into her sleeve, where she could almost feel it burning a hole.

They rode along through the country villages, past fields and churches, houses and markets, woods and streams. The weather remained fair, and the lanes were smooth. Presently, they joined the main road leading towards London, where there were more travellers, in a variety of carriages and driving carts, or on horseback or on foot. All the time, Thomasin was conscious of Rafe outside. Sometimes he overlapped the road, swapping from right to left, appearing through the window on Ellen's side, and at others he surged forwards or hung back, although he always seemed to end up beside Thomasin again. Once or twice, he approached the window to ask how they fared, but the conversation was brief and functional.

After a while, Rafe fell back level with the window again. "Not long now. The outskirts of the city are within sight."

A little stab of disappointment rose within Thomasin, that the end of the journey was almost upon them, but she squashed it down, chiding herself for her folly.

The buildings started to appear more frequently. The road thickened with traffic and noise. The carriage had to swerve to avoid a flooded field that had breached its hedge. Somewhere, a church bell was striking noon.

"We shall have you there in time to dine with your Lady," Rafe smiled.

Thomasin noted that Rafe referred to her mistress as Lady Catherine, not Queen. It rankled — even Lady Boleyn had allowed Catherine her title.

She felt the difference when they joined a cobbled road. The carriage jumped and rattled, sending shocks through the seats and into their bones. Ellen grasped the side.

"London. We're back!"

Mindful of her father's words and the lingering pestilence, Thomasin sat back in her chair. At least they were coming from the west, the right side for Westminster, and would not need to pass through the busy heart of the city. Large houses and farms flew by, interspersed with churches and hospitals. Then the houses suddenly came thick and fast, and the sound outside redoubled. It was not long before the carriage made a sharp turn and rumbled through stone gates. Outside the window, the redbrick walls of stables and outbuildings lined the route towards the palace. A silver snake of river lay beyond, strangely dull between the trees. The wheels rattled to a halt and a distant gateway stood open. Thomasin could smell horses and fire.

"Here we are," said Rafe, his face appearing in the window. "Westminster Palace."

NINE

There was music coming from Queen Catherine's rooms. It travelled along the corridor, drifted down the flight of wide stone steps that were richly carved with roses and heraldic beasts. They could hear a lute or two, a pipe, and the patter of hand drums. Their jaunty rhythm reached Thomasin and Ellen as the guard led them up to the first floor of Westminster Palace. It beckoned them, almost as if it had been expecting them. The long corridor was flanked with paintings, hangings in gold and crimson, braziers burning with hot coals. Underfoot, the rushes were fresh and thick, and the air was scented with cinnamon.

Thomasin twisted the pearl ring on her little finger. She was looking forward to seeing the queen again, knowing Catherine had not forgotten the good service she had done her in the summer. She was excited for what the autumn would bring. Cardinal Campeggio would resolve the royal marriage one way or another, and Ellen would marry Hugh.

The double doors ahead stood open. Servants in livery were manoeuvring armfuls of the queen's dresses, brought up from the wardrobe department: swathes of blue and tawny velvet, gold and silver tissue, black and white taffeta. Behind them, a boy carried what Thomasin recognised as Catherine's jewel box, encrusted with engraved crystals and ballast rubies. It appeared they had arrived at just the right time. The guards ushered them inside.

Although the day was advancing, the chamber was filled with gentle sunshine. Catherine's rooms were also brightly lit, with branches of wax burning on the walls and ledges. The outer chamber they entered first was in a colourful state of disarray, with more crates stacked in the centre and gowns in green, white, red and yellow draped over the chairs. Thomasin recognised the brightest selection of Catherine's wardrobe. A dozen pairs of shoes were lined up, ready to be selected: slippers made from gold cloth, embroidered dancing shoes, leather-stitched boots with red ribbon laces, Venetian silver mules and soft square-toed shoes made of doe skin. Laughter came from an inner room.

"This isn't quite what I expected," whispered Ellen, as they stepped inside.

The antechamber contained the musicians, plying their instruments with enthusiasm. Lady Mary, Countess of Essex, rose slowly from a brocade chair as they entered. She was looking older than she had at their last meeting, approaching her middle fifties now. Her eyes were tired and lined, her greying hair thin beneath the French hood.

"Thomasin, Ellen, it is a pleasure to see you. Our Lady will be delighted at your arrival; she has often spoken of you in your absence, saying she misses her girls."

"Is all well, Mary?" asked Thomasin, placing a kiss upon her papery cheek. "The outer room is in a state of disarray."

"Oh, never mind that. It is a good thing. All is more than well. The queen has just received a letter from her nephew the emperor, which has marvellously lifted her spirits, so she called for the best of her wardrobe to be sent up for the feast tonight. Go, go on in. See for yourselves."

With a gentle hand on Thomasin's arm, she ushered them forwards.

Catherine was a golden cross. Standing between her ladies, her chin was raised and her arms outstretched as a voluminous circle of shimmering gold was lifted down over her head. The dress was adorned with pearls and silver spangles, shimmering where they caught the light. As it moved, it gave the impression that the sun itself was burning bright and fierce within the queen's chamber. The effect was breathtaking. Then, the maids on each side gave the material a tug and the dress settled into place, revealing Catherine's face above it.

Thomasin and Ellen unfroze as she met their eyes. Both dropped a low curtsey at once.

"My girls!" Queen Catherine exclaimed at once, gesturing with a glittering hand that they should rise. "What a good day this is, thanks be to God. He has brought me encouraging news, and then delivered you safely to me. I was starting to wonder whether you might be stuck in the countryside forever."

Catherine was looking well. Her face had the appearance of one who was well-fed and rested, and the former sadness and grey pallor had lifted. She was still etched with the lines of age, being now in her forty-third year, but her blue eyes had regained some life. The long red-gold hair, once the envy of women up and down the country, was thinner and streaked with grey at the temples, dressed in a jewelled net. But she stood like a painted icon on a church wall.

"Please accept our sincerest apologies," Thomasin said at once. "We were driven from the road by the bad conditions, when the axle of our carriage broke."

She paused, wondering if she should mention that they had been rescued by the hospitality of Lady Boleyn, but she did not see how this would improve her apology.

Catherine waved her words away. "But what do you think of this dress? Lady Elizabeth Howard said it will eclipse any other woman in the court, any other — didn't you, Elizabeth?"

Thomasin turned to see a slight, dark woman of about thirty, with pretty, petite features and a wide mouth. She was shorter than Thomasin, but held her chin high as if to appear taller.

At the queen's question, the newcomer smiled. "You will outshine *all* others — how can you not?"

The implication was clear. In this dress, Catherine would not fail to outdo her rival for her husband's affections, the young and vibrant Anne Boleyn. Thomasin wondered at the wisdom of letting the queen believe that a few yards of gold cloth would suffice to change the king's heart.

"You will not know Lady Elizabeth Howard, Duchess of Norfolk," Catherine said to Thomasin and Ellen. "She has just returned to court, with Sir Thomas, the Duke, and is pleased to serve in my household."

The Duke of Norfolk? Only yesterday Lady Boleyn had been speaking of him, Thomasin recalled. Surely this was the brother's wife she had mentioned, Anne Boleyn's aunt by marriage, happy to serve Queen Catherine? It felt like a strange situation, and recalling recent plots and schemes by Sir Thomas Boleyn, Thomasin could not help but question whether this newcomer could be trusted. It would be best that she and Ellen were on their guard around her, alert to any possible betrayals.

Lady Howard dropped a tight curtsey. "It is my honour, my Queen."

"Elizabeth has replaced Gertrude Courtenay, who has returned to the country with her husband."

"Oh, Gertrude," said Ellen at once, recalling their old friend. "I am sorry that she has left us."

Lady Howard shot her a hard look, as if she had taken the comment as a slight upon her presence.

"And you are both well?" Catherine asked. "We feared for you over the summer. I did not wish to leave you behind at Greenwich, but with the pestilence in such force, I had no choice but to leave. People were dropping like flies all around us. I prayed for you both. Many were not so fortunate; good souls were taken."

At once, William Carey's face flashed into Thomasin's mind.

"While others were snatched back from the jaws of death," added Lady Howard pertly. "The disease did not discriminate."

Catherine caught her eye. A look passed between them.

"The Lord works in mysterious ways," said Catherine, pursing her lips. "It is not for us to question his motives. We must trust in his plan."

Thomasin watched as Lady Howard tied the laces on the golden sleeves, then the headdress was brought by Catherine's lady-in-waiting from Spain, Maria Willoughby, formerly de Salinas. They did not work as quickly as she or Ellen used to, when they had worked together dressing the queen.

"And your parents, Mistress Marwood? I hope they are well?" Catherine asked, catching her breath as Lady Howard's fingers pulled too hard.

"My mother is a little indisposed," Thomasin replied quickly, "but they will be arriving in the city in the coming days, and may attend court."

"I do hope she recovers soon. I will send my physician to her again, if you think it will help. They stay in Monk's Place, do they not, with your uncle?"

"Yes, at Monk's Place with Sir Matthew Russell; you are most kind, my Lady."

"Well, we have busy times ahead. I do not feel this intolerable situation will last much longer. I have hope, for the first time in many months, real hope. My cardinal is nearing

England; his last letter was sent from near Calais and he will cross soon, weather and sea conditions permitting. Sir Francis Bryan has been sent to accompany him. What a relief it will be to welcome him here, to make my confession and speak with the envoy of the Pope himself."

"Sir Francis Bryan?" asked Thomasin, recalling the king's gentleman who wore an eye patch as the result of a riding accident. Last autumn he had been part of Anne Boleyn's intimate circle. If she recalled, he was her half cousin, or some similar blood connection. And now he was serving the queen?

"I suppose it matters not who brings him," shrugged Catherine.

"Then this dress is in honour of his arrival?" asked Ellen quickly.

"No, this dress is for the feast today. Have you forgotten the day? It is the feast of Michaelmas. Wolsey has planned a pageant and I am to dance in the lead."

Thomasin was surprised. During her time at court, Anne Boleyn had been the one to dance, in her seductive, sinuous way, even inviting Thomasin and Cecilia to participate last autumn. Queen Catherine had usually sat and watched in silence, or absented herself in disapproval. She had been a great dancer in her youth, but most people had assumed that those days were long behind her. This was why Catherine had been so keen for their return.

Maria Willoughby brought forward a golden coronet. It was fitted with stars and in the centre was a pair of balanced scales.

"I am to play the figure of Justice. Is it not fitting?" Catherine beamed. "I shall stand there, shimmering in gold, dispensing justice to the characters of envy, greed, sloth and lust, and then, within days, Cardinal Campeggio will arrive to rule on my case. The Pope has given him definite instructions. My nephew, the emperor, told me such."

"Shall I remove your hood?" asked Maria.

"Not yet. There are hours still to go, and it is weighty."

Maria withdrew, bearing the golden scales in her hands.

"What assistance do you wish us to give you at the pageant?" asked Ellen.

"You will be in my dressing team, in the antechamber. After the pageant, I will change into the burgundy velvet and hood with pearls." Catherine nodded at the items, draped over the bed. "So you two must bring the gown and be ready with it as soon as Maria and Elizabeth have removed the gold."

"Very good, my Lady."

There was a knock at the door. Lady Mary appeared on the threshold.

"If you please, my Lady, there is another letter."

"Another?" Catherine seemed to jolt upwards in excitement. "From the emperor again?"

"I think it is from Ludlow?"

"Ludlow? Oh, hush, hush!" she cried to the musicians, who promptly ceased their playing. "From my daughter?"

"From her guardian, Lady Salisbury."

Lady Mary held out the folded paper and Catherine sprang forwards to claim it, disappearing into the anteroom for privacy.

It reminded Thomasin of the envelope with the Boleyn seal that was tucked in the folds of her inner sleeve. At some point, she had to find an opportunity to sneak away from the queen and deliver it to Anne, although she had no desire to see that woman.

Laughter came from the antechamber, revealing the queen's delight in what she read.

It was imperative, Thomasin thought, that Catherine did not find out about the Boleyn letter or the Marwoods' impromptu stay at Hever, not even when she was in this buoyant mood. It had not been planned, and could not have been helped, but it would shake her faith in their loyalty.

As she looked up, Thomasin met Lady Elizabeth Howard's eyes, hard now in their gaze, as if she could read her thoughts. Blushing, Thomasin dropped a curtsey, as the woman's rank befitted, and in return the duchess inclined her head slightly in acknowledgement before turning away.

"There's something I just don't about trust that woman," Thomasin whispered to Ellen, as Lady Howard disappeared around Catherine's bed.

"I had the same sense," Ellen breathed back. "She seems so sharp she might cut you."

"Come, girls," said Lady Howard, suddenly returning, "do not stand around gossiping. Help order this mess!"

With Catherine absent, they had little choice but to obey, with surprise and a little reluctance in their hearts.

"You don't think she heard us?" asked Thomasin.

Ellen shook her head. "But are we to take our orders from her now?"

An hour or so had passed. The mess was cleared away and Queen Catherine was again dressed in her familiar tawny and navy blue, resting on her bed before the exertions of the evening. The golden gown was packed away in a chest, shimmering with promise.

In the outer room, Thomasin sat darning a pair of stockings whilst Ellen and Lady Mary polished some of the queen's brooches and chains. Outside the window, the afternoon sunshine was deepening into a warm yellow. The musicians had packed away and a soporific peace settled upon the rooms.

Footsteps approached the door from the outside. Holding her needle still, Thomasin looked up to see the guards admit a man dressed in the livery of Thomas Cromwell, secretary to Cardinal Wolsey. Her first reaction was one of caution towards the servant of a man she both disliked and distrusted, but then she recognised Nico Amato, the Venetian she had met in the spring at Windsor. He stopped at once, spotting her in the alcove, his face lighting up at the sight of her. He hurried a few steps forward, then recalled the protocol and bowed.

"Mistress Marwood, I had no idea you were here at Westminster."

"Signore Amato, I arrived only today, and came straight up to these chambers. How long have you been here?"

"Since the start of July. I came with Mister Cromwell, thanks to your recommendation."

It was Thomasin who had put in a good word for Nico after all the other Venetians had departed in disgrace that summer. By showering the queen with gifts and flattery, they had tried to conceal their involvement in a plot devised by Thomas Boleyn to uncover the queen's secret plans. Alone among them, Nico had shown some integrity, some goodness, so she had recommended him for the role as Cromwell's secretary, even though he had been bold enough to kiss her once in the garden.

"You are well?" she asked, although the answer was apparent.

He was more handsome than she recalled, with his dark hair, his skin tanned golden from the southern sun, and his sensuous lips spreading in a quick smile. And, standing there, she saw again how easy he was in his own skin, his movements graceful and self-assured. How smoothly and seductively he had danced by her side, lithe as a bird.

"Is that a messenger?" Lady Howard came through the antechamber, frowning. She looked Nico up and down. "The queen is resting. Who are you?"

"Signore Nico Amato of Venice, my Lady, secretary to Master Cromwell. I am sent by him to say that the arrangements for the masque will be ready for her arrival at half past the hour of five. The masque itself will begin at six."

"Very good," Lady Howard snapped in a staccato voice, although her eyes lingered on him for a moment longer. "You may go."

Nico bowed and turned to Thomasin. "I hope to see you this evening?"

But Lady Howard intervened. "Mr Amato, I said, you may go."

Without looking at the woman again, Nico turned and left the rooms.

Lady Howard rested her eyes upon Thomasin. "A friend of yours? Don't encourage him; remember your place."

Replies sprang to Thomasin's lips at once, but she knew it was wisest to remain silent. She picked up her needle again, pushing it harshly through the wool. A moment later, Lady Howard withdrew.

"Sour as week-old milk, that one," whispered Ellen.

Lady Mary looked up from her polishing. "Don't let her hear you. I don't like to speak ill of anyone, not without good reason, but I would keep your distance as much as you can from that one."

"Oh dear, is that so?" asked Ellen.

"She is related to the Boleyns, is she not?" Thomasin added. "I wonder at her being here in the queen's rooms."

"She's married to Norfolk, Anne's uncle, certainly," Lady Mary confirmed, "but they hate each other and fight like cat and dog. He has taken his laundress as his mistress, and now the duchess works against him at every turn."

Ellen sighed. "That is very sad."

"It was a marriage of affection that turned sour. Take heed, you two, while you are young. It is a trap you do not need to fall into."

Thomasin stabbed her needle back into the stocking.

TEN

There was a sudden brightness. Gold, dazzling in the candlelight. A body, twirling, glittering through the darkness. The flash of diamonds at her throat and wrist made a mesmerising display.

In a side room off Westminster hall, Queen Catherine came to a halt, laughing in delight, sparkling from head to toe with sequins. The headdress sat majestically upon her hair, pinned in place by careful fingers. Thick gold chains hung about her neck. Upon her feet were slippers embroidered with Venetian thread, soft-soled for dancing.

It was a plain antechamber off the main hall, with white walls, rush matting on the floor, and two lines of benches where servants usually sat awaiting their orders. The air was slightly musty, but thick with the fug of smoke. Standing back to admire the women's efforts, it seemed to Thomasin that the queen, who usually wore her age and sadness so heavily, had been transformed into a star. Perhaps there really was something in Lady Howard's words after all.

"Well," Catherine beamed, throwing out her arms. "How do I look?"

Thomasin joined the other ladies in showering her with praise.

"Now it is time to remind my husband that he married a daughter of Spain. And one with the might of the entire Empire waiting behind her!"

Thomasin was surprised. Was Catherine really suggesting that her nephew, Emperor Charles, would use his "might" in her cause? Was a Spanish army preparing to sail up the Thames?

Wisely, she kept her own counsel, and only clapped her hands as the queen basked in her own radiance.

The curtain twitched at the door. A male voice asked, "May I enter?"

Maria Willoughby pulled the tapestry aside and Nico appeared, his eyes earnest. Again, Thomasin thought of frankincense and myrrh, precious things, just as she had when they'd first met. In that flickering light, he struck Thomasin again as one of the most handsome men she had ever seen.

"My Lady Queen, ladies, you are ready?"

"We are," replied Catherine.

"Everything is set. The court is in attendance. You may send out your ladies now, and leave the curtain a little aside so that you might hear your cue."

"I have been performing in pageants since before you were born," Catherine replied, half in jest. "I do not need to be schooled now."

"My apologies," said Nico, bowing his retreat and shooting a quick smile of appreciation in Thomasin's direction.

"It's time," said Catherine, turning to the group around her, her excitement mounting. "You heard him. Now go."

Maria Willoughby led the women out in single file, through the parted curtain and into the great hall. They moved slowly, sedately, as if their dignity could further enhance the whirling gold performance about to be unleashed upon the court. Deliberately placing herself at the end of the line after Ellen, Thomasin suddenly felt nervous at the thought of being before the king again, and all those familiar faces — friends, foes and indifferents. But it was inevitable. Best just to emerge, like this, without having a moment to worry.

The hall was immense and burning bright. Yet its enormous dimensions offered some privacy among the excitement and chatter of the hoards. With such high rafters, so many people talking and the musicians playing, a line of four or five women heading to their seats might, possibly, go unnoticed.

But once she was plunged back into that world, buzzing with voices, Thomasin remembered. Of course, she was a fool to think that anything would escape attention here, no matter how small. People were already looking their way, pointing at the queen's ladies, whispering behind their hands. Like hunters waiting at the mouth of a den, they knew how to be patient, and where exactly to focus their attention. It was the speciality of this court of vultures.

A space at the end of the hall had been cleared for the pageant. It gave them a clear destination to head for, and Thomasin followed Ellen gratefully. Servants were rolling out a huge tableau of the heavens; the sun and moon painted on canvas against a backdrop of stars, all mounted upon smooth wheels. Luckily, it drew some of the eyes away from the women, who slipped onto a bench at the side, sitting back in the shadows.

"All is ready?"

Baron Mountjoy, Catherine's distinguished, white-haired chamberlain stood waiting for them.

"Quite ready," replied Lady Howard.

He inclined his head towards Thomasin and Ellen, ever gracious. "Welcome back, ladies. Be seated."

From her vantage point at the side, Thomasin dared to look around. The layout of the hall was reassuringly familiar. Hierarchical to the last, and therefore, predictable. Down each side of the hall, people sat at trestle tables covered in pristine white cloths, the lowliest at the bottom and the king's servants at the top. At the top end, far away on the raised dais, a golden cloth was thrown over the royal table, which was filled with plates and goblets. There was a matching gold drape above, upon which the royal coat of arms was embroidered large for all to see. Two carved chairs of state were positioned below, also painted in gold, with cushions in purple satin.

King Henry sat resplendent on one side, a distant figure in furs and scarlet, but instantly recognisable. With broad shoulders, a thick neck and red hair under a pearl-sewn cap, he was every inch the king. The other chair was empty, waiting. Thomasin was relieved to see it, half fearing that Anne Boleyn might have dared to occupy the space in Queen Catherine's absence.

Thomas Cromwell stood at King Henry's side. A thick-set man with clever eyes and a quick brain, he wore his habitual plain, dark cloak. He was a lawyer known for his cunning, a servant of great men, willing to get his hands dirty doing tasks that great men shunned. It was rumoured at court that he was the son of a smith from Putney, that he had been a mercenary, a merchant in Italy and the Low Countries. Thomasin recalled how he had tried to pressure her father into supporting the king's cause, reluctant to take Sir Richard's polite rejection and visiting Monk's Place in person. The sight of him made her shiver.

There was no sign of Cromwell's master, the formidable Thomas Wolsey. Similarly elevated from the lowly ranks of a butcher's son, Wolsey was Archbishop of York, Lord High Chancellor and the other cardinal required to sit with Campeggio in the coming papal court. He had been responsible for planning the evening's events; no doubt he was behind the scenes somewhere, making the last arrangements. Thomasin felt ambivalent towards him. He lacked the menace of Cromwell, and she had witnessed first-hand that his relationship with the king's paramour was strained. She'd seen the glimmer of fear in Wolsey's eyes as he'd tried to please Anne, to no avail.

And, just as she had expected, Thomasin saw a cluster of Boleyns close to the throne. Sir Thomas looked impatient, stroking his silvery beard and darting his dark eyes about the hall. He was the Boleyn patriarch, the descendant of a Lord Mayor of London, who had risen through the ranks by making judicious marriages, to become a skilled linguist and diplomat. Funny, Thomasin thought, how the king had surrounded himself with men of humble backgrounds.

Anne stood beside him, resplendent in a vivid dress of emerald green silk, embroidered with some intricate design. It hung about her in folds like water, shimmering in flattering waves as she moved. One thing Thomasin could admit: besides Anne's sensual attraction, she knew how to dress. Her style and palette always drew the eye, making her stand out in a crowd. She wondered what Lady Boleyn would have thought of it.

Anne turned to speak to her father, her laughter ringing out down the hall. Tonight, the long raven hair for which she was known was swept back under a hood, but that hood was pushed back higher than ever upon her head, revealing more of her face. The top curve was studded with diamonds that caught the light. As she spoke, she threw her huge dark eyes about the hall, as if casting spells — first upon Thomas, then up towards the king. Watching as he shifted in his seat and connected with her gaze, Thomasin saw that King Henry was far from immune to her presence.

"Look, there's Mary, too," whispered Ellen, nodding to the side.

There sat Mary Boleyn, in solemn grey and black, towards the back of her family. Her headdress was severe, her face pale and drawn, her eyes tired and heavy. Her colouring and expression couldn't have made a starker contrast with those of her sister. It gave Thomasin a strange jolt to see William Carey's wife, dressed in formal mourning for the husband she had not loved. Memories rushed in. Will's words, Will's smile. A flush of emotion rose to Thomasin's cheeks.

Other dancers were appearing near the pageant, slipping into their places. In black and silver costumes, sewn with stars, they held poses around the tableau, waiting to be brought to life. The hall noticed. It hummed, pointing, whispering, then the voices began to fall silent.

A drummer began to sound out a rhythm, slow and steady as a heartbeat. King Henry leaned forward in his seat and the Boleyns ceased their talk. Their faces were expectant. Did they know what was coming?

The drum faded and the musicians started a melancholy refrain. Then a white-bearded poet in a long, furred gown stepped forwards to recite a preface in rhyming couplets. It was all about the virtues: faith and love, charity and humility, patience and hope. Thomasin let the words wash over her, keeping her eyes fixed upon the curtains where Queen Catherine was waiting to emerge.

The dancers began to twitch and sway. A head turned, an arm stretched out, a hand fluttered. Then they found their feet, circling around a central spot on the floor, while flashes of light appeared behind them, made by a dozen wax branches carried in the arms of servants. The narrator spoke about the inevitability of justice, of light bringing hope into darkness. Then, suddenly, the curtains parted and Catherine appeared in a blaze of gold, heading for the stage.

The hall let out a collective gasp. Their queen had never appeared in quite this light before, far outdazzling any other pageant in recent memory. She stepped into the space as the goddess of Fortune, and her costume and demeanour leant her a radiance that made the rest of the dancers dim as they moved about her.

There were more words from the poet and more movement from the dancers. Then the music quickened in pace, rising to a crescendo before falling into a void of silence. And into that silence, Catherine spoke her lines. The hall was spellbound.

"Fortune I am, goddess and dame, bringer of justice, leveller of humankind, instrument of our gracious God's divine will…"

Thomasin's eyes wandered over to where Anne Boleyn stood, wide-eyed, staring at the blazing queen.

"I see your ways, your thoughts and deeds, the motives and truths within your hearts. And I promise you that each man and woman shall one day receive their just deserts, the true salvation or damnation which their souls deserve."

Thomasin flinched a little at the uncomfortable words. But then Catherine turned to the dancers.

"Here, upon this stage, observe the characters of peace and war, drawn into conflict, with jealousy and lust, truth and virtue among them. You will see how they fare, and how each receives their fate, when Justice is dispensed."

"Goodness," whispered Ellen, "I have never seen her like this. I do not doubt it will give the Boleyns pause for thought, but they will not like it."

It may touch their consciences, thought Thomasin, looking over at Sir Thomas, unless they were smirking behind their hands at their round, middle-aged queen dressed in spangles. To her surprise, though, they were not mocking her, but stood solemn, their faces unreadable. It was King Henry's face that was the strangest. Thomasin could not decipher the mixture of emotions there, but thought she read anger, shame and discomfort. No doubt it would be Wolsey who would suffer for this. Where was the cardinal? Thomasin looked around, because this should be the moment he appeared, but there was no sign of him.

It was then that she saw Anne Boleyn make a slight movement. Standing beside her father, she turned aside, so that her flank was facing the pageant. It was a simple but decisive move that signified boredom. Anne did not quite dare to turn her back on the queen, but this was as far as she could go. Fortunately, no one else, including Henry, appeared to notice, for they were all motionless, transfixed. And Catherine herself was too intent upon her performance. As she continued her lines, walking slowly and regally round the pageant, the hall had no choice but to watch. This was her moment. And Anne could not stand it.

The pageant came to an end with thunderous applause. Even the king was moved to clap with a degree of sincerity. Catherine stood glowing, basking in the radiance of approval. Before it had entirely died down, Baron Mountjoy stepped forward and, offering Catherine his hand, led her up to the dais. She curtseyed low before the king, who inclined his head in greeting, then took the throne beside him.

"It was well done," whispered Ellen, her voice muffled by the sound of the pageant being dragged away.

"We saw the true queen again," Thomasin agreed, "although it was not to everyone's liking." She nodded towards the Boleyns, where Anne was deep in conversation with a tall, broad man in his fifties. He had a shaved, red face and a prominent nose. He looked important, fearsome, as if he would stand no nonsense.

Servants were hurrying out to prepare the tables, and all were now taking seats ahead of the feast being served. Catherine's ladies were directed to their places on a table near the top, but Lady Howard declined to join them and walked boldly down towards the top of the hall. Thomasin and Ellen watched her in awe, reminded again of her rank. She drew up beside Anne and curtseyed, before offering her hand to the clean-shaven man. He took it and inclined his head over it, as if to kiss it, although Thomasin noticed his lips did not touch her fingers. They did not exchange a word, but Lady Howard then seated herself at the Boleyn table.

"That man must be her husband," said Thomasin.

She and Ellen stared at the Duke of Norfolk, Anne's formidable uncle.

"You don't think his arrival will change anything?" Ellen asked.

"Only that they have another strong voice to speak for their cause, but he can no more rule against the marriage than any of us."

"He doesn't look very nice," observed Ellen, wrinkling her nose.

"We only know the rumours about his marriage, and those are none of our business."

"Well, I don't really care so long as his wife doesn't try to boss us about. Can you see Hugh anywhere?"

"Not yet, no."

Thomasin looked about the hall. Down at the dais, she could see Sir Charles Brandon preparing to take his seat. He caught her eye and raised his hand in greeting, a gesture which pleased her greatly. It was an honour to be recognised publicly by someone seated at the top table. He was placed beside his wife, Mary. A former Queen of France, she was the king's younger sister, once a great beauty and a mother of four, although one son had been lost early. She was little more than thirty now, striking in a gown of ochre velvet, but had experienced much illness in recent years that kept her away from court. She was also well known to disapprove of Henry's infatuation with Anne, having known Catherine since childhood.

All four seats at the dais were now taken. It seemed a cue for Anne to withdraw and, muttering to her father, she joined the Boleyn table between her sister and Lady Howard. With surprise, Thomasin noticed that Rafe was behind them, previously obscured by the crowd. Her former dance partner, Sir Henry Norris stood there too, solid and handsome, just like when he had partnered her in Anne's pageant last year.

Then Thomasin remembered the letter that Lady Boleyn had given her. It was tucked in her sleeve, ready to deliver to Anne, although that would be very difficult to achieve without Catherine seeing. Perhaps she should have disobeyed Lady Boleyn's direct instructions and put it in Rafe's hands instead. That way, Anne would have had it by now, and Thomasin would have nothing more to do with it. But she had made a promise. She had not mistaken Lady Boleyn's liking for her at Hever; how would Anne feel about that? It was a problem she would have to resolve later; perhaps she could catch Anne as she was leaving. It was her duty, and hers alone.

As the trumpets sounded to announce the arrival of the food, a slight movement caught Thomasin's eye. Cardinal Wolsey had stepped into the hall from between the curtains, dressed in his red robes, his face unreadable as he surveyed the hall. As Henry's closest advisor over the past years, he had served the king well until the arrival of Anne. Now the expectation that he would deliver the long-desired divorce hung heavily about his rounded shoulders. Thomasin recalled that splendid evening she had spent at his house on the Thames, York Place, a place of unparalleled luxury.

As Thomasin watched, King Henry spotted the new arrival and beckoned the cardinal with a stern finger. Wolsey obeyed the summons with as much dignity as he could muster. Mounting the dais to stand close to the king, the cardinal bowed his head while Henry delivered a few sharp words.

"Wolsey's in trouble," Thomasin whispered to Ellen.

"I'm not surprised, allowing Catherine to take a role like that."

They watched as the cardinal bowed his head then retreated, leaving the hall.

"It was misjudged on his part," Thomasin added, "if he wishes to keep the good favour of the Boleyns."

"Perhaps he no longer cares for them."

"If he ever did."

Servants produced dishes of steaming beef and lamb, patties of minced meat, pheasants and rabbits. A huge plate bearing a glazed, suckling pig was carried through the length of the hall, trailing its delicious scent, and placed before the king. Thomasin unfolded her napkin on her lap as platters of beef and rabbit were placed between her and Ellen. There was more food than they had seen in months, and both were starving after their busy day.

It seemed such a long time since they had left Hever that morning, only eating bread and cheese in the carriage for lunch. Thomasin scooped up chewets of beef, and there was a dish of almond cream, richly spiced sauces and fritters. Her glass was filled with wine, and quickly emptied, although she admitted to Ellen that it was not as good as Sir Hugh's favourite burgundy. The distraction of food made the mood lighter, the evening more manageable.

Thomasin looked back towards the dais. Queen Catherine was still glowing, chattering away to her sister-in-law Mary. To the side, Anne Boleyn was eating quietly, listening to Sir Henry Norris talk, but there was something about her demeanour, the placidity with which she accepted her rival's moment in the light, that put Thomasin on edge. By now, she knew Anne well enough to judge that this was no real, lasting victory for Catherine. It was a brief, golden moment, before the return of the darkness that had plagued the queen this past year. Sadly, Catherine did not seem to realise it, riding high on the unexpected thrill of it all. Either Anne was confident about the forthcoming papal court, or she had another trick up her sleeve.

She looked thinner after surviving the sweat, as Thomasin did. But in Anne, the pronounced cheekbones and thinner neck gave her an air of vulnerability she had not previously had. Perhaps that was the reason for her mother's concern. She had been touched by death, had feared for her life, had prayed, wept and returned to the living to watch them feast and dance. And yet she seemed separate from them. There was more purpose in her dark eyes — a paradoxical fragility and certainty in her position.

"You're staring!" whispered Ellen. "Is it at Mr Danvers?"

Thomasin smiled, dragging her eyes away from Anne. Once upon a time she might have been unable to keep her gaze away from Rafe, but she had learned to overcome that impulse the hard way.

"I was just wondering what Anne Boleyn's next move might be. She looks so aloof today."

"Impossible to tell with her."

Ellen handed her plate of patties.

"Be careful with those," said Lady Mary on the other side. "They have some heating spice in them. Cinnamon, I think, and something else. Almost set my mouth on fire."

Undeterred, Thomasin took two and turned the flavour round on her tongue. Lady Mary was right; they were heavily spiced, but not unpleasantly so.

"So," began Lady Mary, looking to Maria Willoughby, who was seated opposite them with her daughter, Catherine, "what other news is there? The letter from Ludlow?"

Maria Willoughby turned her black Spanish eyes upon them. She had been with Queen Catherine all her life, since she was a girl in the hilly castles of Castile, and had journeyed with her over the sea to England as a young bride. Her loyalty was always first to her queen, but she was willing to share information with the women she trusted, who shared her desire for Catherine's happiness.

"It is hoped," she answered, "that the princess will come to court in a while, to be with her mother during the trial."

"That would make the queen very happy," replied Lady Mary, "but the king less so, I fear."

"She is awaiting his permission, yes. But it is only a daughter visiting her mother." Maria shrugged. "No father can refuse that, surely?"

"And the letter from the emperor?" risked Ellen. "Is there really an Imperial fleet poised to invade if the Pope rules in the king's favour?"

"Now that I cannot answer," Maria Willoughby replied with a smile, "but the Pope will not rule in the king's favour, when he has been asked not to by the emperor."

"Is that behind the queen's new confidence?"

"Of course. Now, let me eat, before it grows cold."

Thomasin looked down the hall to Queen Catherine, a middle-aged woman with grey hair and lines about her eyes, sparkling from head to toe in gold. Was she to be given new hope, or was her time truly over?

ELEVEN

The women waited in the draughty antechamber for Queen Catherine. The feast was over. The pageant had been cleared away and the dancers had vanished. It was late. Candlelight flickered wanly from two wax sticks on the table, but there was no fire here to take the chill from the autumn air. Guests and courtiers passed by the doorway, heading for their chambers. The hall was emptying quickly, but the queen was taking her time. No doubt, Thomasin guessed, she was tired and her feet were aching. Their task after undressing her would be to take turns rubbing ointment into her heavy soles. But why was she taking so long?

Lady Mary was peeping through the curtain that opened onto the hall.

"Oh, she is talking to the Suffolks still. We might be here all night."

"I will go to her," offered Maria Willoughby. "We do not all need to wait. Mary, you stay with me. The rest of you go back to her chambers; build up the fire and prepare her clothing, her ointments and her drink."

Stepping out into the corridor, Thomasin shivered. Then it struck her that this might be exactly the moment she needed to deliver Anne Boleyn's letter.

"I have an errand to run," she said quickly to Ellen. "Go ahead, I will join you shortly."

"Rafe?"

"No, I am done with him. It's an errand I promised to fulfil."

Ellen nodded, recalling Lady Boleyn's last words. "Do not forget you promised to write to your father, too, as soon as you arrived."

"I will do so tonight. Now go."

Thomasin turned back. Through the gap between the curtains, she could see the dais with Queen Catherine, King Henry and the Suffolks. Her view of the side tables was partially obscured, but she knew Anne Boleyn had not left yet. Perhaps she might call to her as she passed by, hand her the letter and be gone.

A fluttering sensation filled her belly. She was nervous about coming face to face again with Anne, nervous about doing something other than what she had been told. The words of her friend, the scholar Thomas More, returned to her, which he had spoken that spring at Windsor Castle, concerning the idea of free will. It was a concept that had deeply affected Thomasin, dwelling in her mind ever since. Taking one's own path in your hands, pursuing one's destiny, following one's desires. Depending on how you understood it, it could be either blasphemous or liberating. After all, it was what Cecilia had done last year, in her attempt to evade her arranged marriage, but that had turned out badly. Although, Thomasin considered, it had failed because William Hatton had betrayed her, not through any fault of Cecilia's. Had Hatton been a truer lover, they might have been married by now. Outcast at court, perhaps, for a while, but wedded according to their inclination. Had it only failed, after all, because Cecilia had chosen the wrong man?

Thomasin had been bold, waiting here, seizing the moment. She had stepped outside her prescribed path for the evening, in order to deliver the letter. As she stood, shivering in the cold antechamber, she knew she would be in trouble if she was found. Catherine would be displeased. And yet, she had no loyalty to the Boleyns, no motive to deliver the letter she now pulled out of her sleeve. She had made a promise, yes, but the risk to herself was greater than it was worth. So why was she standing here, peering through the curtain, tempting the queen's wrath?

If she was honest, she already knew. It was some foolish, lingering desire for excitement, for danger. Something inside that she had felt before, with Rafe, some urge to prove that she was truly alive, not an indentured servant, not a tethered falcon as Nico had hinted at Windsor. She needed to feel that she was able to influence her own destiny, not merely to follow a path.

The Duke and Duchess of Suffolk were approaching. Thomasin drew back from the curtain to avoid being seen, waiting until they passed by. Soon after, Sir Thomas Howard, the new arrival at court, came stalking along as if under a cloud. Lady Howard hurried behind him, reaching out to take his arm.

"Take your hand off me," Thomasin heard him bitterly reproach her as they passed the curtain. "I wonder that you try to reconcile after the way you saw fit to insult me on the way here."

"You spoke more harshly to me!" she retorted.

"Get away from me!" he replied, through gritted teeth, breaking away.

"May devils torment you all night," she cursed, hurrying away to the queen's rooms, before the hall fell silent.

Thomasin dared peep out again. Queen Catherine was still seated at the end, speaking with the round, bejewelled form of Bishop Mendoza, her compatriot and friend. Once, Thomasin had discovered him at Windsor, unable to move due to the pain in his feet. Perhaps the queen was keeping him company because of his condition.

Then, a familiar, bubbling laugh rang out. It might be, Thomasin realised, that Catherine was unwilling to leave before Anne. She was reasserting the protocol that placed her above her rival. No doubt Anne was aware of it, and was clinging on as long as she could. In which case, Thomasin might be waiting in the antechamber for a long time.

"Thomasin Marwood?"

A voice behind her made her jump. Spinning round, she saw the tall figure in the back doorway, dressed in his habitual black velvet, his dark hair falling over one eye. He had the look of mischief about his face that came from too much wine.

"Rafe!"

His appearance was unexpected. Her heart leapt at once, as it always did, but his presence complicated things. He opened his mouth as if to speak but she held up a hand, wishing that he would go away.

"Ssh, be quiet, do not speak my name!"

He came tiptoeing into the chamber, grinning as if he had agreed to participate in a game. "Why are you lurking down here so late, after all the ladies have gone to bed?"

"Why are you, I might ask?"

"I was on my way back, and I passed the door. You know, it's easier to go undetected if you close it behind you. But then you would have been in complete darkness, I suppose."

He crept forwards to the curtain, parting it slightly with one finger. As he leaned in close, she caught that heady scent of spice and masculinity. Her senses reeled with a sudden rush of desire.

"Who are you spying upon? The king, Lady Catherine, Anne? Who has sent you to spy, Thomasin? I thought that was my role."

"Hush!" His words annoyed her. She did not wish to be reminded that he was always the agent of the Boleyns, reporting everything back to Sir Thomas.

"Who, then? I don't mind. It is quite merry, you and I, hidden in here like this. Are you merry, Thomasin?"

"Not as much as you. I am here for one reason only. I have a letter to deliver."

"A love letter?" There was a laugh and a question in his words.

"No, it is from Lady Boleyn to her daughter. She gave it to me this morning at Hever."

"Oh." He straightened his shoulders. "Well, that is easily done. Here, give it to me."

"Why?"

"I will deliver it for you."

Thomasin hesitated. "I promised Lady Boleyn that I would put it in Anne's hands myself."

"What is the difference? What matters is that Anne will receive it. Why are you hiding if it's that simple?"

"Can't you tell? I do not wish Queen Catherine to see. Or to know about our stay at Hever. It would seem disloyal to the queen."

"But that was the result of an accident. It wasn't your fault. Anyone would have done the same."

"Perhaps. But the situation is delicate."

Rafe frowned, looking dejected. "Perhaps you do not trust me. After everything, I can hardly say I blame you."

"No," she replied, shutting down talk of the past, "it's not that. Not at all."

"Then what will you do?"

"Wait until she passes by, of course."

"And if she does not?"

"She must, sometime soon."

"What if Catherine leaves first?"

"I don't think she will."

Rafe thought for a moment. "I have an idea. Wait here." And he strode through the curtain before she had the chance to stop him.

Thomasin had little choice but to wait. She clasped her hands together, wondering if she had enough time to flee, or whether she should trust him.

Rafe soon returned. She could hear his voice, and that of Anne. It sent panic shooting through her. Within moments, the curtain was pulled aside and Rafe stepped inside the room. Anne followed, her head held high, her eyes wide with surprise. It had been months since they had seen each other close up, or spoken, and now the strain in Anne's face was more apparent.

Thomasin felt the indignity of meeting like this, wishing she had arranged it differently.

"Thomasin Marwood?" Anne Boleyn said suspiciously.

For a moment, Thomasin was struck dumb. But she told herself that at least this was an opportunity to deliver the letter, then she need have no more dealings with Anne. She reached inside her sleeve.

"Danvers told me that you were waiting for me, but I think he must have been mistaken, surely?" Anne laughed. "Because there is nothing that *you*, Mistress Marwood, could have to say to *me*."

Thomasin drew in her breath at Anne's rudeness. To add to her confusion, Queen Catherine paused in the doorway, seeing the parted curtains.

"Well?" Anne demanded, without seeing the queen behind her. "What is it you could have possibly wanted to say to me?"

Even Rafe blushed at her tone.

It was impossible to deliver the letter now. Thomasin had to think quickly.

"You are right," she said, loudly enough for Catherine to hear. "I am waiting here to accompany my Mistress to her chamber. If you would please excuse me."

"My apologies, my Lady," she heard Rafe say to Anne, "I must have misunderstood Mistress Marwood's situation."

Without waiting for an answer, Thomasin hurried away and dropped a curtsey before Queen Catherine. Maria Willoughby raised her eyes in a question, but there was no time to explain now — better to let her think there had been a miscommunication.

The queen smiled, still glowing from her earlier triumph. "Thank you for waiting, Mistress Marwood. I am well-appointed with caring ladies. Let us depart."

As she walked away, carrying Catherine's long gold train, Thomasin could feel Anne's eyes shooting daggers into her back. If Anne had not already loathed Thomasin, she surely did now.

The queen's chambers had been prepared for her bedtime routine by the time they had slowly climbed the stairs.

Catherine stood quietly as her ladies undressed her. The dazzling costume was being dismantled, piece by piece. Slippers and stockings, headdress and pins, mountains of skirts. The sequins glinted in the candlelight. Each item was folded and stored in the chest, revealing the tired, grey-haired queen in her simple white shift beneath it all.

"You were the centre of the hall; all eyes were upon you," said little Catherine Willoughby, dancing about the floor in delight.

"I was, wasn't I?" Queen Catherine smiled at the child's excitement.

"It was like you were the sun, bright as day." The little girl skipped around the chest, watching it fill with gold: sequins, fabric, ribbons.

"Come, Catherine," called her mother, "fetch the brush then get yourself ready for bed."

When her daughter had passed over the silver-handled brush, Maria Willoughby teased out the queen's long hair, thin and greying. She drew out the tangles, stroke by stroke until it lay soft and fine about her shoulders like silk. Thomasin and Ellen's job that evening was to smooth down the sheets on Catherine's bed, wiping away any remaining traces of the lavender that had been used to refresh it. Ellen gathered the pillows and plumped them up, while Lady Mary fetched her nightgown.

They had little warning when the king strode into the chamber. Henry had appeared silently, unannounced, breaching protocol by entering Catherine's private rooms without knocking. He was the king, Thomasin reminded herself, so technically these chambers were his and he might do as he pleased, but it was still intrusive, especially at such a late hour.

The women froze, dropping into curtseys at once. This did not bode well.

King Henry surveyed the scene. Thomasin could see his trimmed ginger beard with its grey flecks, his small blue eyes, his red, bullish throat. Once she had feared that this man might be her father, but she no longer felt that was a possibility.

"Madam," he said shortly, "that was quite a performance."

Thomasin was amazed. Had he come here to compliment Catherine? Had her intention to impress him yielded such immediate results?

"Thank you, my Lord." Queen Catherine raised her eyes.

"But it must not happen again. Given your position and age, it is not seemly for you to appear in such a role, or in any masque. Your appearances in public must be sombre and dignified, nothing else."

The women were all struck by a terrible realisation.

Thomasin willed that Catherine would not reply, would not try to argue her position.

"But my Lord, I have always…"

"Things have changed. It is far more suitable now that you take a more dignified position. Remember your years and the wrath of God. You are not to dance. Not in the hall, not in these chambers."

Everyone waited for her response, but Queen Catherine was quiet.

King Henry took her silence as acquiescence. "Good. That is understood. Then I shall bid you goodnight."

No one rose until he had left. The women exchanged glances, sensible of the blow that had just been inflicted.

Maria Willoughby went towards Catherine and helped her to her feet. "My Lady?"

But the rosy face had turned pale. The dancing, glittering Catherine had turned cold. "Maria, stay and help me into bed. The rest of you, go."

"Oh, my Lady," began Lady Mary, her sympathetic heart reaching out to Catherine.

"Go, I say, go!" There was steel in her tone.

Thomasin dared not wait. The women hurried out of the bedchamber into the anteroom, where the truckle beds were being pulled out.

"That was cruel," said Ellen, "such a cruel thing to say."

"He might have just kept his tongue," added Lady Mary. "The mistress is quite broken by it."

"She was so happy before. I have never seen her so happy."

Lady Mary nodded. "Where is his compassion for a woman he once loved? The woman who bore him so many children?"

The chamber door clicked. Thomasin turned to see Lady Howard being admitted by the guards. She looked at the gathered women quickly and read their mood.

"I passed the king. What has happened?"

Lady Mary frowned at her. "You would know if you had been here, attending to the queen."

At once, the pert little figure stiffened. "Countess, it is not your place to speak thus to a duchess."

But Lady Mary simply turned her back and began to unfold blankets.

Lady Howard went to the queen's closed door and rapped on it sharply. Maria Willoughby appeared, but solemnly shook her head, sending the woman away with a flushed face. Lady Howard turned back to the room, feeling the other women's eyes on her.

"The queen does not require me tonight," she announced, "so I will sleep in the Howard chambers and return in the morning."

Lady Mary stared down at her blankets. No one else spoke. Thomasin busied herself with the layout of the truckles.

The door closed.

Lady Mary stood up, flexed her back and breathed a sigh of relief. "I remember his first wife," she said. "Anne of York, daughter of King Edward IV. She was the sister to the king's long-dead mother, God rest her soul. Anne and I were born within a twelvemonth of each other and were girls together at court. She was so kind, so thoughtful, such a gracious lady. She never had a cross word to say to anyone."

"What happened to her?"

"It was a good match for him, but they were not happy. I could see it in her face. And like our dear queen, she suffered from the loss of many children. Four, if I recall, lost at birth or soon after."

"That is very sad."

"Her health was never good either. She died of some complaint in her mid-thirties. I was a chief mourner at her funeral. Sir Thomas married just over a year later. That one — " she nodded at the door after Lady Howard — "was only fifteen at the time of the wedding and had already been promised to someone else."

"Only fifteen?"

Thomasin was only eighteen herself, and the idea of having been married for the past three years filled her with horror.

"She was in love with the Duke of Westmorland, her father's ward, and it was long understood that they would be a match; then Sir Thomas Howard swept in and took a fancy to her."

"But that fancy has not lasted?" added Thomasin, thinking of what she had overheard in the hall.

"Long enough for her to bear five children, but it seems it did not prevent him taking a mistress."

"I can see why that would cause a rift between them," said Ellen.

"But it happens," said Lady Mary. "I am not saying it is right, but it does happen. Some men, well, that is what they do, and the wife can do little but turn a blind eye. Our queen learned that the hard way."

Thomasin flushed, thinking of her own mother's former closeness to the king.

"And it must be doubly hard," Lady Mary added, "if the mistress is younger than yourself, or bears a child."

"It must have been awful for the queen when the king had a son with Mary Boleyn."

Lady Mary nodded. "It was nine years ago. Catherine had just lost a child, for the final time, although none of us knew that then. It almost broke her when she learned of it. And Mary's child was a son, of course — that was the worst of it. He is nine now, little Henry. But come, we cannot stand around gossiping. We must get to bed."

Thomasin straightened the blankets on her bed and took one of the bolsters from the box, shaking it out for air. A stray feather floated up, then came to rest by her feet.

The letter from Lady Boleyn was still in her sleeve. Now, though, she felt disinclined to deliver it in person, and face another round of Anne's rudeness. Slipping it under her pillow, she resolved to find another way.

TWELVE

Incense hung heavy in the air. The painted walls of St Stephen's chapel rose up high on each side, topped with colourful stained-glass windows. Queen Catherine had been kneeling at the altar for almost an hour, her hands clasped in silent prayer. Behind her, the row of ladies remained as still as they could, knees numb and stiff, despite the layers of their dresses. No one dared speak of the events of yesterday evening, the bright, glorious pageant, followed by King Henry's cruelty. But they all knew it weighed heavily on the queen's heart. She had risen with solemn compliance, dressed in grey and come straight to chapel, a different woman. None of them had broken their fast yet, and Thomasin could feel the growls and contractions of her empty stomach.

Finally, Catherine rose slowly to her feet. Maria Willoughby and Lady Mary hurried forward to offer her an arm on each side. It took a while to get her up. The pain in her back had returned, and her legs were cramping and needed stretching out. The queen struggled to keep her dignity in such a holy place: the twirling, golden figure of Justice had been claimed by old age overnight. Once Catherine had passed them, the other women were free to rise, rubbing their knees and eyes.

"At last," whispered Ellen, as they processed outside into the mild sunshine. "I felt as if I was turning to stone in there."

They followed Catherine through the gardens and back into the palace. A dimly lit corridor led past antechambers towards the hall, but instead the queen turned away to a side chamber, where a table had been prepared for a meal. There were places enough for a dozen diners, and here, Bishop Mendoza, Bishop

Fisher and Thomas More were awaiting her arrival. Thomasin was delighted to see More, and Catherine did not prevent her from taking a seat at the humanist's side. The queen herself sat between Mendoza and Fisher at the head of the table. It was a relief, Thomasin thought, to see her among friends.

"Mistress Marwood, a pleasant surprise to see you again. I hear you have recently returned to court?"

Thomasin could not help but smile at More's warmth. He was old enough to be her father, grey-haired and lined, but the eminent scholar had always spoken to her as if she was his equal.

"Ellen and I returned yesterday. We have been in the country, after I had the sweat."

He looked at her in alarm. "The sweat? Goodness me, yes, I remember now. Well, I am glad to see you quite recovered, thanks be to God."

"I am well enough."

"And your parents?"

"They should be arriving in the city soon. Father has some legal business to assist my uncle with. They are all staying at Monk's Place again, but Father, at least, will definitely attend court."

"That is good news. I will be sure to catch him."

"And you?" Thomasin asked. "And your family?"

Thomasin had struck up a particular friendship with Margaret Roper, More's married daughter, who was as intelligent as her father, and as devout.

"We are well, thanks be to God, and all keeping busy, especially Margaret," he said with a twinkle in his eye. "Between the children and her latest translation, she has no idle time. I left her in Chelsea this morning, as Will has gone down to Canterbury to see about their estates there."

Thomasin had always thought Margaret's husband Will a solid, dependable, good sort of man. He took his duties seriously, but he lacked the playful wit of his wife and father-in-law.

"What is she translating?"

"Erasmus again. Currently his *Colloquies*, but I think it is a dry subject and she may turn to his divine works. I wish she would write a treaty of her own; she has many ideas about the nature of good works and salvation and expresses herself so eloquently, but she will only write them in poetry! What can I do?" He chuckled to himself.

"I have been thinking," Thomasin began, as bread and cuts of meat were set before them, "about the question of free will."

More scooped up a pat of butter with a spoon. "Go on."

"Since we discussed last year, it has fascinated me."

"What is free will, and what is God's grace? How far do we, as reformers, pursue the needs and ambitions of ourselves, and where does it conflict with the needs of society?"

Thomasin nodded. He had summed up her thoughts to the letter. "Well, yes."

"And what do you conclude?"

"I don't know if it's possible to reach a conclusion. How can we really know what is our will, and what was intended?"

She thought of last night. Her decision to wait for Anne Boleyn had felt like an act of will, but her aim had been thwarted. Was that the result of circumstances or some divine plan? Had Rafe's actions prevented her from presenting the letter for a reason? Perhaps to protect Catherine's feelings? She looked to the queen now. Catherine was eating little, her face a picture of sadness as she listened to Bishop Mendoza.

"Take the queen," Thomasin said, lowering her voice. "She believes it was God's plan for her to marry and reign. She was prepared for it from the age of three, educated and guided, dispatched to England and widowed. Then she overcame great obstacles and has been queen for nineteen years. But King Henry now sees their lack of surviving sons as a punishment from God, the same God. They can't both be right. Which one is following the true path, and which is exercising their will against it?"

More followed her eyes. Catherine had now turned to Bishop Fisher, who despite his sunken cheeks and grey appearance, had the sharpest wit of all the bishops at court.

"Perhaps there is no written plan," More suggested. "Perhaps both of them are following their own will and God is more distant than we think. What if He does not direct us in such an involved way, but is at one remove, allowing us to make our own choices?"

"Without intervening in any way?"

"Trusting us as His creatures to make the right decision."

"But what if we don't know what the right decision is? Or if there are many conflicting right decisions?"

"We must all live according to our consciences."

"As both King Henry and Queen Catherine are now doing, but there can be no resolution between their opposing views."

More nodded. "No, there can't, so as is always the case in conflict, each will dig their heels in, push and push until one side backs down. Usually the side with less power."

Catherine was staring into the middle of the table, listening as Fisher reeled off a swathe of information. Thomasin got the impression he was advising her about the legalities of her situation.

"Is there nothing she can do?"

"Beyond submit to his will? She can keep holding out in the hopes of a change in his affections, or some circumstance beyond their control."

"Like the sweat."

"That ship has sailed, I think," he replied.

Thomasin paused to eat, recalling how excited and happy Catherine had been yesterday afternoon.

"But I suspect you were not just thinking of the king and queen," said More astutely. "It is a question that affects all our lives. Is there a personal matter that makes you ponder the circumstances of free will?"

Thomasin blushed. As usual, her companion had seen through her query. "It is central to all our lives, as you say."

"You are happy serving the queen, despite her situation?"

"Indeed I am. Court can be a dangerous place, but I found that I missed it during my absence. I am grateful for the chance to serve my queen."

"Then I suppose it must be a matter of the heart that moves you. No," he said, raising a hand, "you are not obliged to confide in an old man, but if I may give general advice, the same tensions apply. Duty and desire. I believe we are happiest when we can make the two match. If we can make ourselves desire our duty, or else seek approval for our desires from those to whom we owe duty, that is the way to resolve the conflict."

Thomasin felt the wisdom of his words.

"Think about it," said More. "Marry the duty and the desire, and that is the path to happiness, both earthly and spiritual."

Happiness. Thomasin turned the word over in her mind. That was the other question. Last year she had believed Rafe was the man who could truly satisfy her, body and soul, heart and mind. Hadn't Queen Catherine started out with the same hopes, even though the match had been arranged for them? She had loved with all her heart, devoted herself to her husband, borne his children and lost them, been the best wife she could and overlooked his infidelities. Yet she had been pushed aside for a younger woman. The same was true of the Duke and Duchess of Norfolk.

But then, she thought, there were other examples. Her own parents, still committed despite all these years and differences, Charles Brandon and Mary Tudor, still very much in love, and More himself, whose wife Alice awaited his return home to Chelsea. No doubt some people went into marriage reluctantly, as Cecilia had almost done, but other than that, why did some marriages fail and others thrive?

Queen Catherine was rising to her feet now. The brief meal was over.

Seeing that she was about to depart, More took Thomasin by the hand. "Remember, my deep-thinking friend, this life is merely the prelude to that eternal life that comes after. I am always your counsellor, should you ever be in need of advice."

"Thank you," Thomasin replied, touched by his kindness and seeking some way to respond with equal warmth.

But Catherine was on the move. With Fisher at her side, she headed down the table and out into the corridor. Thomasin was bound to follow.

Catherine headed to the presence chamber, where King Henry was hearing petitions. The space was busy with people from all walks of life. Once in a while, they might approach the king in person and request his intervention on legal questions. Only one chair had been placed on the dais at the far end, as this was a matter for the king alone. King Henry was sitting in the centre, wrapped in furs, with Cardinal Wolsey at his side.

Thomasin was relieved, though, for the queen's sake, to see that none of the Boleyns were present.

The petitioners bowed as Catherine passed them, to take a chair set in an alcove beside the dais. Bishop Mendoza was awaiting her. A number of those waiting turned to the queen and diverted their course from the king, trying to voice their requests. Guards stepped in to limit their access, and they approached one at a time, on bended knee. From his raised seat, King Henry looked across and frowned.

"Thomasin?"

Thomasin turned to see her father and uncle standing before her.

Sir Richard gave his daughter a kiss on the cheek and Matthew Russell beamed to see his favourite niece again. He was tall, grey-haired and distinguished, with the same delicate skin and bone structure as his sister Elizabeth.

"Father, you reached London so soon?"

"Your departure stirred your mother to action. She could not bear that you were heading to court whilst she remained in the country, so she made us leave in the afternoon. We arrived at Monk's Place just after nightfall. She is in bed there, recovering, with Cecilia waiting upon her."

Thomasin smiled to think of her impatient sister having to take that role.

"Your journey was uneventful, then?" Sir Richard asked.

"Very smooth, with no trouble whatsoever. Mr Danvers proved a trustworthy chaperon."

Her father nodded, as if he did not wish to acknowledge this.

"It is a good thing you arrived when you did," said Sir Matthew to Sir Richard. "You see that pair by the second fireplace? I believe those are the Aston children, come to press their suit."

Thomasin turned to see her cousins by marriage. The first thing that struck her was how tall they both were, even the woman, who was taller than many of the men present. They were dressed plainly, in what appeared to be the best clothes they possessed, or had borrowed, although the styles were years out of date. They were standing close together, both dark in colouring, with sharp features, perhaps in their mid-twenties. Although they stood tall, and with dignity, they were ill at ease, and Thomasin could almost smell the fear coming off them. It reminded her of her first time at court.

"Should we go over and introduce ourselves?"

Her father and uncle looked at her in surprise.

"It can't hurt, can it? If we start on good terms, it might make them more amenable."

"It will not change the case one little bit," said Sir Matthew, "but we have the advantage here at court, so as you kindly suggest, we should go and do the gracious thing."

Thomasin followed them across the floor towards the Astons. Both turned at once as they sensed their approach, with startled eyes. The similarity between them was so striking that Thomasin realised at once that they were twins.

"Mr Aston, Miss Aston," began Sir Matthew, "I am Sir Matthew Russell, the counter-claimant in your case, and this is my brother-in-law Sir Richard Marwood and his daughter Thomasin."

The pair exchanged a glance that Thomasin found impossible to read.

"Russell?" said the gentleman. "We have heard your name."

It was a surprisingly abrupt reply that contained no greeting. Sir Matthew did not flinch.

"I hope you have secured suitable lodgings. If you require any assistance in this matter, or in general matters at court, you may come to me, at my house in Thames Street. I hope we can resolve this question as swiftly and painlessly as possible. After all, we are family."

It was a generous speech, given the circumstances. Thomasin felt sure that two friendless, illegitimate claimants, arriving at court for the first time, must be pleased to receive such a warm gesture from a man they might have feared meeting.

But Master Aston lifted his chin and spoke down to them. "The only assistance we require is for the king to approve our petition."

Sir Matthew refused to take affront. "Very well. Then I wish us all God speed in this case." He gave a brief nod, and they left the Astons in peace.

"Goodness, what a self-important fool," pronounced Sir Richard. "To throw back such generosity in your face. Him, a nobody, from nowhere. Let us hope he treats the king in the same manner, then this matter will be resolved today."

"It was strange," said Sir Matthew. "He looked afraid."

"You are too generous," corrected Sir Richard. "It was downright insolence, nothing more."

Thomasin looked back at the Astons, who had bent their similar heads together and were whispering animatedly. There was something that set them apart; their social difference, obviously, but also the very strong connection they shared. And that aloofness, whether it was fear or insolence, was disappointing, but it was also intriguing. Did Gilbert Aston really think he might stride into court and take exactly what he wanted, with no assistance?

"Borrowed robes, too," added Sir Richard. "We could at least have advised them there, had them over to dine."

"It is their choice," Sir Matthew replied. "We have done our duty; now we must let the law run its course."

Ellen was beckoning Thomasin.

"It looks like the queen requires my presence," Thomasin apologised to her father and uncle. "But we shall meet again soon."

"Is that Ellen?" asked Sir Matthew. "Is she well?"

"Well, but uncertain, I think, of her welcome with you."

"She is always welcome," he replied quickly. "Has the matter between her and Barnaby not been concluded?"

"It has not, to the best of our knowledge, and she has the most particular reason for wishing it to be."

"I will write to Barnaby, asking him to pursue the matter. She was a good daughter-in-law, a little too fond of ribbons, but she did not deserve the wrong he did her."

"Thank you," said Thomasin, "she will appreciate that."

Ellen was waving again, as Queen Catherine was rising to her feet, heading towards the king with Bishop Mendoza at her side.

"I must obey the summons. Oh, and More is here, I breakfasted with him just now. Until next time."

Catherine stood facing Henry. A humble man was on his knees before the king, cap in his hand, as he spoke of the difficulties experienced by his business. Catherine waited until he had finished and handed over his petition, with a final desperate plea.

Henry did not look at the scroll but passed it over to Wolsey, who stood at his side. "I will see that the matter gets looked at."

The man in grey hurried away, although there was immediately another, then another, moving forward to take his place.

Henry turned to Catherine. His narrowed eyes and thin lips indicated his barely concealed impatience.

"My good Lord," she began, "I wish to beg your gracious forbearance in a matter relating to a ship of Spanish sailors, who were forced to surrender at the port of Rye. Their captain has been corresponding with Bishop Mendoza to help retrieve the goods taken from them, or receive the equal amount in compensation."

Henry looked from her to Mendoza, amazed at their intrusion.

"My Lord?"

Henry was forced to answer civilly before the crowd. "Spaniards were in our waters, you say?"

"On legitimate business, trading with our ports."

"What reason did the customs give for the confiscation of goods?"

"No reason, my Lord, other than that they were Spanish."

"Why do they not come here and speak for themselves?"

"They are falsely imprisoned in the castle at Rye. Will you extend them your justice and mercy, as foreign traders in your realm, and permit the bishop to write under your authority, to redress these wrongs?"

It was a clear plea, with a simple request. The king was caught in public, bound to answer. Henry's mouth turned down at the corners. "I am surprised that you seek this role, Madam."

"Any petitioner may ask for assistance from the king."

"And there is a long line of them waiting. I am also surprised that you seek to champion the Spanish cause, when you are aware that relations between myself and the emperor are at a delicate stage. Have you forgotten your allegiance?"

Catherine was stunned. "I speak on behalf of a few sailors, my Lord, for the sake of justice. Their nationality and mine should not be significant."

"And yet you cite their Spanish identity as the reason for the incident. Perhaps your bishop could write to the emperor for assistance in the matter."

There was a stunned silence in the hall at Henry's lack of civility.

Catherine understood it was not wise to push the matter further while the king was in such a combative mood. She offered her arm to Mendoza, who took it, and together they walked from the hall.

"I will write to the customs men in Rye myself," Thomasin heard her tell the bishop.

THIRTEEN

Thomasin could hear her own breathing as she strained to listen. Along with Ellen and Lady Mary, she waited at attention in the antechamber. Early morning light filtered through the window and their limbs were heavy with sleep. The insistent knocking had woken them well before the appointed hour.

The door to the queen's chamber was firmly closed and a guard in livery stood before it. Leaning a little forwards, Thomasin could hear a flurry of movement from within: footsteps and voices, the flutter of linen or curtains. The unwanted visitor had stirred up a wasp's nest inside.

Suddenly, the door was flung open. Thomas Cromwell appeared, frowning in anger and passing quickly through the chamber. Catherine braced herself in the doorway after him, a robe thrown over her nightgown, her face like thunder.

"And do not think to return again, Thomas Cromwell, blacksmith's son from Putney! How dare you enter the bedchamber of the Queen of England!"

She closed the door firmly, and they heard the key turn in the lock, leaving Cromwell looking sheepish outside. He pulled his cloak over his rounded shoulders and turned to the women, displacing his irritation.

"You are the queen's ladies? You dress her and assist her at night, into and out of her bed?"

Thomasin could only look upon him with disdain, and Ellen seemed dumbstruck by his audacity. It was left to Lady Mary to mutter a monosyllabic acknowledgement.

"Have you, in recent months, seen any indication of her monthly courses? Any blood in her underclothes or sheets?"

The intimacy of the question sparked Thomasin's fury — and it had been asked by this coarse, intrusive man, who had turned up before the queen had risen and blundered his way into her private chamber. She might have been sleeping, or dressing, or at her prayers. It was a gross breach of court rules, but one which he would never have dreamed of committing, unless confident that he had Henry's backing to do so.

"Well?" he asked again.

To answer would have been an absolute betrayal of Queen Catherine.

"Speak up!" he demanded. "Have you seen any signs that she is still capable of bearing a child in the last year or more? It is of the utmost importance."

"You would be better asking the laundresses," replied Lady Mary in a steely voice. "We do not strip the beds."

Cromwell looked closely at her. "No. Think yourself too good for that, do you?"

But Lady Mary held her own. "It is not part of our role, as gentlewomen."

"Your role is to obey the king's orders."

"We are part of the queen's household and follow her instructions."

Thomasin was impressed by Lady Mary's bravery, but feared for her with this reply.

"Well," said Cromwell, with undisguised menace, "perhaps you will not be for much longer, once the king hears of this insolence."

"What greater insolence can there be, than forcing your way into a queen's bedchamber unbidden?"

Cromwell looked like he might explode, then he mastered himself. "We all have our orders, Madam."

He stalked from the chamber, and the women collapsed with relief.

Moments later, Baron Mountjoy came striding in through the door.

"What has happened? I passed Cromwell in the corridor."

"He came bursting in here, without warning," explained Lady Mary, "demanding to examine the queen's bedding and her linen. He was asking all manner of intrusive questions."

"On whose authority?"

"He gave none. But surely he would not have dared to act in such a way without the knowledge of the king?"

Thomasin had never seen Mountjoy angry before. He was always serene and dignified in his bearing, as befitted his station and years, no matter what challenge he was faced with. It was one of the reasons the queen valued him, besides his long years of service. Now his cheeks flushed scarlet with rage.

"He will not get away with this breach of etiquette — a man of such coarseness and brashness! Surely it is enough to secure his dismissal!"

He rapped sharply on Queen Catherine's door and was admitted. Inside, there followed an intense ten minutes of discussion, which drifted out into the antechamber in odd words of outrage, before Mountjoy left again and set about his mission of Cromwell's downfall.

A short while later, Catherine's door opened again and Lady Howard appeared.

"The queen is going riding. Quick, quick, ladies."

Thomasin and Ellen looked at each other in surprise, but obeyed the summons. Catherine was waiting, with perfect composure, to be dressed in her green checked riding habit.

"Riding?" whispered Thomasin, as she gathered up the dress. "Where can you ride at Westminster?"

Ellen shrugged.

"Aldgate pastures," supplied Lady Mary, her fingers fumbling to untie laces ending in silver aiglets. "It is not for us to question why."

Once they had dressed her, they walked solemnly after Catherine along the corridors and out to the inner gateway of the palace. One ostler held a horse for the queen and another for Lady Howard. A group of mounted guards in livery stood ready to accompany them, along the street and out into the fields that lay to the west of the city. It was hardly hunting grounds, thought Thomasin, or even especially pleasant to look at, but perhaps the queen wished for the air and exercise.

Catherine stopped. "This is not my usual horse. Where is Pipkin?"

The ostler looked uncomfortable. "This is a steady, reliable mare, who will do you good service."

"No doubt, but where is Pipkin?"

"That horse is already out this morning."

"Already out? Who would take out my horse?"

The poor man clearly did not wish to answer.

"Speak, I implore you. Who is riding my horse this morning?"

"The king has ridden out early to inspect the docks at St Katherine's."

Catherine frowned. "But the king is not riding Pipkin, is he?"

"No, my Lady."

"Then who is?"

"One of his party, I believe. I'm sorry, my Lady, those were my orders. If we had known of your intention to ride, I would have ensured that Pipkin was reserved for you."

Catherine coloured. The thought of Anne Boleyn riding her horse was an affront she had not imagined. "Tell me your name," she began. "Is it Walker?"

"Yes, my Lady."

Thomasin felt sorry for the poor man.

"Tell me, Walker, how many mares there are in the stables this morning that are suitable for riding?"

"Half a dozen, my Lady. This is the best of them all."

Catherine stroked the creature's silky flank.

"Her name is Chestnut," Walker added, nervously.

"Half a dozen. But my Pipkin was chosen. Was she requested specifically by name?"

Walker dropped his eyes. "I believe so, my Lady."

Catherine asked no more questions. She climbed the stone steps and allowed Thomasin and Ellen to assist her into the saddle, both legs at the side, arranging her skirts so that they hung becomingly. Without a word, she pulled on the reins and the little party rode away. The horses' hoofs clattered over the paved yard and through the outer gateway into the street.

Thomasin took a deep breath and turned back to the palace.

They were passing back through the old painted chamber, when an idea occurred to Thomasin. With both Catherine and Anne absent from the palace, this might be the perfect opportunity to rid herself of the troublesome letter she carried in her sleeve. If she could find Mary Boleyn, she might leave Lady Boleyn's words with Anne's sister, which was almost as good as Anne herself. Otherwise, she might have to wait a long time for another opportunity, and there was a chance that the contents of the letter might be urgent. Thomasin simply wanted to fulfil her promise and have no more to do with the Boleyns.

Telling Ellen that she would join her shortly, Thomasin hung back, wondering where, amid the vast palace, she might find Mary Boleyn. There was a chance she was not at court at all, but if Anne had already ridden over from Durham House, there was a chance Mary had come too.

She looked around at the painted chamber. Once an important room, with many colourful murals that gave it the name, it had been badly damaged by fire fifteen years earlier. A few of the former paintings remained, but much had been whitewashed over, to cover the smoke damage. Now embroidered hangings covered the walls and the king preferred to sleep in one of the newer, riverside chambers.

Thomasin retraced their steps through the larger White Hall, toying with the idea of entering the grounds again. Where might Mary Boleyn be?

Footsteps were approaching. A line of servants appeared, carrying items through the hall — cushions, goblets, bowls, books, a pair of shoes.

"Excuse me," Thomasin said to the last servant, a thin man in his middle teens. "Where might I seek the Boleyns in this palace? Where are their rooms?"

"They go where the king goes, Lady, or else on the first floor, to the east."

"Thank you."

She was heading for the main staircase, daring herself to climb up and seek out her adversaries, when another pair of figures crossed the hall before her. It was Nico Amato and another of Cromwell's men, young Ralph Sadler. Nico spotted her, made his excuses and sent Ralph Sadler on his way.

"Thomasin, what are you doing here, wandering about? Is aught amiss?"

"The queen is out riding. I had hoped to deliver a letter."

"To whom? Might I help you?"

"Thank you, you might guide me; I seek Mary Boleyn. I was told she might be in a first floor room."

"I don't know about that, but she has taken lately to walking in the cloister garden about this hour. Shall we?"

Thomasin followed Nico gratefully, through the twists and turns of the palace and out through an arched side door. It was a cloudy, mild day. To the side of the cloisters, the little garden was a haven of autumnal colours amid all the buildings. The leaves were turning from green to yellow, orange and red, before falling to make a brown carpet on the floor. A few gardeners were sweeping them up and pruning the heads off dead flowers, dropping them into their baskets. The setting put Thomasin at ease at once.

She sensed that Nico was looking at her.

"So you are a deliverer of letters, now?"

"Just this once. It is not an office I enjoy."

"Sometimes that is our lot, is it not? Due to our station in life, to perform those tasks our masters do not wish."

She looked at him sharply, and those golden, dancing eyes met hers. "How is your service with Cromwell working out, then?"

"I have that place of influence that I craved. It is important work and a steady position, so I will not complain. He has me copying letters, seeking out references and precedents, compiling lists. I am certainly kept busy."

"He was the most insolent he could be this morning, insisting upon entering the queen's chamber at an ungodly hour. And he was quite rude to her ladies, myself included."

"I am truly sorry for that." Nico made a small bow, his words and voice sincere. "The king has stepped up his search for evidence against his marriage, now that the Italian cardinal has almost arrived. He seeks to prove the queen incapable of further childbearing, and my master has no delicacy or scruples when it comes to getting results."

"Evidence or not, the case will go against her, will it not?"

"Even if it is a fair hearing, that is likely. The king will try to ensure the outcome he wants, but he has to weigh against the authority of the Pope. But your Lady should engage her good friends to speak for her. They should prepare their defences, if they have not already done so."

Thomasin nodded. The thought of the upcoming legal battle filled her with dread. "And King Henry will really go ahead with this?"

"He hopes to put the decision into another's hands, whilst professing his grief at the loss of his queen."

Thomasin shook her head.

They turned a corner on the path, their faces now bathed in warm, gentle sunlight.

"And what of you, Thomasin?" Nico asked, in his gentle, lilting way. "How do you fare?"

"Well enough, I suppose, given everything."

"You are not unhappy?"

"No, not unhappy."

"But not happy, I think, or not happy enough?"

Thomasin turned towards a patch of late roses, their drooping pink heads catching the light. There was still no sign of Mary Boleyn.

"Was that your father I saw yesterday?" Nico asked.

"Yes, he was here with my uncle. He has some legal business, a private matter about an inheritance."

"So what would make you happy, Thomasin? What is missing?"

His words struck a chord with her musings of the day before. What was happiness? Belonging, duty, youth, health, a sense of being useful and needed by the queen: all these things gave her a sense of satisfaction, but none of them quite amounted to happiness. It had been that intense spark of hope, of joy, when she had realised that Rafe desired her. That thrill when she first came to court. The excitement of being invited into Anne Boleyn's chambers. Or were those things just novelties? Had she confused lust and pleasure for happiness?

"Thomasin?" He put his hand lightly on her arm, drawing her out of her thoughts. "You know that I have always held you in the deepest regard. My feelings for you are unchanged."

She had not expected such a speech. The confusion must have shown in her face.

"Do not be alarmed," he said quickly. "I mean nothing dishonourable. I have been reflecting myself upon the state of happiness, of what it means. When we met at Windsor, I was too forward, carried away by our mission and Venetian manners."

She remembered the way he had flattered her, sought her out, stolen a kiss.

"Now I have been at the English court for a while, I can see how things are done here. Differently," he smiled, "to the way my hot Italian blood would dictate."

Thomasin could not help but smile a little at this.

"I was wondering," he continued, "now that my circumstances have changed, as has my understanding, whether you might permit me…"

Thomasin stopped abruptly on the path, frowning and wondering what was coming next. Another kiss? A proposition?

He turned to face her, his handsome face open. "Thomasin, would you give me your gracious permission to pay court to you, with only the most honourable intentions on my part? I wish for no secrets, only discretion, so that I might better get to know you and how I might serve you."

His words left her stunned. They sounded like something from one of the old French Romance tales, so formal and respectful, quite unlike anything she had encountered before at court.

Nico took her by the hand. "I want to do things right, Thomasin. Let me show you my pure intentions, and then you can make up your mind if you wish to accept me as a suitor."

His words were pleasing, respectful. His tone was melodic, his eyes enchanting. She recalled dancing with him at Windsor, the lithe rhythm of his body, the easy way he had led her through the steps, the curve of his back and thighs.

She smiled. It would not hurt to let him prove his worth to her. "Well, Nico Amato, I will give you the chance to show me how you Venetians woo."

He pressed her fingers to his lips. "You will not regret it, I promise. You may consider me your humble servant from this point forwards."

Then he stood up, at his full height again, his eyes just a little above hers. "Pleasant as this has been, and I must admit my heart is soaring at your graciousness, we have not yet achieved your purpose. We have not found Mary Boleyn. Come, let us go and search inside, as she proves not to be here."

As they turned back towards the palace, Ralph Sadler appeared in the doorway. He was a slight youth with a hungry look.

"Have you heard?" he asked Nico as they approached.

"Heard what?"

"Cardinal Campeggio has crossed the Channel and landed at Dover!"

"So, he is here at last," Nico replied. "This is when our real work begins."

"And you, Miss," said Ralph Sadler, turning to Thomasin, "I think you are lady-in-waiting to Queen Catherine? She's back already from her ride."

"Already? But she only just left. I'm sorry, I must leave you for now, Nico."

And Thomasin hurried back towards the palace entrance, with Anne Boleyn's letter still scratching in her sleeve and the Venetian's words still ringing in her ears.

FOURTEEN

Queen Catherine was sitting with her back to the door, facing an open window. Still dressed in her riding habit, she had pulled off her headdress and let out her long, greying hair, which hung in wisps down her back. Maria Willoughby was brushing it gently, with a big silver-handled brush that bore the Spanish coat of arms.

The women turned as Thomasin slipped through the door, as if expecting someone else, or resenting the intrusion on their privacy. They seemed relieved when they saw who it was. Ellen beckoned Thomasin over to stand beside her.

Catherine was holding herself with taut poise, chin high, spine rigid, her eyes fixed on the window panes. Outside was a view across the Thames, with its little craft heading back and forth to Lambeth, but the queen saw none of that. Even from the side, where Thomasin stood, it was clear that she was barely containing her emotions.

"What happened?" Thomasin whispered to Ellen.

"Apparently they encountered Henry."

"And…"

Ellen nodded. "And her. They were … close."

Thomasin looked back at Queen Catherine, who sniffed quietly, holding back a flood of tears. She wondered what her cousin might have meant by "close." Had they been riding side by side, or had Catherine witnessed the king and Anne touch or kiss? And, of course, to add further insult to injury, Anne would have been riding Catherine's horse. Thomasin would have to ask more questions when the opportunity arose.

"Here we are," said Lady Howard, emerging from the inner chamber, carrying a glass. "Spiced Spanish wine." She handed it to Catherine, who sipped gratefully. When she had drunk enough, the queen rose to her feet and turned to face her ladies. Her eyes were steely with resolve.

"This state of affairs cannot continue. I am calling a meeting of my most trusted intimates. You must summon them to attend me here, this afternoon: Bishop Mendoza, More and Fisher, and the Duke and Duchess of Suffolk, if they can come. Only those we can rely upon for their discretion. Go!"

Then Thomasin remembered. "My Lady?"

Catherine half turned her head.

"I have just come from the white hall, where I heard news that the Italian cardinal has crossed the Channel. He is at Dover as we speak."

Thomasin thought she saw the queen smile a little in response. Catherine drew in a deep breath and expelled it slowly.

"Campeggio is in England, at last. It must be a sign." She turned back to them. "Go, do my bidding. Tell those loyal to me to assemble here at four of the clock."

Thomasin hurried after Ellen down the corridor, until they were in a quiet corner.

"What happened on the ride?" she asked.

Ellen turned. "What happened to you? You said you were right behind me, then you disappeared. I had to cover for you. I said you felt unwell and needed fresh air."

"Oh, I am sorry. Thank you. I didn't plan to be so long."

"What happened? What secrets are you hiding?"

Thomasin sighed. "I had to deliver the letter. The one that Lady Boleyn gave me."

"You still have that?"

"She told me to give it directly to Anne, and I promised, but I have not had the chance. I don't want the queen to know that we stayed at Hever."

"No, I understand why."

"I still need an opportunity. I thought to deliver it to Mary Boleyn, but I could not find her either."

"Do you know what is in the letter?"

"No, it is sealed still. I would not read a sealed letter!"

"Of course not. I only wonder if it might be urgent. Perhaps put it into the hands of a servant?"

"I will have one more try. If that fails, then I shall do so. But what happened while the queen was on her ride?"

"Maria said that they came upon the king's party, who were hawking at Aldgate. The king was assisting Anne, with his arm about her waist, speaking into her ear. She says the queen gave a little cry, then turned her horse about and returned."

"That must have been humiliating for her."

"You saw her just now," added Ellen. "That was her composed. When she first came back, she wept a good deal."

"Did they see her?"

"We don't think so. They were quite engrossed in themselves."

"I am glad I was able to bring her tidings of the cardinal's arrival. That seemed to give her a little hope."

"And now this meeting?" Ellen looked up and down the corridor. "Shall we go and seek out the Duke of Suffolk?"

Charles Brandon's chambers were close to those of the king. Guards let them into the outer room, where his wife, Mary was reading from a leatherbound book. She looked up at their entrance, her arched eyebrows forming a question. Her cheeks were drawn from illness and her blue eyes had lines around them, but this could not conceal the great beauty that had once led her to be described by poets as the fairest woman in the land. Mary Tudor's red-gold hair and angelic face were similar to that of her brother in his youth. Thomasin could see the likeness of the king in her face, but there was also something softer there. She and Ellen curtseyed low.

Mary Tudor closed her book.

"My Lady," Ellen began.

"You are seeking my husband?" Her voice was low and languid.

"Yes, my Lady, but also yourself."

"Myself? You have business with me?" Mary Tudor looked closer. "You are Catherine's ladies, are you not?"

"We bring a message from her, for your Ladyship and the Duke of Suffolk."

"A message? Pray, do deliver it."

"Queen Catherine desires your company in her chambers this afternoon at four."

"Is she hosting a dinner?"

Ellen faltered. "A dinner?"

"It's more of a meeting, I believe," Thomasin jumped in. "Of her allies. The queen finds the current situation intolerable and wishes to find a solution."

"As do we all," echoed Mary Tudor. "Well, I shall certainly attend."

At that moment, the door behind them opened again and in strode Charles Brandon, in his riding boots and cloak. His arm was flung about a second figure, tall and broad. He was dressed in russet brown, and his head was thrown back in laughter at whatever the duke had just said.

Thomasin was taken by surprise to see Hugh Truegood again so soon, having left him behind at Raycroft just a few days before. She could sense Ellen's response — the sudden quickening of her pulse, the smile spreading shyly across her face.

"Well," beamed Brandon, "what have we here? How pleasant a reunion this is."

The women curtseyed, but Hugh came forward to take each by the hand.

"This is a pleasure indeed. I had not thought to see you both again so soon."

"Nor we you," replied Ellen, "although we have been expecting you."

"I have come up for the tournament tomorrow," Hugh explained. "I hope you will be able to attend."

"Of course they will!" Brandon replied. "The whole court will be in attendance."

"My Lord," said Mary Tudor, "the ladies have brought us an invitation to attend the queen at four this afternoon."

"For dinner?" Brandon beamed.

"For the pleasure of our company and our good counsel."

"Why, then, of course. Do tell the queen that we shall be most pleased to attend."

"We shall," smiled Thomasin. "And we shall now leave you in peace, as we have other messages to deliver."

"I will walk out with you, if I may," Hugh beamed, his eyes fixed upon Ellen.

"Remember, Sir Hugh, to seek an audience with Wolsey. Do not leave it much later."

"I won't, my Lord Suffolk. I thank you for your kindness."

But Hugh did not direct his gaze away from Ellen, nor did he see that Brandon was looking at him with concern. Only Thomasin saw the look that passed between husband and wife.

Thomasin bid farewell to the Suffolks, then followed the pair out into the corridor. Hugh had bent his head low to whisper to Ellen, whose face was turned up to his, so close that it might have led to a kiss. They were so absorbed in each other that Thomasin was struck by an idea.

"Ellen, I will go and try to deliver my letter again, and seek out Thomas More, if he is here."

"Are you sure?"

"Yes, of course. Why don't you try to find the bishops, as they are likely to be together?"

"Very well."

Thomasin leaned in and lowered her voice. "And I am sure you would wish for a little time with Hugh."

Her cousin blushed, mouthing her thanks.

Thomasin headed away to the chapel, where More had mentioned he intended to pray during his visit.

The richly painted St Stephen's Chapel protruded from the main palace site towards the river. Thomasin felt its solemnity at once, as she opened the door into darkness and the smell of candles and incense. Even though the sun had disappeared behind clouds, the light shone through a horseshoe of stained-glass windows encircling the altar.

All was quiet within. She peered through the dim light, hoping to catch a glimpse of More's rounded shoulders and bent head. Instead, to her surprise, she spotted Mary Boleyn herself, sitting close by the entrance, her eyes lifted in contemplation of the light. Finally, here was her chance to get rid of the troublesome letter.

"Mistress?"

Thomasin halted, unsure whether to address Mary by her family name of Boleyn or by her married name of Carey. The latter felt too uncomfortable to voice.

Mary Boleyn turned. It was strange to see that face again, the pale mask with pretty lines, the full mouth that both the king and her husband Will had kissed. She looked Thomasin up and down, but did not reply.

"May I speak with you, please?"

Still silent, Mary Boleyn rose majestically. She was still dressed in mourning, wearing a pale grey and black gown with a plain bonnet. Only the gold chain about her neck gave the slightest hint of colour or warmth.

"Outside."

Thomasin was surprised by her clipped tone; perhaps it was because Mary Boleyn did not wish to break the penitent air of the chapel, but something in her voice made Thomasin's stomach turn to knots. She followed her outside and round the corner into a little space of bushes and trees that led down to the river. There, Mary turned and faced her.

"I was offering prayers for the soul of my late husband."

Thomasin froze at the words.

"So your timing is a little inappropriate, but here I am. What can you want to say to me?"

A pair of defiant eyes stared at Thomasin. Mary Boleyn was not tall, but she was well built, and knew the power of her position and beauty.

"My apologies, my Lady, I would not have interrupted your prayers for anything."

"Well, you did," said Mary Boleyn sharply, "so let's have it."

Thomasin thought of the supper party she and Cecilia had attended last autumn. The laughter and the smiles, the flowing wine and conversation, the dancing. It had seemed then that like Anne, Mary was offering her friendship. Clearly that good will had now been withdrawn.

Thomasin reached into her sleeve and held out the letter. "I wish to deliver this to Anne. I hope you will be so good as to pass it to her, with my regards."

Mary Boleyn looked at the letter but did not take it. "That is my mother's hand."

"Yes, yes, it is. She entrusted it to me. I promised to hand it over to Anne in person, but it has been difficult to find the opportunity."

"How did you come by it?"

"My family were travelling to London, when the axle broke on our carriage, and amid heavy rain, your mother was kind enough to offer us shelter at Hever."

"You were at Hever?" Mary Boleyn looked at her long and hard.

"Yes, my Lady. By your mother's kind invitation. Otherwise we would never have intruded upon her privacy."

"You are Thomasin Marwood, are you not?"

The conversation did not seem promising. Thomasin lowered her arm. "Yes, I am. Daughter of Sir Richard of Eastwell, Suffolk."

"And sister of Cecilia. I remember you from last year."

Thomasin waited, still gripping the letter.

"And I hear that you were close to my husband before his passing."

Thomasin flushed hot at this unexpected turn, unaware that Mary Boleyn had known anything of it.

"We were friends, my Lady."

"Oh," Mary Boleyn laughed. "I think it was a little more than that, wasn't it?"

Thomasin made no reply, but steeled herself for the possibility of accusations. Will had always been insistent that the marriage was one of convenience and that Mary's affair with the king had prevented any real intimacy between them. No recriminations or apologies could bring him back, now, though.

"It's funny that you should speak of letters," Mary Boleyn continued. "You see, Will left behind an unposted letter when he died. It was handed to me, of course, as his wife."

Her words were painful. A last letter. Thomasin could not imagine what it contained, and it was a blow to her heart that she would never get to read it. Had it been anything like the one letter that reached her in Suffolk, it would have been full of protestations of love and plans for them to build a future together, for Will had hoped he would be able to part from Mary.

But then it struck her that Mary might be bluffing. There may be no letter after all. Thomasin should not give herself away. She held out Lady Boleyn's letter again.

"Would you be so kind as to hand this to your sister? I do not wish to leave it any later, in case the contents are significant."

Mary Boleyn did not even look at the letter. Thomasin noticed that she had not asked after her mother.

"You were close to him, weren't you?"

Thomasin looked away.

"There was some kind of understanding between you, I think? What did you expect would come of it? He was a married man."

Thomasin held out the letter one more time.

"No," said Mary Boleyn, finally, "pass on your letter yourself. Did you think I would run your errand for you?"

Cheeks burning, Thomasin stuffed the envelope back up her sleeve yet again, despairing of ever fulfilling her promise to deliver it.

"I hope there is nothing important in it. I am sorry for your mother."

"Then do as she requested. Pass it to Anne yourself. Or are you simply a coward?"

The pressure of those words bore down upon Thomasin, giving rise to an unpleasant mix of guilt and shame. Tears threatened, so she turned on her heel and walked away with all the dignity she could muster.

"Did you sleep with him?" Mary Boleyn snapped after her. "Am I to endure Will's bastard about the place?"

FIFTEEN

Queen Catherine's chamber was brightly lit with candles, although there were still a few hours of daylight left. A table bore jugs of red and white wine, and dishes of spiced cakes and wafers. The chairs had been scattered with gold and purple cushions embroidered with the joint arms of England and Spain, a legacy from the happy days of the royal marriage.

Catherine had placed herself in a central chair, having changed into a blue and yellow dress with gold embroidery, her hair under a pearl headdress. Her emotions had been brought under control, and she offered the room an expression of queenly determination.

Thomasin, Ellen, Lady Mary and Maria Willoughby were placed behind her, standing to attend to her needs, but also because the chairs were taken by her visitors. Each had obeyed the queen's summons, compelled by their loyalty.

Charles Brandon and Mary Tudor were by the hearth, with Lady Howard beside them, her face intent. Mountjoy stood by the doors, alert and ready to prevent any other admissions. Elsewhere, Bishop Mendoza and a group of other Spaniards were deep in conversation, whilst two new figures sat at the table: the white-haired Archbishop of Canterbury, William Warham, a trout-faced man well into his seventies, and the Bishop of London, Cuthbert Tunstall, a serious scholar in his fifties. Close by sat Thomas More and Bishop John Fisher, both well-known champions for the queen's cause.

Catherine had already welcomed her guests and launched her appeal for their assistance.

"In addition to my letter from the emperor," she was saying, "I have also heard from our good friend and scholar Juan Luis Vives, who is in Oxford, but considers my cause to be of the utmost urgency and will write to the king on my behalf."

"I am in constant correspondence with the emperor," said Mendoza, "and continue to press your case and beg for his Imperial assistance. He cannot allow this suffering to continue."

"And I will write to Erasmus," added More, "whom the king has long admired since childhood, and implore him to return to England, to guide him back to his senses."

"At least Cardinal Campeggio is in England now," Catherine continued. "Reports say that his progress is slow, and he suffers terribly from the gout and cannot put his feet in the stirrups or hold reins. Sir Francis Bryan is with him. A litter has been dispatched to carry him, and his arrival is anticipated shortly. It is slow, but it is progress, at least."

"Now that the cardinal has finally arrived," said Fisher, "it means that preparations can begin in earnest. No doubt Wolsey will keep the arrangements as secret as possible, but we must prepare ourselves to defend the royal marriage before the court — to build our arguments and write our speeches. Mine is almost complete. But we must go into this with hope, in the certainty that the queen's cause is right and true. So much favours our cause."

"We shall all be called as witnesses," explained Tunstall, looking round at the room. "And the court will be all ears, listening out for any advantage. We should be discreet among ourselves, and not speak or declare ourselves in public, so that the king does not know how much support there is for the queen, right until the point that we each are called. Surely the numbers must be overwhelmingly on her side, as are the entire

Catholic church, the Pope, the emperor, centuries of tradition and faith, almost three decades of habit, and our consciences before God."

Fisher was nodding. "The king will not be surprised by my defence, nor that of More, but the rest of you have that advantage. The sheer numbers alone might make him rethink. In these coming days, we should sound out the opinions of our clergy, question untried men and resolve any concerns that may arise in them. Vives is now in Oxford, as he writes to me, and between us we are searching all the texts we can, to find precedents and earlier rulings that will go in our favour."

"The king will have Cromwell and his team scouring the Bible," said More, "but I left my Margaret at home with Leviticus, and I warrant she has more brains than all of them."

Queen Catherine smiled gently. "This is a battle we can win. I am confident that God hears our prayers and that when the king, my husband, is faced with the legalities of the case, and the possible danger to his soul, he will see the error of his ways. But it will take preparation and care. You should definitely write your speeches now, those of you who will be called."

"We must be wary of his servants, too," added Mountjoy. "The king may be dissatisfied, but he wishes to do the right thing by the queen, and in the eyes of God. It is those ruthless men around him, Cromwell and Wolsey, who will talk him out of his duty. Men who have no scruples about barging their way in here, like the other day."

Eyes turned to him in surprise.

"Yes, Cromwell barged his way in here without an invitation and behaved with great indelicacy. I complained to Henry, and normally he would never have tolerated such a slight, but he merely shrugged it off, as it suited his purpose."

"Terrible behaviour," said Mary Tudor. "I will speak to my brother. A lady's privacy must be sacrosanct."

Thomasin's attention wandered. As the queen continued to speak, Nico crept back into her thoughts, and she turned over the words he had spoken earlier in the garden. There was a formality about his proposal, a formality that was full of respect and honour, unlike the raw, animal passion of Rafe, who had simply sought to satisfy his desires. She recalled Nico at Windsor. No one could dance like him, move with such elegance. It would not hurt to see how he would go about wooing her, and what offer he might make. To be courted by a Venetian could be very exciting.

Lady Howard was speaking. Thomasin was surprised to hear her expressing such determined views, but returned to the conversation.

"The situation has become so severe," she was saying, "due to the hold Anne Boleyn, my niece-in-law has over the king, almost like an enchantment. It is that hold upon him that we must weaken. The king is of a resolute and stubborn mind, but Anne herself might be the chink in his armour. We must consider her history in France, our natural enemies, her forwardness, which could cause awkwardness at court, and her reformist views."

"Do you think Henry will listen to reason? Agree to just walk away?" Catherine snapped. "That woman is as ruthless and ambitious as a man, and has set her sights upon him."

"So she is," agreed Lady Howard, "but another woman might not be. Listen, with apologies to those present, men are easily charmed by a pretty face. They barely see beyond that until they are hooked."

The room murmured, some in protest, others in agreement. Thomasin watched their reactions with surprise and a little amusement.

"We must be realistic about this. The king has been bewitched by young, vibrant woman, a novelty. Lacking the stamina and patience for longevity, he has been diverted. But this can work in our favour. It means that he can be diverted again. If we can find another young woman, vivacious and beautiful, more so than Anne, who can offer what she does, but is more pliant and amenable to our cause, then we might prevail. What matters is to break the spell she has over him."

There was silence for a moment.

"My goodness," said Charles Brandon, stroking his beard. "I think you might be right. We need to beat Anne at her own game. We need an Anne of our own."

"All she need do is be attractive and available. Distract Henry from Anne, wounding her pride and breaking her hold. Then, once the damage has been done, our Lady can simply withdraw — leave court or marry elsewhere."

"If she were to promise him a son," said Mary Tudor, thoughtfully, "but stop short of sharing his bed."

Lady Howard shrugged. "She would need to secure his interest in whatever way she could, using her feminine charm. It might be that she needs to do so, to make the break with Anne complete. Henry must see that another woman can give him what he requires."

"What would prevent him from returning to Anne afterwards?" asked More.

"Anne herself," said Lady Howard. "She has a character that, once scorned, will show her spite. We need do nothing. Her unpleasant side will be her undoing. Once she knows he has strayed, she will scold him and become intolerable: he will not wish to unite himself to such a woman. It will break her hold. What do you think, my Lady?"

The room turned towards Queen Catherine, who had sat at attention throughout, listening to the idea unfold.

"It is an interesting approach," she said at length. "If it were to happen, all would depend upon the choice of woman. It must be someone we can trust completely, who understands the intention of this move and seeks to serve us."

"I will say now," chimed in Mendoza, "that it can be none of your good ladies. They are too well known to the king and he will see their motives at once. It must be someone on the outside."

Thomasin felt some relief at this and smiled at Mendoza, who inclined his head in return.

"But that also lessens her motivation to assist us," said Catherine. "This woman cannot be too distanced from my cause, or else there is no reason for her to remain loyal. She shall be rewarded, of course; we shall arrange a good match for her once it is over. But she must be noble and willing, and although not completely new to the court, she must have knowledge of its ways and our cause."

"We are asking a good deal of this woman," said Mary Tudor. "It makes me a little uneasy on her behalf. She stands to risk her reputation for this cause, and lose her good name. She must understand what it is she does, for it is a very dangerous game and she runs the risk of making some powerful enemies. First she will anger Anne and her faction, and then, when she withdraws, she will enrage the king. She must be attractive enough, and yet have the edge over Anne, and be completely trustworthy."

Fisher looked around the room. "Does anyone know of such a woman?"

No one made a sound.

"Then that is our immediate task, if the queen is willing." He turned to Catherine.

"It is less than ideal. I do not like the subterfuge of it, nor the use of the woman; it feels wrong to me in many ways. And yet, knowing my husband as I do, this may be the only way to break the spell this Boleyn woman has over him. I give my consent, although we must tread carefully. Let nothing be done without my consultation."

After the others had left Catherine's chamber, Charles Brandon and Mary Tudor lingered. The queen called for more wine and a blanket to cover her legs. Thomasin and Ellen withdrew to the antechamber, where a pile of mending awaited them. One burgundy coloured dress needed the hem turning up, having become scuffed from use. Lady Mary sat with them, clicking her knitting needles, but Maria Willoughby took her little daughter away to read some improving works.

Lady Howard lingered between the rooms, poking her sharp nose into the main chamber, then back into the women's business.

"Can you not stitch faster than that?" she asked Ellen, looking over her work. "The dress will not be ready before the year's end otherwise."

Thomasin bristled at her words, and felt Ellen and Lady Mary do the same. But Ellen had a reply ready.

"Well, I can sew faster," she agreed, "but those stitches would be an untidy mess. I prefer to go slow and steady, to achieve a more reliable result. The queen is happy with my work."

"Happy enough to wait that long? She may wish to wear it."

"Is there a rush for the dress?" asked Lady Mary. "Because if so, you are most welcome to take over the sewing, if you can do the job both faster and better."

Lady Howard decided not to engage further, but turned away with a smirk to rejoin the queen.

"Did you see that?" Lady Mary muttered. "No answer, but she's as smug as a cat that got the cream."

"It is a pity that Gertrude needed replacing," Thomasin said.

"I agree, but poor Gertie had a longing for her children. They are so young and court is no place for them."

"Does the duchess not have children?" asked Ellen.

"Oh, she does," said Lady Mary, "five of them, born before things turned sour. Eldest one must be nine or ten, I think, left with a governess in Norfolk." She paused and listened. "Ssh." She pointed her needles towards the open door. The women turned their attention to the conversation within.

"This scheme worries me," Mary Tudor was saying. "There is potential for it to backfire and draw Anne even closer to my brother. If they sense that there is a plan, laid here, within these walls, they might string the woman along, play her to their advantage."

"The success of it must lie in Henry's vanity," said Charles Brandon. "Anne must sense his interest in the new woman. It will pique her jealousy and cause them to row. We must throw this woman in the king's path whenever possible, but you are right: Henry must not suspect her in the slightest."

"The Boleyn woman must be kept out of his way," said Queen Catherine, thoughtfully. "Perhaps, like I did at Greenwich, I could summon her to my chambers to wait upon me."

"That would be a duty you would not seek, sister," Mary Tudor said sympathetically, "and it may suggest a pattern to her. If every time she is summoned, this new woman appears with Henry, she may make the connection, and trace this back to us."

"Unless," said Lady Howard, entering their discussion, "she is not summoned by the queen but someone else of high rank."

"You think to suggest myself?" Mary Tudor's voice had an edge to it.

"Only if you wished it, my Lady."

"It is a task I do not wish for, but then none of us would wish for this situation. If it helps you, dear Catherine, I will devise some occasions to summon her."

"You might present it as a your wish to get to know her better," added Brandon.

"It would stick in my teeth, but I would do it."

"So, you don't think that any of your ladies would be suitable?" asked Lady Howard. "At least you could guarantee their trustworthiness."

"No," said Catherine quickly, to their relief. "As the bishop said before, it would be too close to home. Besides, I would never ask it of them."

"They are not suitable, either," added Mary Tudor. "Both are nice girls and I do not doubt for a moment that they would do anything you asked of them, but you are right not to. They do not have that hard edge, that worldliness. The woman we seek must have some slyness and cunning about her, and the ability to manipulate and captivate a man."

"Thank goodness for that!" Ellen mouthed in the antechamber, with a wry smile.

"No, we must keep our search going," Mary Tudor continued. "It may be that we are best served by an entirely new face. Play on the novelty. Perhaps we might invite someone suitable to court for the purpose."

"But the question remains as to who," sighed Catherine. "In the meantime, we must keep up our prayers and hope that the good Lord will bring the king back to his senses without the need for such action."

The silence that followed showed that the others did hold out much hope of this.

Tired of their talk, Catherine called for a servant and a boy came running to pick up the lute. Sweet, soothing chords reached Thomasin and Ellen through the door as they sewed.

"What do you think of this plan?" whispered Lady Mary, as her needles clicked and whirred.

Thomasin had been plying the dress hem with pins. "It all depends if it works, I suppose. But if it breaks the spell that Anne has over him, it may not necessarily propel the king back into the arms of the queen. He may well end up obsessing over this new affair. We might just be swapping one adversary for another."

"And what if she has aspirations of her own, this woman?" Ellen added. "What if she decides she likes the king's attention and plays us false, and takes the prize for herself?"

The others looked aghast.

Lady Mary broke the silence first. "She must be a false mistress, not a true one."

"But false to the king," said Ellen, "and true to us."

"This is a puzzle indeed," said Thomasin. "All this doubt and concern, and yet no woman has yet been mentioned by name, let alone asked."

"You are right," agreed Lady Mary. "We should wait and see who is chosen before we voice our fears. The choice alone may put our minds at ease."

Or the opposite, thought Thomasin.

"You girls are lucky to not be asked," Lady Mary continued, "being of the right age and beauty, and of good breeding! I am glad that you are not being drawn into this matter. I do not think your suitors would be pleased, either."

Thomasin laughed, but Ellen blushed deeply.

"Don't think I didn't notice you and young Truegood making eyes at each other," the older woman smiled. "In this very chamber, under the queen's nose. Do you have expectations of him?"

"I hope so," Ellen said coyly, "although it all depends upon my circumstances. I hope he will be patient."

"Still no progress on your divorce?"

"Barnaby has gone silent. After sending those unpleasant letters to Windsor, demanding that I return to him, I have heard nothing more."

"Uncle Matthew is looking into it," said Thomasin, "so with any luck it will happen soon."

"I hope so," Ellen looked wistful. "This waiting feels endless."

"And you, Thomasin?" asked Lady Mary. "Is there a suitor waiting for you somewhere?"

Nico's words came flooding back to her. The women seized upon her hesitation.

"Thomasin?" said Ellen, laying down her needle. "There is someone! Why have you not told me about this? Who is it?"

The desire to confide bubbled up within her, tempered only by her blushes.

"It may come to nothing, so I don't want to speak too soon, but…"

Ellen was too keen to know. "Who? Not Rafe Danvers?"

That name made Thomasin feel more sober. "Not him, no. Someone far nicer, a thoughtful, careful gentleman."

"Here at this court?" asked Lady Mary. "You have us intrigued."

"You can't guess?" Thomasin asked Ellen. But her cousin shook her head. "Well, I was asked by Nico Amato if he might pay court to me."

"The Venetian with the golden eyes? He is almost perfection! What a leg he has."

Thomasin blushed. "He is also considerate and kind. He was most respectful in his approach and wishes to do things the right way."

"Goodness," said Ellen, "a rarity indeed. I suppose you will marry him and go off to live in some castle in Venice and dress from head to toe in silver."

This hadn't even occurred to Thomasin. Nico was a foreigner, of course. Yet she had not considered the possibility that he might wish to leave England one day, and take her to live in a foreign country.

"No," she said softly, with hope. "I am sure he does not intend that."

"You would be lucky indeed to escape this place. Nico Amato. Well, I never!"

"I must lay eyes on this man," added Lady Mary. "Point him out to me when you can, and I will give him my blessing."

"No, no," Thomasin smiled. "It is very early still. Let me tread with caution and see how it goes."

"Caution," tutted Lady Mary. "You young people think you've got all the time in the world, then in the blink of an eye, you're married with five children."

"Not yet, not yet," Thomasin protested. "No, not yet."

SIXTEEN

Thomasin inhaled deeply. Smoke and candles, spices and meat. Currents of warm air enveloped the queen and her ladies as they headed down the steps and approached Westminster Hall. The corridor rang with the sound of footsteps as people from all over the palace made their way through to dinner. Darkness had not yet fallen but shadows were long in the corners, and servants were carrying long tapers, setting fire to the lanterns.

Queen Catherine had changed into a dress of deep marine blue, trimmed with white and silver. The skirts swept along the floor in a constant, rippling motion as she made her way down from her chambers. Lord Mountjoy led her by the hand and the pair seemed to glide ahead down the corridor. They had dressed her hair carefully, adding a diamond trim to the silver headdress and hood that hung behind, conscious of her need to appear as dignified as possible. The queen's mood was solemn after her meeting earlier. No doubt she was pondering the question at the heart of the plan, the identity of the false mistress, as she swept serenely past waiting courtiers and into the hall to take her seat.

King Henry was already positioned under the embroidered canopy. He was freshly shaven, his hair neatly trimmed and hidden under a broad flat cap set with jewels, yet his face looked pensive. He rose with dignity and offered Catherine a slight bow as she approached to take her seat. Thomasin noticed Bishops Fisher and Mendoza, seated on the left, with Wolsey and Cromwell on the right, although there was no sign of the Boleyn faction yet. She guessed that her father and uncle had returned to Monk's Place, on account of their absence. It was a quiet, routine dinner, no celebration, no masque, no feast. Thomasin sincerely hoped that it would remain that way.

As the women took their seats at the table set aside for them, Lady Howard cast her eyes along the length of the hall. Servers began to appear with dishes, while others walked about carrying ewers, filling the glasses with wine.

"My Lord is not present," said Lady Howard, her eyebrows twitching. "Nor his family. I wonder where they are tonight."

A steaming plate of pork in mustard and honey was placed between Thomasin and Ellen, followed by a flat tart with a pastry lattice case.

Thomasin's mouth watered at the sight of her favourite dish, but she handed the serving spoon to Ellen so that she might take her portion first.

"Do begin," said Lady Howard stiffly. "We don't need to wait for the latecomers, I suppose."

On her other side, Lady Mary took a knife to the tart. "Latecomers are latecomers. No one should have to delay their meal for them, no matter who they are."

"Not even the king?" Lady Howard retorted.

"The king is dining already," Lady Mary replied, nodding at the dais, where King Henry was reaching for slices of beef. "But if you are concerned for your husband, perhaps you should go and seek him out. Perhaps he has forgotten that the dinner hour is upon us."

"If he has, I am sure it is because he is about some important business."

Looking across, Thomasin saw that plates of food were being placed on the empty table that was usually occupied by the Boleyns. She looked again, then turned in surprise to Lady Howard, but the duchess kept her pert little face turned away.

Taking the spoon, Thomasin scooped up the tender cuts of meat before her. New plates of boiled chicken with lemons, and braised hare and leeks, were brought by the second round of servers, and soon Thomasin had lost interest in Lady Howard entirely.

"Such sweet lemons," smiled Ellen, "bottled, I suppose, and a hint of ginger."

Thomasin nodded, turning over the flavours on her tongue, grateful again for the fare that life at court could offer.

A group at the back were coming in late. Yet it wasn't the Boleyn faction, as Thomasin expected; these figures were hurrying respectfully, slipping into place at the side. She recognised Henry Norris, followed by Cromwell's men, Ralph Sadler, Nico and a few other young men, in haste, as if they had come from some serious matter. Nico caught her eye and flashed a smile, but the only seat left was one with his back to the hall.

"Still no sign of the Boleyns," whispered Ellen. "It is most unlike Anne to leave the king and queen in peace, like this."

Thomasin looked back up to the top of the hall. Under the glittering canopy, King Henry and Queen Catherine sat side by side, in solemn enjoyment of their meal. As they watched, the king looked up and gestured to the musicians, who began to play a gentle, melodic tune.

Letting her eyes travel down towards the players, Thomasin spotted two figures seated at the bottom table, nearest the door, the place reserved for newcomers, temporary visitors, and those of lower status. So the Astons were still here. Gilbert and Ursula sat side by side, eating stiffly and watching the hall with wide eyes.

"Those are the illegitimate cousins," Thomasin whispered to Ellen, "down at the end."

Ellen followed her gaze. "Goodness, they are a matching pair!"

"Twins, I believe."

"They don't seem very happy."

"Uncle approached them and offered them a welcome, but he, Gilbert, said the only assistance they needed was that of the king."

"Did they? How very brave of them. Perhaps they are regretting it now. It's not quite a tavern here, as they are used to."

Thomasin watched the pair, eating slowly and silently. Although they did not exchange words, they were perfectly in rhythm with each other.

Ursula was a prim, proper-looking young woman, Thomasin decided. She had a modest look about her, for someone in her situation, although it might have been the circumstances she found herself in. The brother, Gilbert, was bolder and outward-looking, and his face had a harder edge. Both were very dark-haired, although their skin was pale and their features regular enough. What they lacked, Thomasin realised, was animation. Those faces could become pleasant, even attractive, with a little warmth. Dared they even smile at each other? Surely, when they were alone, out of sight of the world, they softened?

"How long are they staying?" asked Ellen.

"I suppose until their business is concluded, however long that may be."

"And there is your Nico." Ellen gave her a nudge. "He's trying to catch your eye."

The Venetian smiled broadly at being acknowledged and nodded towards the exit, as if to hint that they might meet later.

"Oh, he will have to do better than that," sighed Ellen in disappointment. "Not at all romantic."

"But where is Hugh?" Thomasin asked, realising that she had not seen him yet.

"Over with the Suffolks. They seem to have taken him under their wing a little, which might be of use to us, I hope."

Charles Brandon was seated beside Hugh Truegood, who had paused his meal to listen intently to whatever the man was saying. Brandon seemed to be delivering a lecture of some seriousness, with the occasional anxious look from his wife. Then Mary Tudor looked up, directly at Thomasin, leaving her convinced that their conversation related to herself, or to Ellen. She pulled her gaze away with an uneasy sense of being single out. Ellen was chattering away to Maria Willoughby, and appeared not to have noticed. When Thomasin looked back a moment later, Mary Tudor was staring determinedly at her plate. Perhaps she had been mistaken, but still, that glance weighed heavily on her.

The meal was almost over when Thomas Howard appeared. It was impossible not to notice him stride towards the dais, brimming with anger. The sound in the hall dimmed briefly, and all eyes followed him, but he continued as if he were the only one there. Reaching the front, he leaned forward and spoke a word in the king's ear. Henry paused, frowned, then gave a curt nod. Howard seated himself alone at the empty Boleyn table and began to eat as if he was ravenous.

At once, Thomasin could sense Lady Howard beginning to twitch. She felt it was only a matter of time before the little duchess made her excuses and headed over to him. For all her professed dislike, and his rejection, she was irresistibly drawn to her husband. And sure enough, a minute later, she muttered something about it "looking bad" that he was alone and crossed the hall to sit with him. As Thomasin watched, he ignored her initial greeting, but answered directly, seeming cross, when she asked him a question.

"Do you really think we can trust her?" asked Thomasin.

"Who? The duchess?" Ellen shrugged. "I wish she had not been included in this plan. She seems to be driving it now, when I don't even feel confident in her loyalty."

"I thought the same," agreed Lady Mary. "What if she is only pretending that she dislikes her husband, and is passing on information as we speak?"

Thomasin looked to Catherine. "The queen seems to trust her. They have known each other a long time."

Lady Mary nodded. "I just feel uneasy about her, with that sharp tongue. She might truly hate the duke now, but what if they are reconciled? What then?"

And as they watched, Lady Howard smiled, as if her husband had said something amusing or pleasant.

The meal over, they stepped out into a gentle twilight that bathed the gardens in softness. The moon was visible above the twisted chimneys, a blotted white amid the watery clouds.

"Look, there," said Ellen, pointing towards the trees.

Nico was waiting in the shadows, keeping well back out of the light so that the queen wouldn't see him. Thomasin looked round, reassured by the sight of Queen Catherine's back disappearing ahead; she was deep in conversation with Bishop Fisher.

She half expected to see Hugh Truegood as well, waiting for Ellen, but there was no sign of his broad shoulders and bright shock of hair, so she concluded he must have left with the Suffolks.

"Go on," said Ellen, looking disappointed. "Just don't be too long."

Once Thomasin was alone, Nico approached her with his dazzling smile. He still wore his livery, but had removed the obligatory black cap. His hair had grown quickly since the spring and was starting to form dark curls. Coming forward to meet Thomasin, he swept up her hand and pressed it to his lips.

"My Lady, a few stolen moments with you; an unexpected pleasure."

She couldn't help but smile.

"Shall we walk a little way?"

"Very well, although I can't be long."

"Of course, you have your duties. I am content with a few moments of your time."

They walked round the flowerbed into an avenue of trees. There was a seasonal edge to the air — the mixture of dying blooms and falling leaves.

"Was the meal to your liking tonight, my Lady?"

"Oh yes, indeed," Thomasin began. "It was all so good. I have missed court food. Pork and mustard is my favourite dish, and…" She stopped and laughed. "But you will think me a terrible glutton."

"Not at all," he smiled. "I like a woman to enjoy her food. Back home in Venice, food is an art form, taken most seriously. We have the most delicious and plump partridges and woodpigeons, and the sweetest suckling pigs, along with fresh olives, ripe figs and sweet oranges, grown on our trees, and fish caught in our streams. All set amid the most beautiful landscape. You would love it there."

Thomasin could not deny the appeal of the image he presented. "Is Venice the place you still think of as home?" she asked cautiously, mindful of Ellen's words.

"Of course, I was born and raised there. It made me who I am."

"So London is not your home?"

"No more than it is yours, I think, my Lady. Where does your heart lie? In the countryside?"

"In Suffolk, yes. But I am no longer the girl who grew up there."

"I should think you are not." His eyes gleamed in the darkness. "Travel changes us, even a little way. Venice to England. Country to city. It is enough."

"And the court, too — it makes you see things differently."

"And so you can return home, but you can never go back."

Thomasin looked at him in surprise.

"You don't think?" he asked. "You can never visit your Suffolk again, as the girl you were. You can only visit it, and see it, as the new you, now. The you who knows other places, other experiences. It does not mean you won't return, or even live there again, but you will do so with new eyes and a new heart."

"And Venice?" she asked softly. "How long is it since you last saw it?"

"Six months now. But it is not the first time I have left. I have spent time in France and Spain. Venice is more like a mother, welcoming me when I return to visit."

Thomasin smiled. "What of your family?"

"There are so many of them. I am the eldest son of twelve, and I am sure my cousins run into the hundreds."

"Really? That's such a large family."

"It is indeed. But I'm closest to just a few. My mother, my eldest sister, you know."

"Don't they miss you?"

"Of course they do. And I them. Italian families are close."

"So will you be seeing them soon?"

Nico stopped and took both her hands in his. "Is this the reason for all the questions? You wish to know if I plan to leave you and return to Venice, before you get too involved with me?"

Thomasin shrugged. He had seen right through her. "I suppose."

"Well, believe me, I have no plans to return to Venice soon. I am happy with my position here, grateful to be at court. And now I have even more reason to stay."

"Would you want to make your life there, though, one day? Settle down?"

"In Venice? In the summer it stinks to high Heaven. My place is here now. I will be an honorary Englishman for as long as you wish it. I am not about to disappear. Is that what you wanted to hear?"

Thomasin blushed and tried to turn away, but Nico kept hold of her hands.

"But what of you? What guarantee do I have that you will not rush off to the rolling fields of Suffolk, and leave me here?"

"It's less than a day's ride away."

"That's more than an eternity if I was stuck here alone. Come, you must give me your word. Promise you will stay at court."

"I am here as long as the queen needs me."

"No, no, no." He pulled her a little closer. "You must make your promise to me, to stay for my sake."

"Well, I have no plans to leave."

"You know that is not the same thing at all. You are teasing me." His hand crept about her waist. "Promise me."

She felt a little reluctance, as if she was being cornered. It felt too soon to be making promises, but he had led the way, and he was so insistent.

"I promise."

"Not good enough. Promise me more."

"More? How can I promise you more than that?"

"With your lips," he breathed, his face close. "Give me your lips in promise."

Then, as she hesitated, he leaned forward and softly pressed his mouth against hers. He took her by surprise, but after a moment, she yielded and let him kiss her. It was different to that first, stolen kiss at Windsor; it was tender and gentle.

"There," he said, drawing back. "Now you can't leave me."

"What should I tell the queen when she asks why I have not returned to her service?" she asked. "Why I am living in Cromwell's quarters, and following you about like a shadow? I shall have to tell her I made you a promise."

Nico threw back his head and laughed. "Thomasin, I had not realised you are such a wit, but in truth, you do amuse me."

"But seriously," she added, changing tone. "I must return in a moment, as I will be needed."

"One more kiss, then," he said, bringing his mouth down on hers again. "So that I have something to keep me warm at night. And I shall see you again. Tomorrow, at the tournament?"

The tournament. Hugh had mentioned it, but Thomasin had forgotten. "Yes, of course. Are you taking part?"

"A humble man like me? No, no. I can sing and dance, and fight if I need to, but such displays are not for me." He smiled. "The king secretly knows I would outshine him."

"Well, good night, then."

"You must leave so soon? With nothing more?"

"I must. The queen will be needing me. What do you mean?"

"There is nothing else you wish to give Nico?"

He looked up at her slyly from under his long lashes, and she could see what he was driving at: a kiss, at least, or more, if she dared. But it was not the right moment, and she felt that it was wrong of him to have asked.

"I am already here on borrowed time."

Still he held her gaze, then stepping forward, pursed his lips at her. She felt obliged to meet them, but retreated quickly, after a mere peck.

"Now I must go."

Nico remained under the trees as she hurried away to the stairs.

"Good night," he called after her. "Good night, good night."

SEVENTEEN

Overnight the lists had been made ready in the new Palace Yard. The long, railed area where the competitors would perform was covered with a blanket of sand, and wooden stands had been erected ready for spectators. Buildings flanked them on all sides, with towers in the corner, and more faces thronged at the windows, watching as the court assembled below. It was still early, and there was a chill in the air, despite the autumn sunlight that played upon the ground.

Queen Catherine led the way to the royal enclosure, with the two duchesses and her ladies following. Her box had been hung with embroidered drapes on three sides, in rich reds, greens, and browns, depicting a hunting scene, with ladies on horseback chasing after a deer. There was a large, carved chair for the queen, covered in furs, and benches for Thomasin and the others, set with russet-coloured cushions. Behind them, braziers stood loaded with coals, waiting to be lit, should Catherine feel the cold. Servants hovered by a small table set with wine and pastries.

Thomasin watched as Catherine made her way to the front of the box, spread out her skirts and took her seat. The ever-attentive Mountjoy was already in position, to ensure all her needs were met. Then Mary Tudor and Lady Howard seated themselves on either side of her. Upon that signal, the rest of the ladies scrambled to find a spot with a good view of the action. Thomasin and Ellen eagerly looked out at the scene, where the crowd were gathering and horses trapped in bright colours and silver bells were being led up and down by their grooms. At both ends, bell-shaped tents housed the teams that were ready to compete; one black, red and yellow, decorated with heraldic beasts, the other green and white, with hands and hearts sewn into the design.

"What does that mean?" asked Ellen, nodding at the strange choice.

"It must be a hidden message," Thomasin guessed. "A declaration of love? Giving someone your heart and wishing to have their hand? In marriage, perhaps?"

"But who would make such a bold and personal declaration as that?"

For their answer, the tent flaps parted and out stepped the king, wearing partial armour, his hands on his hips as he surveyed the ground.

"There you have it," Thomasin whispered.

"But where is Anne? His message will be lost if she is not here to see it."

They scanned the crowds opposite. A mix of court faces and visitors stared back. Wolsey and Cromwell had a box together, where Nico and Ralph were deep in conversation. Another box contained bishops and a third held ambassadors, while others were filled with women in colourful dresses and men with feathers in their caps.

Eventually, Thomas Howard and Thomas Boleyn appeared in the box beside Cromwell, who shooed away Nico and Ralph. Then, Thomasin felt the uncomfortable sensation of Mary Boleyn arriving, remembering their nasty scene in the garden. However, there was no sign of Anne. Had she been present, she would have made a grand entrance, ensuring she was impossible to miss.

"Anne is definitely not here," Thomasin whispered to Ellen. "Not at dinner last night and not in the box, although her family are."

"Rafe is here too. Look at the far tent."

Thomasin couldn't help looking where her cousin directed, and seeing Rafe Danvers preparing himself to ride, with a squire tightening his saddle. Henry Norris was beside him, pulling on gloves. But she drew her eyes quickly away.

"They are all here but her. I wonder what it can mean?"

"Perhaps the king has already moved on. Perhaps the love message is for one other than Anne?"

"It can't be. Perhaps she is indisposed."

King Henry was preparing to ride. Beside him, Charles Brandon, Henry Norris and Hugh Truegood were selecting their lances. It struck Thomasin that if Anne was not present, that meant she could be back at the palace alone, unless she was at Durham House. That presented another obstacle for Thomasin to overcome, if she was to deliver Lady Boleyn's letter.

Then Thomasin saw something that gave her an unexpected start. At first she could not believe it, but she squinted and looked again at the array of faces. She put her hand out and touched her cousin's arm.

"Oh, but Ellen, look who has come, on the end."

In the far box sat a group of familiar figures. Her father was with Thomas More, nodding sagely as the scholar explained something. Her mother and sister had co-ordinated their ash-grey silk dresses and leaned forward to watch in excitement. There were scarlet touches to the sleeves, bodice and cuffs. Cecilia looked especially proud, her profile almost sculptural in its perfection. Thomasin was surprised to see them at court so soon, given her father's ill-concealed reluctance to bring them with him, but she knew just how persuasive the pair could be. No doubt they would meet up after the tournament.

A little way behind them was Uncle Matthew, and to Thomasin and Ellen's horror, next to him was a pale, portly figure with a sour expression. It was definitely Barnaby, Ellen's estranged husband.

Thomasin felt her cousin's intake of breath as her eyes found him.

"God in heaven, what on earth is he doing here?"

"I have no idea," said Thomasin. "Nothing was said of his attendance. But don't fear, he cannot approach you, and you are under the queen's protection. We will keep you apart."

"What if he asks to speak with me?"

"We shall warn the queen; she will allow you to remain out of sight, or else send him away."

"I can hardly bear the sight of him. I feel sick to think of him here." Her hands were trembling as she spoke.

"I wonder at Uncle Matthew and Father, agreeing to allow him to come to court."

"Perhaps they had little choice. What on earth can he want?"

"Unless it is to do with the inheritance case?"

Thomasin had also spotted the Astons at the other end of the terraces. "The hearing might be scheduled soon, and there is a lot of money at stake."

"I suppose so. I am tempted to feign illness and return to the room."

"You would not be feigning. He is enough to make anyone ill. At least he has the decency not to bring your sister with him."

"She lost the baby, did you know?" said Ellen softly.

"I am sorry for that, but it doesn't excuse their deception."

A trumpet sounded. Loud, long peals thrust through the air like arrows. The crowd fell silent. Charles Brandon and King Henry had mounted their horses and were ready to ride. In the centre of the lists, a small hoop hung above the ground, tied with colourful streamers. It swayed very slightly in the breeze. Setting his eyes upon it, Henry lowered his lance, kicked at his horse and began to charge. The horse's hoofs thundered down the lists, building momentum. As he approached the ring, he leaned in to direct the tip of his lance. The crowd followed his progress with bated breath as the distance closed. But the king's lance only glanced off the side of the hoop, sending it spinning away in a mass of colour, and the king rode disappointedly on, kicking his horse in frustration.

"Well, that won't please him," said Thomasin, although everyone broke into applause. "He will have wanted to be the first to take it. Let's see if Suffolk can do any better."

Brandon was ready, resplendent in red and gold, looking even more regal in the saddle than Henry. He waited until the crowd were quiet again, then lowered his visor and began to ride forwards. His pace started slower than the king's but increased until his lance was level with his shoulder, pointing forwards to where the ring dangled temptingly. The breeze stirred again. It looked at first as if Brandon was going to miss his mark, and Thomasin felt a sting of disappointment for him. At the last moment, though, he corrected his lance and speared the ring through the centre, lifting it in triumph, with the streamers flying. The audience went wild with applause.

"Look, he's impatient."

Thomasin had spotted King Henry, waiting at the side. It was Henry Norris's turn, but the king had told him to stand aside. Ushers rushed forward to reattach the ring as Brandon circled round.

King Henry awaited the signal, then was off again at once, the moment the lists were clear. But his energy was too intense, too tightly wound, and Thomasin could feel that he was not rightly placed for success. He rode furiously at the ring, but again it glanced off his lance and was left swinging in the air as the horse and king passed by. An awkward silence followed.

"Suffolk should not succeed again," whispered Ellen. "The king would be furious."

"You're right. If he must ride again, he should deliberately fail, and pass off his first success as a lucky strike. I'm sure he knows the king well enough."

But it was not Brandon who lined up to take the next ride, nor Norris. Hugh Truegood, in his tawny orange and black suit, made a dazzling figure on horseback, his ride also dressed in the same colours.

"It's Hugh," said Ellen, blushing.

"So it is," smiled Thomasin.

They watched Hugh lift his lance effortlessly to his shoulder and position it with ease. Like Brandon, he gave the impression of a man who was in command in the saddle. When he began to ride, all eyes were fixed upon him, as he headed towards the ring. His lance was positioned perfectly for success.

"He will take it for sure," beamed Ellen.

But at the last moment, the lance shivered slightly and Hugh carried on serenely past the ring.

"He did that on purpose," said Thomasin. "He wouldn't take it, so as not to upset the king."

"Yes," said Ellen, still smiling. "He did, didn't he?"

Over on the other side of the stands, Thomasin spotted that her mother and Cecilia had got to their feet and were applauding Hugh most enthusiastically.

King Henry was lining himself up to ride for a third time. The other riders waited at the sides, allowing the king to take their places in his quest for success. Thomasin glanced over at Catherine, but her eyes were set firmly ahead, as if she was oblivious to her husband's efforts. Anne still had not appeared to witness the display.

A groom adjusted the king's stirrups, while another slipped in and replaced the original ring.

"Is it me, or is that ring slightly larger than the one before?" asked Thomasin.

"I believe it is," nodded Ellen, "although the ribbons are there to try and disguise it. Surely a bigger target? He can't miss it now!"

Henry rode again. Head bent forward, shoulders hunched, squat in his saddle, he hurled towards the ring like the embodiment of anger. Thomasin felt herself curling up inside. If he did not take this ring on this strike, the embarrassment would be almost palpable. The crowd shifted with discomfort.

The king bore down upon the lists, lowering his lance, driving the tip through the air. The ring came closer, closer, and then finally, to everyone's relief, he pulled it clean away on the tip of his lance. A cheer went up, but no one celebrated more than Henry. Instead of returning the ring to a groom, he slowly rode back the length of the lists, proudly displaying his achievement.

"Now at least he is equal to Suffolk," Ellen whispered.

Rafe was to ride next. Dressed in the livery of the Boleyns, on a horse trapped in blue and silver, he lifted his lance in one hand and took the reins in his other. Thomasin had never seen him perform this way before. He wasn't skilled in the sense that Charles Brandon and Hugh Truegood were, after their chivalric training, but there was a connection between him and the animal, and a clear sense of mastery. The horse moved as if it was an extension of him.

When the ring was replaced, Thomasin noticed that the original, smaller circle was being used. She couldn't help wondering how well Rafe would fare with the challenge.

At the sound of the trumpet, he began to urge his horse forward, sleek and fast towards the ring. The hoofs clattered in rhythm, reverberating against the earth, thundering down as he neared the bright, streaming circle. Aiming his lance, Rafe strained forward in his saddle and pierced right through the centre, carrying the ring away with him. The crowd applauded and he made a short bow of triumph. Then he turned and rode back down the lists on the opposite side, so he had to pass the queen's box. He went slowly, displaying his success, looking into the faces of the people, and Thomasin had the sudden conviction that he was doing this for her benefit. As he approached her seat, she pulled her eyes away, turning her head so as to look at the royal tent, until he had passed by completely.

"That was rather obvious," commented Ellen.

"Oh, do you think so? You think he noticed?"

"He absolutely did, and looked most disappointed at it."

Thomasin felt guilty. "I hadn't meant to snub him, only not to acknowledge him. There's a difference."

"Of course there is. And you may have intended that, but I think he took it as a snub."

"Oh dear, I shall have to apologise, if the right moment arises."

"But you don't want to encourage him?"

"No, especially after Nico. But I don't want to hurt his feelings either."

"You are too nice, Thomasin. Consider whether he would have the same delicacy of feeling for you."

Thomasin shrugged. "We shall see. I need not think of him any more."

"Of course not," said Ellen. "You will be entirely free to think about your Venetian instead. Where is he, now I come to ask?"

"He's over with Cromwell," Thomasin replied at once, betraying her interest.

"He may have been, but he has gone now."

Thomasin looked over to see that Ellen was correct. Ralph Sadler stood beside Cromwell alone and Nico was nowhere to be seen.

"Never mind," said Ellen. "I am sure he will reappear at the feast."

The feast! Thomasin shuddered at the thought of Rafe, Cecilia, Barnaby, and the Astons all together in the same room. But would Anne Boleyn also show?

EIGHTEEN

The way back to the hall was littered with ribbons and ropes, gloves and brushes, debris of the tournament. Servants hurried about, picking up the pieces, while others raked over the sand. Queen Catherine sat serenely until the way was clear, then she rose to her feet, giving the signal to Mountjoy. Once she was on the move, her ladies rose to follow. As was fitting, Catherine was the first to leave the tiltyard, placing her feet carefully, her long skirts dragging a smooth trail through the sand. Thomasin felt all eyes turn to watch them as they headed back inside, before the crowd surged after them like a wave.

"Thomasin!"

They had barely set foot inside, when her mother's voice pierced her like a needle. It occurred to her to pretend she had not heard, or that she was busy, but Catherine was already seated and content; doubtless, Lady Elizabeth Marwood's calls would only have become louder and shriller had her daughter ignored them. Thomasin turned, putting on a smile.

"Mother, how unexpected."

Lady Elizabeth and Cecilia had somehow got to the front of the new arrivals.

"There you are! We saw you outside; you did not see us waving? Never mind. We are here now; we simply had to come."

"We have sat in Monk's Place long enough," added Cecilia, looking around. "And when we heard there was a tournament, we just had to come. Father said we would be tired by it all, but it's actually so exciting."

"You look well, Thomasin," her mother continued. "You must remember, though, not to eat too much at court. I saw you at Hever, quite gobbling your food. Mind your manners here, won't you? It's not attractive."

Thomasin sighed, deciding not to even reply.

"And make sure you brush out your hair at night. One hundred strokes."

"When would I ever have the time to do that?"

"Before you sleep, just as I used to when you were a child."

"More often I am brushing out the queen's hair, before we fall asleep exhausted."

Lady Elizabeth's nose wrinkled. "If you do not take care of your looks, do not complain to me when you lose them."

"Is the king here yet?" Cecilia was looking around.

Thomasin had never been so grateful to her sister for changing the subject.

"I imagine he is getting changed out of his armour."

Lady Elizabeth sniffed. "Should we go and greet the queen now? Is it still the done thing?"

Her question made Thomasin's blood boil. "Why would it not be?"

"Well, you know, because of how things stand."

"How things stand? How they stand is that my mistress is your queen and your gracious hostess today. She has not changed in her person or her merits, regardless of anyone else's inclinations."

"Well, I wasn't suggesting…"

"Of course you should give her the respect she deserves."

Cecilia moved forward as if heading towards Queen Catherine, but Lady Elizabeth put a warning hand on her arm. "Wait, we should be careful."

"Careful?" asked Thomasin. "Of what? Showing proper respect?"

"You never know who is watching. We don't want to be seen to be taking sides."

Thomasin felt her rage rising and fought to control it. She lowered her voice. "You can't mean this, Mother. You spent a night at Hever and suddenly you are of the Boleyns' faction?"

"It's not that," said Lady Elizabeth.

"Then what, exactly?"

"Caution, prudence, for the sake of Cecilia. For a new marriage."

"Well, unless you plan to marry her to a Boleyn, of which there are none available, your prudence is misplaced. Excuse me, I am busy, serving my queen."

Lady Elizabeth and Cecilia exchanged a glance, but Thomasin was already walking away.

"Your mother?" asked Ellen, as Thomasin took her place beside her cousin, who was serving the queen from the buffet.

"Yes, my mother," Thomasin replied in such an irate tone that Ellen looked up.

"Oh dear. Not already?"

"I'll tell you later."

Thomasin was mindful of the queen's proximity. Catherine was speaking with Bishops Tunstall and Fisher, with Mendoza already seated on a plump velvet cushion. The old man was looking tired and pained, and Thomasin remembered seeing him suffering in a similar way one evening at Windsor.

"Might I fetch you anything, Your Grace?"

Mendoza's face lit up at her kindness. "Thank you, a little wine. It's my legs again."

"Of course, one moment."

She poured out a large glass of wine and brought it back to him. As he reached up to take it, he spotted the pearl ring she wore upon her little finger.

"Ah, the queen's ring. I remember now." He smiled up at Thomasin. "You have served the good Lady well, I think, Mistress…?"

"Thomasin Marwood."

"Mistress Marwood." He lifted the cup to his lips. "I drink to your good health."

"Why, thank you. Can I bring you any more cushions? Are you comfortable?"

"Comfortable enough, my dear. Don't worry about me. God will ease my pains."

Suddenly Ellen was at Thomasin's elbow, her eyes and cheeks bright with alarm. "Barnaby is here, in the hall."

Looking round, Thomasin saw her father and Thomas More, followed by her uncle and his odious son. Ellen's estranged husband looked particularly pale and round, his skin sallow as if it had not seen the sun all summer.

"Oh, Ellen, this is intolerable. Why not say you have a headache and ask to retire? The queen does not need all of us here."

"I think I will do so. I have no desire to see him or speak with him. The very sight of him makes me feel ill."

"I can't imagine what they were thinking, bringing him here. Go, go now while he is still at a distance. Speak to Mountjoy; do not disturb the queen."

Ellen went to speak to the baron, and a moment later, Thomasin was relieved to see her leave the hall.

"Is she well?" asked Lady Mary, seeing Ellen go.

"Just a headache, I think. Does the queen require more food?"

"Some of the sweet sauce, I think — you know, the one she likes? There seems to be none on the table."

"I will ask for it."

Thomasin headed across the room, to make her request of a servant. As she turned back, Nico was approaching, dressed smartly in green and gold trim, with a crisp white shirt collar and a jaunty cap, quite exotically Venetian amid the greys, blues and browns of the court. At once, she felt a little bad for having hurried away from him the last time they had met.

He made a shallow bow. "My Lady, you are looking lovely as ever."

Thomasin curtseyed and smiled. "You enjoyed the tournament?"

"The little I saw of it, before my master dispatched me on errands!"

"Oh dear, I am sorry. Anything important?"

"Well…" He stepped closer, took her gently by the elbow and steered her towards a corner. "I should not say it aloud, but Cromwell sent me about the king's business."

"Oh?"

"The king and his paramour have quarrelled. Yes, Anne Boleyn. She is refusing to attend, even though this tournament was devised for her entertainment. I had to dispatch a messenger to demand her presence, but still she has not come. The king is in a fury."

"That would explain much," Thomasin nodded. "She was not present at dinner yesterday, and the king was most distracted throughout the tilting."

"It is not yet resolved," said Nico, turning to see King Henry enter the hall, which erupted in applause. "She remains defiant at Durham House. Be discreet."

Nico took advantage of the disruption by seizing Thomasin's hand and pressing it to his lips. "I hope I shall see you later?"

"Yes, indeed," she said, smiling, but her mind was already turning this news over. If the king and Anne had quarrelled, and Anne was refusing to come to court, what better time to launch the queen's new plan to divert him?

She turned to find Cecilia coming towards her again, her eyebrows arched.

"So, who was that very fine young man who kissed your hand?"

"That is not your business," Thomasin snapped, annoyed at having been observed with Nico. "Where has Mother gone? Shouldn't you be following in her shadow?"

Cecilia ignored the insult. "Mother is waiting to greet the king, with all the others, but I thought perhaps you could introduce me to some people, which would be far more interesting."

"It would be my pleasure," Thomasin replied with a smooth smile. "You can meet the queen's ladies-in-waiting, busy about their duties, or an ancient bishop with aching legs. Take your pick."

"You are quarrelsome today. You know that I mean gentlemen, like the one who just left."

Some raw emotion reared up in Thomasin. Suddenly she felt able to speak openly about what they had been dancing around. "Is that your purpose in coming to court? To chase men? To make a spectacle of yourself again? Have you learned nothing?"

The ice-blue eyes hardened. "I had thought to seek an ally in you, sister. That perhaps after all this time you might have grown up a little, that we might even be on the same side. But I see you are the same quarrelsome little girl. I wonder how the queen tolerates you."

"Oh, she tolerates me well enough," Thomasin snapped at once, holding up her hand with the pearl ring. "This is the mark of her favour."

She turned and walked away from her sister, seething with anger. It was the first time they had clashed so bitterly since they were children, and it was worse for having been unexpected, and in public.

Queen Catherine was retelling an anecdote about her daughter dancing for the ambassadors when she was a child. When Thomasin looked back to see if Cecilia was still there, her sister had already gone, having spotted Hugh Truegood among the young men. She sauntered over to shower him with flattery.

"Who was that young woman you were speaking with?"

Thomasin turned to find Lady Howard beside her, all wide-eyed and sharp-nosed. Her heart sank.

"That was my sister."

"Your sister? I would not have guessed. Her colouring is so different from yours."

"She takes after our mother."

"She is visiting court? Unmarried? How old is she?"

Suddenly, Thomasin realised the duchess's motivation. "No, my Lady, do not think of her in that way."

"It what way? I merely enquired."

"She is not suitable."

Lady Howard leaned in. "Not at the moment, no, but after she has been schooled, perhaps. And while Anne is absent from court, what better time?"

Thomasin decided to play dumb, annoyed that Lady Howard had thought the same as her. "Anne is absent? I thought I had not seen her. Why would that be?"

"She says she is indisposed, at Durham House, but my husband says otherwise. She has quarrelled with the king and last night, she tried to forbid her whole family to attend dinner."

So that had been the reason why Thomas Howard had arrived late and alone.

"My husband is not the kind of man to take instructions, especially not from that headstrong girl."

Thomasin thought it better not to reply.

"What is her name? Your sister?"

Again, she kept silent.

"Oh, don't be so ridiculous, girl. I can simply ask someone else."

"Her name is Cecilia."

"Unwed?"

"Yes, unwed, but please, my lady. Leave her be. She is already known to the king, so any deception would not work."

Lady Howard twisted her lips into an unpleasant smile and drifted away in the direction of the king.

The hall was almost full now and the plates of food were rapidly being cleared. Heat was mounting from the candles and all the bodies, and Queen Catherine appeared to be tiring. It had been a long day, with wrestling and swordsmanship after the jousting, and darkness would be falling soon. King Henry was striding about, hands on hips, beaming with pride in his performance, and drenched in compliments. It was strange, thought Thomasin, that one man could be the centre of the world like this, the sun and moon, with the powers of happiness, life and death within his gift. What would a court be like, where the king was quiet, modest, reserved? Would such a man even remain king for long?

A movement drew her gaze. On the other side of the room, her mother and father were standing together, with Sir Matthew and Barnaby. Her father was beckoning, as if he wished Thomasin to join them. She had no desire for her mother's company, and still less to come close to the odious Barnaby, so with a nod of her head she indicated to the left, where an alcove would shelter them. Her father understood at once, and made his way across the hall.

"Thomasin, I am pleased to see you," Sir Richard sighed, apologetically. "I had no choice but to bring them, after the terrible fuss they made at being left out. You have already bid your mother greeting?"

"I have indeed, Father."

"And I must explain, and apologise, about your awful cousin. Matthew wrote to him a while ago, asking about Ellen's cause, and never had a reply, until he turned up at Monk's Place yesterday out of the blue. You can imagine our surprise."

"Ellen was most disconcerted to see him. She has made her apologies and left."

"Poor Ellen. We did our best to dissuade him from attending, but he would not listen. The case is being heard tomorrow, and he wished to see the Astons in advance. Are they here? I will use them to distract him from the company."

Thomasin could not wish that fate upon anyone, even the aloof Aston siblings. "Actually, I have not seen them enter the hall. They may have returned to their lodgings after the tournament ended."

"Well, it is probably for the best. He will see them tomorrow."

"He will."

"I was having a pleasant conversation with More earlier. He is full of praise for you."

There was a stir at the far end: voices, banging, excitement. Thomasin and her father turned to see what all the commotion was about. The outer doors stood open to reveal an older gentleman in travelling clothes, dusty and tired from the road. His hair was white and he had a foreign look about him, gazing around the room in surprise.

Even from afar, King Henry paused his conversation to inspect the new arrival. His voice boomed down the hall.

"And you, Sir, who might you be?"

The man bowed low and rose slowly. "Do I have the honour of addressing the King of England?"

"You do. Speak your mind."

"My good Lord, my name is Campeggio…"

A gasp burst out from the crowd, followed by a cheer. The long-awaited cardinal had finally arrived to investigate the king's marriage. Thomasin looked around at Catherine, but she was staring at him with a frown upon her face.

The man held up his hand and waited for the noise to die down.

"That is a most generous welcome, but do not mistake me for my brother. I am Antonio Campeggio and my brother Lorenzo, the cardinal, lies tonight at Canterbury. He bade me ride ahead to inform you of his progress, as he suffers greatly from gout in his feet and must travel slowly. He sends his best wishes and hopes to be with you soon."

"Why, this is still good news," said King Henry. "Canterbury is not so far; surely he will be here within days. Bring more wine — this calls for celebration. Soon we shall uncover the truth of this great matter."

In dignified silence, Queen Catherine rose to her feet. The cardinal's approach was good news indeed, but Henry's blatant delight at the prospect of his separation from her stung her deeply. Thomasin nudged Lady Mary, who was still picking the spices out of a dish of custard, and they hurried out of the hall after her.

NINETEEN

"The queen will be missing you soon, I think," said Nico, shooting a look back to the palace.

They had walked through the gardens down to the river, where the boats butted up against the wet steps. Other craft hurried back and forth, battling upstream past Lambeth to Chelsea or being carried with the current towards the London Bridge rapids.

Thomasin doubted her absence would make a difference. Queen Catherine had Lady Howard buzzing in her ear about the dresses and jewels that they would prepare for her to wear at the cardinals' court, so she had just waved her hand at Thomasin's request to take a walk.

"Do you wish to turn back?" Nico asked, noticing her thoughtfulness.

"No, we can stay a little longer. It's pleasant to be out of doors."

"My thoughts exactly," he replied. "The fresh air, the view, being out in nature; these are all things that I long to experience more of. We used to visit the countryside around Venice, near Padua and Treviso. I had cousins with vineyards and we'd be outdoors all day long, from sunrise to sunset."

"You must miss that."

"I do. It's a good, honest way to earn your bread, but I always wanted something more. To travel to foreign places and witness the lives of great men."

"And here you are."

"I always had a burning ambition," he said, his face lighting up, "since I was small. Once, I saw the emperor riding through the city, and I used to sit and watch the ships arriving from all over the world. It made me long to travel and see other places, to serve great men."

He was looking fresh and crisp that morning. Thomasin thought that he might have just jumped up from his bed, raked his fingers through his curls and put a cap on top, but somehow he always managed to look beautiful and effortless. It was his neat jawline and long eyelashes, his curved lips and his perfect, glowing skin. Like a classical sculpture. Thomasin both adored and envied his good looks.

"Does your master keep you busy?"

"Cromwell? Always. But he has travelled into Kent this morning, to greet Campeggio, so what is your English saying … while the cat is away, the mice will play."

Thomasin smiled.

"And after I have played, I will have to copy out his letters."

Thomasin's eyes were focused on a small boat, a river ferry, that was approaching the steps. As they watched, it drew alongside the palace quay, and she recognised the Astons climbing out. They looked a little shaky after their journey on the choppy waves and took a moment to breathe. Ursula straightened her headdress and skirts while Gilbert paid the ferryman.

"These are my distant cousins, through marriage," Thomasin explained, watching them approach. "They come to have their case heard today."

The pair drew closer. The garden paths were laid out in geometric shapes, so it would be impossible for them not to pass her.

"Good morning," Thomasin said, as they drew near.

Gilbert looked at her sharply, as if surprised. His sister looked frightened.

"I'm Thomasin Marwood, niece of Sir Matthew Russell, so we are related through marriage."

As soon as they heard the name Russell, the pair turned inward.

"And this is my friend, Nico Amato, secretary to Lord Cromwell."

At Cromwell's name, though, Gilbert's demeanour changed. Ignoring Thomasin, he turned to the Venetian. "You serve Cromwell? Is he here today? Might you take us to him?"

Nico raised his eyebrows at this presumption. "I am at the service of Mistress Marwood."

Realising his mistake, Gilbert turned to Thomasin. "My apologies, a very good day to you, cousin."

"I found my first time at court daunting," Thomasin replied generously, trying to make eye contact with Ursula, "so I am happy to help, to show you around, regardless of the outcome of the case."

A slight smile touched the young woman's lips, lifting her expression at once. "That's nice — isn't it, Gilbert?"

Her brother did not answer her, instead turning back to Nico. "Is Cromwell in his rooms today?"

"Sadly he is from court."

"Not here at all?"

Nico shook his head. "Not at all."

"When do you expect him back?"

"Whenever he chooses to return. I am merely his secretary."

Gilbert gave a curt nod and took hold of his sister's arm. "Very well. Good day."

He led Ursula away before she had a chance to speak further. She looked back once, over her shoulder, and Thomasin thought she glimpsed a little hope in her eyes, before they disappeared inside.

"What an intolerable man. Such rudeness," said Nico, once they were out of sight.

"They were raised in a tavern, I think, but there is more to it. I think Gilbert takes the stigma of illegitimacy very hard."

"I can see that. Unfortunately, it is no way to get on at court. You are good to extend the hand of friendship to them."

"I didn't want them to feel that everyone is against them. This court case is likely to go against them, although in truth I hope it does not. It may be a harsh lesson. The sister doesn't deserve it."

Nico nodded. "You have a soft heart, I think. Your kindness is one of the things I admire about you, besides your beauty."

Thomasin blushed at the unexpected compliment.

"Now," said Nico, "shall we walk down and sit in the arbour a little, before we have to return to our duties?"

Thomasin smiled and put her hand in his. The arbour was secluded by large, overhanging shrubs; no doubt he had suggested it to give them some privacy, in order to steal a kiss or two. This time, she found she did not mind in the least.

Later, as Thomasin crept into the queen's chambers, she was dizzy with Nico's sweet words in her ears and the warmth of his mouth on hers. Ellen came hurrying forward to meet her, with a face full of concern.

"You have been gone a long time."

"Was I missed?"

"No, it's not that. Come and see."

Thomasin hurried after her through the outer chamber into the next. There, Cecilia was standing in a dress made of scarlet and cream silk, adorned with gold embroidery and aiglets. A gold and white headdress was perched upon her tumbling hair. Lady Howard was fussing about her, with two of her friends, while Queen Catherine stood looking on, flanked by Charles Brandon and Mary Tudor.

"This has been going on all morning," whispered Ellen.

Cecilia looked down at them disdainfully. "Do you like this dress, sister? The red and cream, or should I go with the blue? Which one would the king like?"

"This red one definitely suits you better," said Lady Howard, ignoring Thomasin entirely. "The colours make your skin warmer, and it's more flattering about the waist. We want to show off your figure, not conceal it."

"Whatever you think, Duchess," Cecilia simpered.

"And you are sure about your purpose?" Lady Howard continued. "About how you must behave?"

"I think so, if you are certain."

"You should not be too obvious, nor exercise your charms in the sight of the Boleyns, but take every opportunity you can to show the king what you have to offer."

"It's more than that," added Brandon, striding closer to examine Cecilia better. "The king's relationship with Anne is stormy. She contradicts him, questions him, and makes him doubt himself, which is something he has never experienced before. You will gain his attention through flattery, compliance, and submission."

"You need to make him feel like a man again," summed up Lady Howard, "and you will be amply rewarded for it."

Thomasin threw an uncomfortable glance at Catherine, but the queen's gaze was fixed straight ahead, like a statue, giving nothing away.

"Remember to talk to him about his favourite subjects. Praise his performance in the lists, his looks, his jewels, his horses and dogs; ask to be told about his exploits abroad. But stay away from politics, do not mention Anne, and if he complains of her, you should say it is a pity he is sad, and that you wish you should make him happy again, as your king and a man."

"Will he really be so easily won?" asked Cecilia.

"Very likely," said Brandon, "but we must strike swiftly, while Anne is absent from court, while the wounds of their quarrel are still fresh."

"Be gentle and soft with him," said Lady Howard, fussing about her sleeves. "But be playful. Show him how a woman can be kind and yielding, without the need for challenge or conquest. Show him it is your duty and pleasure to serve him. Whatever he asks."

"Do you understand?" asked Brandon. "Whatever he asks? You know what you will need to do? How far this might go?"

Cecilia nodded.

"We mean you may have to share his bed."

"Yes," Cecilia replied, "I have understood that."

"And you are still willing to proceed?"

She nodded again, briefly, but unequivocally.

Thomasin felt sick to the stomach. She turned to Ellen. "Does my mother know of this?"

Ellen shrugged. "I doubt it. I think she is still at home in Thames Street. The queen sent a carriage to fetch your sister alone."

Lady Howard turned in triumph to the queen. "There, I think we have an understanding."

Catherine came forward, her hands clasped together. Thomasin noticed that her knuckles were white. The queen was short in comparison with Cecilia and looked up into the younger woman's bright, excited eyes.

"Mistress Marwood, remember your purpose at all times. You are doing this in service to me, to England. You are to break the spell the Boleyn woman holds over him, then quietly melt away, your duty done. We shall arrange you a grand marriage and great rewards for yourself and your family, should you succeed. But in all things, you are mine."

Cecilia dropped a curtsey. "I am grateful for the opportunity to serve you, my Lady. I will do my best for you, and be trustworthy. You may rely upon it."

Her words were in such contradiction to those spoken by their mother at the feast yesterday, that Thomasin was left in no doubt that Lady Elizabeth was unaware of the plan. Probably Cecilia had been, too, until she arrived here, excited at the prospect of being needed. And by the looks of things, she was going to seize the challenge with both hands.

"The problem of Anne will collapse once the king has been weaned off her," added Brandon. "She must remain away from court as much as possible."

"Well," said Lady Howard, "there is no better time to start than at once. I will take Cecilia to walk about the hall, where we may be sure the king will notice us, and engage him in conversation."

"God be with you, for England," said Catherine.

The pair of women curtseyed, then left the room.

A heavy silence followed. Catherine turned and slumped in a chair. Maria Willoughby brought her wine and reassurance at once.

"There, my Lady, you saw how willing and compliant the girl was. All will be well."

Catherine drank but did not reply. Thomasin wondered whether she was thinking about how willing and compliant Cecilia had been a year ago when she had hosted a betrothal feast for her.

As the queen and Mary Tudor sat talking together, Thomasin drew Ellen into the antechamber.

"I feel sick. I can scarcely believe this has happened so quickly, and Cecilia is so keen to get started."

"She arrived soon after you went out. They had her dressed and primed so quickly, before I had the chance to even speak with her."

"Did she express no concerns?"

"None. She was so excited to be summoned. She said yes before she even understood what was being asked of her."

"But she understands now."

"As you saw."

"It turns my stomach, especially given our mother's past."

"I know," said Ellen softly. "I know."

"That man isn't here, is he? At court? I mean William Hatton?"

Hatton's brief affair with Cecilia had been the ruin of her proposed marriage last year, but while Cecilia had returned, disgraced, to the country, Hatton had been received back into the king's household, and had been close to him throughout the summer.

"I overheard it said that he was in the north, seeing to his estates."

"That is a relief, at least. I could not bear for him to witness this, or to think Cecilia is fair game again."

"No," said Ellen, "let the north keep him, for his sins."

Then an unpleasant idea suddenly occurred to Thomasin. There was something in Catherine's quietness, her complicity. "You don't think…"

"What?"

"I don't know. It'll sound foolish. But there's a symmetry about this. Almost as if the queen approved of Cecilia in this role as a kind of revenge for what my mother did years ago. You remember? She once shared the king's bed."

Ellen frowned. "Surely not? Did Catherine even know about that?"

"I don't know. Perhaps I am letting my mind run too much on this. It is Cecilia's choice, not mine."

Thomasin picked up her darning. "Shall we?"

But Ellen paused and glimpsed back into the room, to ensure they were not being overheard. "The queen spoke to me about my absence from the feast. She guessed that it was more than that I was feeling unwell."

"What did you say?"

"I told the truth. I explained that my estranged husband had arrived, and I told her what he has done."

Thomasin felt a throb of pity for her at once. "Oh, I am sorry I was not here to help you."

Ellen sighed. "It doesn't matter. You couldn't have changed the facts."

"What did the queen say?"

"She said that he was my husband, we were united in the eyes of God, and that it was my duty to forgive him, as many others have done in similar situations. She meant herself, of course. And that I should return to live with him and be the best wife I could."

Thomasin looked at her cousin, aghast. "Oh, Ellen, this is terrible."

"She will not, she cannot, force me to, can she?"

"Return to him? No, of course not."

"But she could end my service, remove me from her household."

"I doubt she would do that, but even if the worst did happen, you would always be welcome at Monk's Place, or to live in the country with my parents. You would never be without a home."

"I can't return to my father; he is difficult and the house is secluded. It would be a living death."

"No, no, that will never happen. Remember that you have Sir Hugh madly in love with you. I have seen it with my own eyes. This is merely a bump in the road, then you will become his wife."

"Do you really believe it?"

"I do. When I think of the way he was with you at Raycroft, and how happy he was to see you here, I don't doubt that he loves you."

Ellen looked sad. "I haven't had the chance to see him in the last few days. He is always with the Duke of Suffolk. It is good that he has taken Hugh under his wing, but he seems reluctant to let him go, even for a moment."

"We must speak again with Uncle Matthew. Hopefully after this Aston case is concluded, he can put pressure on Barnaby and get the divorce resolved. If the case goes in our favour, Barnaby will have all that he desires. He can go anywhere else, even marry again, so he should be content."

Ellen nodded. "You're right. The answer is to speed through this matter. I'll go and speak with Barnaby myself."

"What? Yourself? Face to face? Are you sure?"

"Believe me, the last thing I want is to look upon his face again, but it's the only way I can gain my freedom."

"Very well. The case is opening today. I've seen the Astons arrive already. Father, Uncle and Barnaby will be here shortly, if they've not already arrived."

"I'll go and seek them, when the queen takes her afternoon rest."

"Do you want me to come with you?"

Ellen put a hand on her cousin's arm. "Thank you, that is kind of you, but it is something I have to do alone. You would be better going to keep an eye on Cecilia."

"I honestly do not think I have the stomach for that." Then a thought struck Thomasin. "Oh, do you think I should tell our father?"

"He will be angry if you don't," Ellen mused, "but frustrated if you do, because there is nothing he can do if the queen is involved. He can't order Cecilia home again if Catherine commands her to stay. And besides, the queen has already compelled us to silence, hasn't she?"

"Yes. She did make us promise not to tell anyone of the plan."

"So that excludes your father. The question is taken out of your hands."

"I suppose so," Thomasin sighed. "I just hope she doesn't make a fool of herself and the family again."

"There's nothing we can do now," said Ellen, "only trust in Cecilia."

"Yes," said Thomasin, "that's the problem."

As she picked up her needle, Thomasin felt the scratch of Lady Boleyn's letter in her sleeve, like a prick of conscience. There was nothing more to be done, while Anne stayed away, but she resented the wretched letter for the trouble it was causing her. And it was especially cumbersome whilst sewing. As Ellen was fetching her thread, Thomasin whipped it out of her sleeve and stuffed it under the cushion pad of her chair. It was a relief not to have the sharp edges constantly reminding her of her failed duty.

TWENTY

"Thank you for seeing me, my Lady," said Thomas Wolsey as Maria Willoughby opened the door to the queen's chambers.

They all watched him cautiously; the queen, her ladies and Mountjoy were all suspicious of the enemy who had requested an audience.

The cardinal entered slowly, portentously, with the air of one who is careful of his footing. At fifty-five, his holy position offered no protection against all the mortal pains that his life of power and excess had brought on. He carried his jewel-encrusted hands before him and breathed heavily through his thick lips. And yet there was something pitiful about him too, thought Thomasin, watching him make his way towards the queen. Something she couldn't quite put her finger on, but it stemmed from his strained relationship with Anne.

Rumour had it that years before, when Anne had first returned to court from France, she had fallen in love with a young man named Henry Percy, now Duke of Northumberland. The pair had even contracted a secret engagement, even though his family intended him for another. Wolsey had separated the lovers, sending Anne back to Hever and insisting that Percy be wed, a good two or three years before she had caught the king's eye. They said Anne never forgot a slight or let a grudge go, and that her memory was sharp as a knife. She had made no attempt to conceal her dislike of the man who had been by King Henry's side for the last fifteen years.

"A gift, my Lady. Cramp rings, to ease your suffering."

The irony of this, from a man who had brought suffering to the queen, was not lost on Thomasin.

He held out a small cloth bag between thick, shaking fingers encrusted with gems. Mountjoy stepped forwards to take it, then handed it to the queen. She toyed with the ribbon but did not open it. Instead, she waited.

Wolsey understood what was required of him. Very slowly, he lowered himself to his knees. His robes pooled about him as he tried to accommodate his limbs and feet. The queen watched his suffering without offering respite.

Wolsey waited until he was composed and had his breath back. "Good day, my Lady."

"You wished to speak with me?"

"I hope I might, as you have been so good as to grant me an audience?" He looked hopefully towards a chair, but the queen had not forgotten the many times he had taken Henry's part against her.

"What is the matter on which you wish to speak?"

Wolsey sighed in acceptance. "The great matter between you and the king, my Lady."

"Do you mean my marriage?"

"I mean that which you, no doubt, sincerely believe to be a true marriage."

"And which was conducted in the eyes of God, with a dispensation from the Pope, according to the rites of the Catholic Church by Archbishop Warham."

"Yes, my Lady. That marriage."

"What do you wish to say to me about it?"

Wolsey leaned forwards, resting the knuckles of one hand upon the ground. "A moment, my Lady. My apologies."

Still Catherine showed herself little inclined to show mercy. Wolsey's cramp rings sat in her lap.

"My Lady, we have had a long history together, united in the service of the king. I recall back in 1513, how we corresponded when he was in France, how I have always done the best for you as queen and served you as well as I could, as almoner, councillor, chancellor. Do you remember how we celebrated when I was made Cardinal? How I smoothed over the king's anger when his sister wed Suffolk against his will?"

"My memory is quite intact," replied Catherine, coolly. "I ask again, what is your matter?"

"My Lady, it pains me to see this situation arising between yourself and the king, and the division it has caused between us. It seems that God will not allow me to serve both of you, while the king's wishes are so determined. But I pray for you, my Lady, for your health and happiness, for your soul, although here in the temporal world I feel quite helpless." He shifted awkwardly from one knee to the next. "I have tried, on many occasions, to reason with the king. To outline his duty according to the church and yourself, but his mind is set in stone. I cannot see a way forward save but one thing, and one thing alone."

"And what is that?"

"My good Lady, you have already proved yourself in the eyes of God, as a dutiful daughter, a Christian queen and a devoted wife. Is it not time, as the years advance, to think of your own comfort and dignity?"

"Save your breath, Wolsey. I will not retire to a convent."

"Please, my Lady, hear me out. Why are you so set against it? Such a devout soul as yourself has earned the respite of a truly holy final life, dedicated to God. It would appease your struggling soul and allow the king to move forward. He does not wish to cause you further pain, only to care for you, in the coming years, as he would his own sister. It is in your hands to end this suffering we all endure. For the sake of everyone involved."

"You fail to understand me, Cardinal. I am an anointed queen, chosen by God to serve this great kingdom that I now call my home. I was set upon this path at the age of three and I will continue to serve God in the way he intended until my dying breath. To fail to do so would be to reject his calling, to turn my back upon my people and allow my husband to walk into his own damnation. It is my duty to save him from the fate he rushes to embrace."

"I do understand," said Wolsey softly, trying to conceal the hands that had begun to shake. "I have given the king the very same advice myself. His ears are deaf to it. He will proceed regardless. There are precedents for retirement and for divorce. The wife of the king's one-time brother-in-law, Louis of France, became an abbess and lived for years in peaceful seclusion."

"But their marriage was never consummated. There is no comparison."

"The king's own sister then, Margaret, dowager queen of Scots, was granted a divorce not eighteen months ago by the Pope."

"So why does he not give one to my husband, as he is handing them out so freely to whoever asks?"

"My Lady, you know it is not that simple. This woman, Anne Boleyn, will be the death of us both."

Catherine paused. These words brought her up short. "You may rise."

With great effort, Wolsey brought himself to his feet. He stood before Catherine and the pair simply stared at each other.

"We do not have to be adversaries in this matter," Wolsey said after a while. "We could be united against our common enemy."

"But we do not wish for the same outcome, I believe."

"Perhaps not. I am the king's servant and bound to fulfil his wishes. But neither of us will come closer to achieving our goals while we are faced with the current obstacle."

She looked at him with renewed interest. At her side, Mountjoy's frown deepened.

"Go on."

"If I may speak plainly, the king sent me here. He asked me to speak to you as I have, to implore you to enter a religious house of your choice. I have fulfilled his commission, and now, if you will permit me, I will speak on my own behalf."

Catherine nodded.

"Is it safe to speak openly?"

"Close the doors," the queen instructed. Only Thomasin, Ellen and Mountjoy were left within the room. They saw the indignant face of Lady Howard appear in the antechamber, too late to be admitted.

"It is but me and my household. What would you say to me now?"

"Thank you, gracious Lady."

"Get to the matter."

"Between ourselves, I greatly dislike this rise of the Boleyns. Sir Thomas is a man I would never trust, and now that Norfolk has returned to court, I fear they will become overmighty and gain too much influence over the king without properly understanding his needs and character. They are clearly no friends to yourself, nor to me either. Norfolk has a grudge against me that goes back a decade and the woman herself speaks to me as if I was a dog." He paused for breath. "It is in both our interests if the Boleyns fail in their attempt to further Anne."

Catherine took a while to reply, then slowly, she asked, "What would you suggest?"

"That we combine our forces, share our intelligence?"

"I have the ear of the emperor. What additional intelligence can you bring?"

"My knowledge of your husband makes me your natural ally. I know how his mind works, how he can be appealed to, and how dissuaded."

"Then why have you not appealed to him with success?"

"Because we are up against a force we have not met before. Anne Boleyn has him bewitched. I have left him this morning, pacing his chamber in anguish because she will not reply his letters or come to court. It was all I could do to prevent him calling a carriage and riding out to Durham Place himself."

Catherine looked pale. "Is that so?"

"But in Anne's rise, lies our failure, my Lady. If she gains more power, she will not tolerate either you or I to be around the king."

The words stung the queen's pride like daggers. A queen of England, to be sidelined by a creature such as Anne Boleyn!

"What do you suggest?"

Wolsey looked relieved. "I have thought of a few possible moves. We could pretend to seek an alternative new wife — now, wait, hear me out. I could pretend to pursue an alliance with Burgundy or Italy, find a suitable princess, young and healthy, who would bring him wealth and status, even draw up a treaty. Anne could be discreetly married off, before this greater match. Then at the last minute, the alliance will conveniently fold, due to some impediment beyond my control."

Catherine shook her head. "She would not accept that. And you would be playing with fire on a diplomatic front."

"The alternative is more scandalous. Objection could be raised to a marriage with Anne based on consanguinity. We could use his former relations with her sister Mary."

Thomasin stiffened at the thought of involving Mary Boleyn. Surely it would happen against Mary's wishes; she would never consent to the scandal of having her intimate secrets made public.

Catherine shook her head again. "That would reflect badly upon the king. You know what a private man he is at heart. He would not admit it, not even in this case."

"There is also her precontract to Henry Percy, although he is married now, and has no wish to remember the past."

Catherine waited.

Wolsey looked uncertain. "Or we appeal to a higher authority."

"Henry already believes God is displeased with him, and that this new marriage will make amends."

"I was not thinking of God."

"The emperor? He has ships waiting to sail, in case of danger to myself or my child. But we must not be seen to be inciting an invasion of England. We could both be sentenced for treason, and leave a clear path for the woman."

"Then the only option is to remove Anne somehow."

"Yes, yes, it is."

Thomasin shot a glance at Ellen, wondering if the queen would confide in Wolsey about the scheme with Cecilia.

"I have given this matter thought already," Catherine said at length, deciding to play innocent. "It requires a new woman to distract the king's eye, to win his affections away from the Boleyn girl, before disappearing."

Wolsey caught at her meaning at once. "You have hit upon a promising idea, my Lady. Should I happen to see such a woman, engaging the king in such a manner, I would do my utmost to facilitate her efforts."

"I could encourage no such thing," Catherine replied loftily.

"Of course not, my Lady. It would be entirely at my own instigation and discretion."

"Entirely."

"Nor should you wish to hear of it."

"Not at all."

"And if such a scheme should work, then the hold of the Boleyns would be shaken."

"It might."

"If only such a woman existed."

"If only."

Wolsey dusted himself down. "I should return to the king. He is in a most foul temper today and requires soothing. Thank you for granting me an audience, my Lady. Please accept my sincerest prayers for your good health."

Thomasin opened the door to let the cardinal out.

It did not escape their attention that Catherine was looking remarkably pleased with herself.

"You are well, my Lady?" asked Mountjoy.

The queen turned. "Don't you see? Wolsey has given himself away. He loathes the Boleyns and is as against this annulment as I am. Yet whose job is it to pronounce upon the case? Campeggio, who is under instruction from the emperor, and Wolsey himself."

Alarm bells rang in Thomasin's head. Clearly the same doubt had occurred to Mountjoy.

"Do not be too hasty to call him an ally. He may share your dislike of the Boleyns, but as he admitted, it does not mean he desires the same outcome. I do not trust the man one bit."

"I know, and I thank you for your caution and counsel as ever, my Lord. But if the cardinal is now complicit in a plan to divert the king, he is actively working against the king's wishes. He has been seeking to undermine Anne. Don't you see? There we have him! He had placed his own downfall in our hands."

Thomasin was surprised at her ruthlessness.

"Believe me," the queen continued, "I do not like this plan at all. I loathe it. I do not wish to encourage any other woman to pay court to my husband, married in the eyes of God. I detest it. And yet the alternative is worse."

"This is true, my Lady," said Mountjoy. "We must all cut our coat according to the cloth we have."

"And should Wolsey betray us, we will simply point to him as the instigator of the scheme."

"And wisely protect yourself, my Lady."

"The cardinal has been no friend to me, whatever he says about years gone by. Just last year he tried to woo a French princess to replace me. He must think I had forgotten about that, but I do not. I forget nothing."

There came a rapping at the door. Catherine frowned.

"He can't have returned so soon. Open up!"

Maria Willoughby let in a boy of twelve or thirteen, catching his breath and babbling in Spanish.

"Slow down," said the queen. "Aren't you one of Mendoza's boys?"

The dark head nodded and the boy spluttered out a string of sounds again.

"You have run all the way here?" translated Catherine. "House arrest? But why? When?"

The boy burbled some more.

"But it can't be!" exclaimed Maria, the other native Spanish speaker in the room.

"Sit down," Catherine said kindly. "Maria, fetch him some refreshment." She turned, with a face like thunder, barely able to contain her anger. Then, seeing Thomasin and Ellen, she explained, "Bishop Mendoza has been placed under house arrest. The king's men arrived this afternoon and locked him in his lodgings, while two stand permanently on guard."

"But why?" asked Thomasin, horrified for the poor old man.

"Because he is the representative of the emperor. The Imperial Ambassador. And it is the emperor who currently stands between the king and what he desires."

"But that is no fault of Mendoza!"

"No, but it is the final straw. He is writing to Brussels, asking to be recalled. I must send him some supplies: wine and meat, medicine and blankets. This is such an unkindness. I am sure the king has done it because of the friendship Mendoza has shown me over the years."

"It is a monstrous cruelty," added Maria. "I will put together remedies for his feet, and some delicacies for his table."

"Are my friends now to be in the firing line?" asked Catherine.

And Thomasin had the vision of King Henry, standing with his legs apart, a longbow in his hands as he drew back the string and loosed an arrow.

Catherine turned to Mountjoy. "I must go to Henry at once. I must speak to him of this matter, urge him to release Mendoza. It is an outrage. The emperor will hear of it before long."

"Forgive me, my Lady, but I would advise against it at the present time."

The queen looked at him impatiently, but he held his position. "Well?"

"I do not presume to advise you, my Lady, but I recall the cardinal's words about the king, being in an angry state and pacing his chambers. If you go to him now with this request, it is not likely to be received well. He may react in anger rather than listen to reason. Might it be better to wait until he has calmed down?"

"At least the bishop is in his own lodgings," added Maria, "so he can rest. And if you send him the supplies, he will at least be comfortable."

Catherine considered the wisdom of their words. "You have a point," she admitted. "There is no point approaching Henry when he is not in the right frame of mind. And yet again, I must be cautious with my own husband because of that woman. It is because of her that my friends must suffer."

"Patience, my Lady," said Mountjoy, "will yield better results."

"Patience," grumbled Catherine, muttering something that followed in Spanish. "My whole life is an act of patience."

"And God sees all, Catalina," added Maria. "Never forget, God sees all."

TWENTY-ONE

The morning was still young, but Westminster's outer yard was busy with arrivals and departures. Horses, led in and out, attending the smith to be freshly shod. Deliveries of apples and leeks from the countryside, a basket of eggs, a haunch of venison, all headed for the kitchen entrance. Servants were sweeping, and a boy was leading out a dog to be exercised, filling the air with its excited yelping.

Thomasin was carrying a letter from Queen Catherine to Bishop Fisher, when she spotted Rafe riding in through the far gate. He'd been out early, dressed in his boots and cloak, and he cut a dashing figure. At once, her heart gave its predictable, annoying jolt, infuriating her that he still invoked that physical reaction.

Rafe dismounted and headed towards the palace entrance. It would be easier to avoid him than to meet, so Thomasin turned away and sought out a messenger boy for her task.

"Here," she said, placing the letter in the hands of a tall youth with a pocked face. "This is from the queen."

His eyes grew wide as he nodded in earnest.

"Make sure you give it to the bishop directly in his palace at Lambeth; do not give it to anyone else. You know where that is?"

"Yes, Mistress."

"What's your name?"

"Peter, Mistress."

"Peter. Be swift and don't fail. There's a coin for your pains."

He hurried away on long legs, full of eagerness to be of use.

The errand reminded Thomasin of Lady Boleyn's letter to Anne. In what had become an habitual gesture, she clasped the sleeve of her gown, but this time, found only empty folds of material there. With horror, Thomasin remembered the moment when she had stuffed the letter under the cushion in the antechamber, to make her darning easier. A sense of panic seized her. What if someone else was to find it?

"Thomasin? What are you doing out here?"

Rafe had seen her, after all. He strolled up with that easy, powerful gait she knew so well, cloak thrown over his shoulder.

"Good morning," she replied formally.

"A love letter?"

His question annoyed her. "An errand for the queen."

"Me too. An errand, I mean. I've just come from Durham House. The king made me take a letter out to Anne at first light and wait for a reply, but she has woken, read it, and sent me back empty-handed. I dare not tell him!"

Thomasin's ears pricked up. This was interesting information to take back to Catherine. "So she is still angry with him? What was it that they quarrelled about?"

"The usual. The divorce, or lack of it. Anne sees the time passing. She starts to lose faith in the process of the courts."

"Perhaps she should set her sights elsewhere."

Rafe laughed. "Do you want to be the one to tell her that?"

"No, quite."

"Can I walk you in?"

She nodded and they headed back towards the palace.

"I couldn't help but notice you in the gardens the other day with that Italian," Rafe suddenly said in a rush. "I'm sorry if I speak out of turn. I don't mean to chide you. I simply noticed that he was, how do I say it, very attentive."

"Yes," said Thomasin, smiling, "I suppose he is."

"And you don't mind?"

"Why should I mind? He asked my permission to pay court to me, and I granted it."

Rafe stopped briefly and brushed the dark hair out of his eyes. It was a gesture she had once found endearing. "He asked your permission?"

"Yes, he did."

"How very formal. I thought the Italians had hotter blood than that."

"He's a Venetian. And his blood is quite hot enough, thank you."

They had reached the point where they would need to part ways: Rafe to the king's chamber, Thomasin to the queen's.

"So it's serious between you two, then?"

Thomasin couldn't deny the sneaking sense of satisfaction that he cared.

"Not serious exactly, but we are becoming better acquainted."

"But why him?"

She smiled. "He is passionate and respectful, a gentleman and a romantic, considerate and driven."

"I suppose I can't claim to be half those things."

"I hadn't really thought to compare you," she lied. "You are you, and he is he. That's all there is to it."

"Well, I shall be watching him, to make sure…"

"That won't be necessary," she replied quickly. "You are not my father. Now, I had better hurry back to the queen before I am missed. Good day, Rafe."

Thomasin had not quite reached the end of the great hall when she saw two figures engaged in what appeared to be an intense conversation in the doorway. Gilbert Aston was angry about something and while his sister did her best to calm him, he reacted to every gentle word, every calming touch, with pent-up fury. Ursula tried again, speaking softly to him, but he broke away from her, shaking his arm away and sending her staggering backwards. In that moment, her eyes met those of the approaching Thomasin. A silent appeal screamed out of them.

Thomasin redirected her route so as to pass by them. They became still at her approach. Gilbert turned away.

"Ah, good morning, Mr Aston, Miss Aston," she began, seeking something in her mind that might help. She needed an excuse to speak with the woman alone. "Miss Aston, I wish I might have a word with you. I've been meaning to do so, as you are a woman new at court, and there are a couple of practical things I would share with you." She looked to Gilbert, then back to Ursula. "For your comfort, as a fellow woman. Might we speak in the gardens for a moment?"

"We are waiting for our case to be heard," said Gilbert, with force.

"And what time does it start?"

"Ten," replied Ursula quickly.

"Well, then, the abbey bells have only just rung for terce. There is a full hour still to wait, so I might take a little of your time without any disruption." She turned to Gilbert. "It's so important that the women here know what their safe privy places may be, to avoid any embarrassment or compromise."

His face turned sour and he waved a hand between them. "Do not be late back, Ursula. I shall be waiting."

Thomasin led Ursula out through the back door to the gardens. The woman visibly relaxed at the change of scene. Warm sunlight slanted down, lighting up the grey stone walls. Gardeners were pulling up weeds and picking the dead heads off roses.

"Thank you," Ursula said. "I shall be all right now. You may leave me."

Thomasin was surprised. "But don't you want to hear any of my advice about being a woman at Westminster?"

Ursula gave a slight smile. "I appreciate your help, but I do not wish to take up more of your time. You must be busy."

"I am not too busy," said Thomasin, not wishing to make Ursula feel unwanted, but hoping that Lady Boleyn's letter still sat waiting under the cushion.

Ursula looked around her, nervously. "Please don't think badly of Gilbert. He is so concerned about this case, convinced that they will try and take Father's money away from us. We'd have to leave our home, sell the tavern."

When it was put like that, so starkly, Thomasin could see their concerns. "I understand. I hope he will convey that in the court; the difference the money would make to you. It is a substantial sum, but my uncle, Sir Matthew Russell and his son, are already well provided for."

"That's what Gilbert says. It would make only a little difference to them, but a world of difference to us."

"What does your mother say?"

"She is in Essex still. She is too afraid to come to court, and her back troubles her. It would mean we could take over the running of the tavern and afford to look after her properly."

Her reasons were compelling. Thomasin privately resolved to speak with her uncle when she had the chance. She looked sidelong at Ursula. Miss Aston was breathing deeply, her chin lifted in relief. Where the sun fell upon her skin, it warmed her features, making her suddenly seem pretty.

"You like court?"

"I've hardly seen any of it."

"Of course. And I suppose you'll leave as soon as the case has been decided?"

Ursula shrugged. "No reason to stay, so Gilbert says."

"Would you like to stay?"

Ursula picked at a flower. "Doesn't matter, I suppose."

They walked a little further, chatting until Thomasin felt herself compelled to ask, "And Gilbert? Does he often speak harshly to you?"

"Oh that, no. Only when he is in a temper about something."

"But he is not in a temper today with you?"

"No. But he is still in a temper."

"Does he experience them much at home?"

"Sometimes. But only when there is a reason: if the supplier sells us bad ale, or if the roof leaks. He's not bad really. He has a lot of responsibility, especially now Father has gone."

"And does he raise his voice to you, like that? Or strike you?"

"Not very much." Ursula turned away. "I shouldn't speak of him this way."

Thomasin led her down towards the water, past the gardeners. "There is no one to hear us now; you may speak freely to me."

"It's not that." Ursula chewed her lip. "It feels disloyal. It's always been just him and I. And Mother, of course, but we've been close."

"You're twins?"

"Yes. I'm the elder, would you believe?"

Thomasin smiled. "What do you wish to do? With your life, I mean? Are you content to run the tavern with Gilbert, or would you wish to leave your home, to try something new, even to marry?"

Ursula looked back blankly. "My life is simple. I bake for the tavern and take in a little extra sewing. I'm good with a needle, and I like it. I've never really thought of marriage; I just assumed it wasn't for me. And," she said, half-frowning, "I don't think Gilbert would like it."

The idea of free will resurfaced in Thomasin's mind. "What about your wishes?"

"I don't know. I've always been grateful that we don't go without."

"There you are again, saying 'we,' when I've asked about 'you.'"

Ursula shrugged.

"What if Gilbert was to marry, though? How would that change things for you?"

"Gilbert, marry?" Ursula gave a dismissive little laugh. "He's never spoken of it. I can't imagine him with a wife."

"All I suggest is that there's more out there to consider. You could go into service, as I am, at court or in a wealthy household, or sew, or you could marry, although you must choose your husband carefully."

"Would I get to choose, though?"

"You can certainly refuse a man who is not your choice. Otherwise you only exchange one master for another; the right man can bring you freedom and opportunity."

"Are you married?"

Thomasin laughed. "Me? Not yet. I am but young; I have not seen enough of life."

"It would be nice," smiled Ursula shyly, "to not have to do what someone else tells you all the time."

"And if this ruling goes in your favour, you would have the means to do something for yourself. Think about that."

The garden door opened and Gilbert appeared in the distance. He scoured the garden then waved frantically at his sister.

"Oh, I must go." Ursula jumped, reverting to the timid little mouse of earlier. "They must be starting early. I should like to speak with you again, cousin, if I may call you so."

"Cousin and friend, I hope." Thomasin smiled. "Go, and good luck!"

Briefly, the anxious face was lit by something that looked like hope. "Thank you. I had never dreamed that I might come to court and find a friend."

As Thomasin hurried back along the upstairs corridor, her heart was in her mouth. She had lingered too long with Ursula, but the woman's situation was a difficult one, with her illegitimacy, the court case and the way her brother seemed to control her. Thomasin had no choice but to help her, but in the meantime, she had let time slip away. Her absence might have been noted, but worse still, Lady Boleyn's letter might have been discovered.

There was the sound of sobbing coming from the queen's chamber as she entered the main doors, although it did not sound like Catherine. Lady Mary looked up from her book as Thomasin entered.

"Ah, there you are. I just sent Ellen out to find you."

"I am so sorry, I was speaking with another cousin of mine, newly come to court."

"Never mind, Ellen can stay out a little longer," Lady Mary replied with a knowing smile.

Thomasin cast her eyes around. "Is … is everything all right?"

"Yes. Oh, the weeping. It is the Duchess of Norfolk. She and the duke have had words again."

It was Lady Howard! Thomasin couldn't help being relieved that it was not the queen, and that all seemed well otherwise.

"I'll just get my darning."

She slipped into the antechamber. Maria Willoughby was sitting in there, reading to her daughter. The other chairs, including the one Thomasin usually favoured, had been pushed back against the wall.

"Please, don't mind me," she said as Maria looked up. "I'm fetching my work."

The sewing chest had been placed on the floor at the far end. Thomasin hurried there first, lifting the lid and rifling through to find the stockings she had got halfway through: a long, pale, ash-coloured pair, threadbare at the heel and toe.

Maria went back to her reading, telling little Catherine about the life of St. Anne.

The cushion on Thomasin's chair had been straightened. Seeing that slight difference, she felt sick with a presentiment about the letter's absence. Lifting the corner, she quickly confirmed that there was nothing underneath at all. The wooden chair seat was empty. No letter, no scrap of paper. Nothing. She lifted the entire cushion in desperation, but it had gone.

Thomasin paused and took a deep breath to keep the panic at bay. It was definitely the right chair, and no other. She liked that one because of the scallop-carved handles that were smooth to the touch. Perhaps the letter had fallen, when the chair was moved? She looked about the floor frantically. Nothing. Or perhaps someone had picked it up and put it somewhere safe? But there was nothing on the table, nor on the cupboard at the side. The letter had simply vanished into thin air.

"Have you lost something?" asked Maria, noticing her activity.

Thomasin tried to make her tone light. "Just a piece of paper — a letter, actually. I thought I had left it here. You've not seen it? It was on this chair."

"No, nothing like that. The chairs had been moved when I came in."

"Very well, thank you." Thomasin was nodding, but her heart was beating fast.

There was no fire in the grate. Usually they didn't bother in the anterooms until evening, but there was a chance it might have been considered rubbish and thrown into the hearth. She inched closer to see, but the grate had been swept clean that morning and there was nothing there.

"I'm sure it will turn up," said Maria.

"You've not seen anyone with a letter?"

"Only the one My Lady gave you to deliver, no other."

"And who was using this room before you?"

"I suppose we have all been in and out. Was it something important? You seem upset."

"No, no, just something I had to do. Do not worry."

With her heart like lead, Thomasin took her darning back into the chamber and sank into a chair.

Lady Mary frowned at her. "What's up? Cat got your tongue?"

Thomasin sighed. "I don't know. It's either nothing, or else I'm in trouble. I lost something, I think, a letter I was meant to deliver."

"Oh, that's unfortunate. Was it the queen's one?"

"Oh no, I sent that off to Bishop Fisher. This was a personal one."

"Can you get the sender to rewrite it?"

Thomasin shook her head.

"Well, perhaps it will turn up. These things often do. Perhaps someone took it for safekeeping?"

This idea was troublesome. Apart from Lady Mary, Maria Willoughby and Ellen, only Queen Catherine and Lady Howard were left. Mountjoy also may have entered the room at some point, although he was no longer present.

Thomasin forced a taut smile. "Perhaps."

"Don't worry. I am sure it will all work out."

Thomasin sucked at the end of her thread, wishing she had Lady Mary's confidence. She could not shake the terrible feeling in her gut that someone had hold of the letter. Even when the queen and Lady Howard emerged to take a walk in the gardens, and neither so much as looked in Thomasin's direction, her nerves still did not settle, but remained twisting and turning like snakes in her belly.

Presently, as it approached the hour of noon, Ellen returned. Her eyes were rimmed with pink as if she had recently shed tears.

Thomasin followed her into the queen's empty chamber.

"Did you speak with Barnaby?"

Ellen nodded. "He is being as stubborn as ever. Insisting that I return to him and refusing to give me a divorce."

"Oh no, what a vile man he is. I am so sorry."

"He seems to take delight in persecuting me. I just don't know what I can do."

"What does Uncle Matthew say?"

"He has spoken to him, urged him in every reasonable way he can. I'm sorry." Ellen drew in a deep breath. "I am at my wits' end, with that and the queen telling me to return to him."

"No one can make you do that. We need to appeal to a higher authority."

"The king?" Ellen's eyes grew round. "He has enough trouble getting his own divorce."

"I hadn't thought to aim that high, but someone in authority whom Barnaby might fear would work. Like a duke or a person in office. I was thinking of Suffolk, or even Wolsey?"

"Do you think they would favour my cause?"

"Why not? All it would take was a few minutes of their time, a few words to impress upon your husband what his correct duty should be."

"I am scared to ask."

"Then I will. Let me speak to Suffolk at dinner. Hopefully it will all be over soon."

"Thank you, thank you, Thomasin. Perhaps freedom is within sight, after all."

"If we do not chase after it, no one else will."

TWENTY-TWO

The hour was approaching evening. Shadows in the corners lengthened and maids went from room to room in the palace, setting fires in the grates. From the opposite side of the river, Westminster Palace appeared as a host of gleaming windows, sparking into life as those fires kindled, like a constellation overhanging the Thames.

Queen Catherine had resolved to dine quietly in her chamber, and had kept back Maria Willoughby and Lady Howard for company. With a wave of her hand, she dismissed Lady Mary, Ellen and Thomasin, telling them to eat in the main hall and partake in the dancing. Lady Mary rolled her eyes, only longing for a good meal and her bed, but the younger women pulled on their cloaks against the autumn chill and hurried outside.

"Oh no," said Ellen as soon as they entered, looking down the hall.

Cecilia was standing down by the top table where King Henry was seated, resplendent in the red and cream gown lent to her for the part. Thomasin could see at once that she was bent upon seduction, hanging on Henry's every word, smiling widely, laughing at his jokes. If Thomasin had not felt sick already over the missing letter, this was quite enough to put her off her meal.

"Oh, let me have a seat with my back to her, I beg," she groaned, "so I can pretend tonight that I do not have a sister."

"I thought her instructions were to be subtle, suggestive," said Ellen, unable to tear her eyes away. "She is as good as announcing her intentions to the world. People are looking."

"Come, let's ignore her and eat, then we can leave quickly."

They took a place as far down as they could and began to load up their plates. Every so often, Cecilia's laughter reached them, sounding forced to Thomasin's ear. And yet, the king did not dismiss her. He kept recounting his stories, pleased to hear her response.

"Can it really be that simple?" Thomasin groaned.

"I believe that men are especially susceptible to flattery," said Ellen, "and as the king likes to remind us, he is a man like any other."

Thomasin looked back, drawn by the ghastly spectacle of her sister's flirtation, and she spotted Baron Mountjoy close by the pair, eyes turned towards them with a frown to which Cecilia was oblivious.

"Oh," said Ellen, "there is Hugh, with Suffolk."

The two men had strolled in, deep in conversation. Hugh Truegood looked at ease, dressed in soft dark grey, smart and expensive, as Charles Brandon appeared to be explaining something, ever the elder statesman. They took a seat closer to the king, where both appeared to notice Cecilia. Knowing of the plan, Brandon glanced over briefly, then proceeded to ignore her as he dug into his dinner.

"I hope to speak with him later," Ellen continued. "Perhaps he will stay to dance. But honestly, I hardly know what to say. I can only tell him again of my husband's stubbornness."

"Then we shall speak to both of them. You must spend some time reconnecting with Hugh; reassure him, dance, talk. I will tackle Suffolk at the same time and, hopefully, the matter will be resolved tonight."

"Do you really think it could be so soon?"

"Suffolk is not a man whom Barnaby would dare disobey."

"But would he speak on my behalf?"

"He is the queen's brother-in-law, and we are her ladies."

"I had heard," Ellen said softly, "that he was married before, as a young man, before Duchess Mary. He had one marriage annulled, and another betrothal cancelled too. He is a man who knows the importance of these things."

"Where did you hear this?"

"I overheard the queen and the Duchess of Norfolk talking, a while back."

Thomasin looked over at the handsome Duke of Suffolk. "I suppose a man like that can do whatever he wants."

"He thought so. But the king was furious when he married Mary in secret. He banned them from court and fined them; it took a long time before they were taken back into his favour."

A servant leaned between them to refill their glasses. It was a dark, brackish sort of wine, with a woody taste that the spices couldn't disguise.

"What is this, new wine?" asked a gentleman sitting further down the table. "By my eyes, it has a strong kick!"

"It's imported from the New World," replied the servant. "To Spain, and then to here."

"The New World," whispered Thomasin. "We are drinking New World wine!"

Ellen smiled. "I can't imagine a new world. This old one is quite trouble enough."

Presently, the meal came to an end. Servers appeared to remove the dishes, and the minstrels began to play softly. As they waited, Ellen nudged Thomasin in the ribs.

At the top table, King Henry had risen and extended a hand to Cecilia. Tossing back her hair, she accepted, her face all smiles, as he led her onto the floor in preparation to dance. A few other couples joined them, but Thomasin hung back.

"We should wait and watch Suffolk and Hugh, and take our chance when it arises."

The pair were still deep in conversation and did not look as if they would welcome an interruption.

"I wonder what they can be saying all this time," said Ellen.

The first chords of the dance began and the couples made their bows and curtseys. All eyes were upon Henry and Cecilia, who stepped together into the first pairing, then began a pattern of double steps.

"I can't watch," Thomasin groaned.

"It's almost hypnotic," Ellen replied, her eyes fixed upon the couple. "She's really giving all she has, trying to outdo Anne."

"I'm sure it will hold his interest this evening, but surely it won't be enough when Anne returns?"

"Then let us hope Anne stays away much longer, to allow Cecilia to get a foothold."

Ellen was staring again, and even Thomasin felt her gaze pulled in the direction of the king and his dance partner. Henry's expression was one of interest and amusement. He offered Cecilia his arm and they walked about together in a circle.

"I danced to this tune with Hugh at Greenwich," Ellen murmured. "I wonder if he recalls."

"That's something you can ask him later. Remind him of that time, when you get the chance to speak in private."

The dance was picking up pace. The couples were moving closer, then parting, back and forth, with claps of the hands. Thomasin knew what was coming next: a passionate moment where the usual restraint was put aside and the pair would spin each other off their feet. In some cases, it had led to dancers falling over, even injuring themselves. As the key changed, all eyes were upon Henry and Cecilia, as he put his arm about her waist and began to spin. Faster and faster they turned, until, predictably, Cecilia staggered. Henry stepped in to save her balance, pulling her close against him. His face was near to hers.

"Oh," Thomasin muttered, "I just can't look."

"I know what you mean," Ellen agreed. "It's painful."

"I really think that I should inform Father about this. He would be furious if he learned of it, and I had not told him."

"True, but remember the queen demanded our secrecy. If your father is at court, and she carries on this way, he will learn of it soon enough."

"Well, he is present at the moment, engaged in the Astons' case, so I suppose it is only a matter of time."

"What would he do? Take her back to the country?"

"He can't if the queen forbids it."

Then, as the dance dropped down to a more sedate pace, Thomasin noticed movement. "Look, Suffolk is leaving. I'll go to the right and head him off by the door. You go to Hugh and get him to dance to the next tune with you."

They parted, picking their way around the side of the hall. With relief, Thomasin saw her cousin reach Hugh Truegood, who stood and bowed to her in greeting. Now all she needed to do was catch up with the swift-moving Charles Brandon.

She had only gone so far when Baron Mountjoy crossed her path, blocking her exit.

"Your sister," he whispered tersely, "is making a spectacle of herself. This is not the approach we advised. You must speak with her."

"Me?"

"Who else?"

"Just because we are sisters, it does not mean she will listen to me. Quite the opposite, in fact."

Mountjoy ignored this. "She must be spoken to. She is drawing too much attention. The plan will be over before it has begun. Do it, please."

It was a direct order that Thomasin dared not disobey.

She gave a nod and turned back to the hall. Brandon was already out of sight.

The dance was drawing to an end. Henry was leading Cecilia through the final steps with a look of amusement on his face. Thomasin saw that Mountjoy was right. Cecilia was in danger of making herself seem too available, too eager, when she should have whetted his appetite and then withdrawn, to preserve an air of mystery.

She positioned herself close to the dais, where they were likely to pass.

Cecilia was laughing, head thrown back, following Henry.

"Sister, will you come?" Thomasin asked as they passed by.

"Not now," she hissed, and nodded towards the king. "See?"

"Do come. It's by order."

Cecilia looked at her sharply.

"I mean it," Thomasin insisted. "You must come. You've done enough for now."

Henry had reached his seat and turned to watch them. Thomasin dropped a curtsey and extended her hand to Cecilia. For a moment, she thought her sister was going to defy her, but under the king's gaze, she complied with only a little visible reluctance, sulkily taking Thomasin's hand and following her down the hall.

"What are you doing? Whose orders?" Cecilia fired at Thomasin as soon as they were out of earshot.

"Mine," said Mountjoy, approaching them. "That is enough for tonight. Withdraw now and you leave him wanting more. You must not overplay your hand."

Cecilia could not argue with Catherine's chamberlain. No matter how little she liked it, she bowed her head in acceptance. "Can I not stay and dine?"

"No, you should go entirely. Disappear from his sight, so he has time to think of you. You may go to the queen's chambers now."

Thomasin saw Cecilia's lips go thin, and the slight downturn in the corner, the familiar signs of disappointment. But she was playing a game that was bigger than her, and there was no room for private feelings or disobedience.

"I will go too," Thomasin said, with some sacrifice, "as it will look more natural for sisters leaving together."

"Very good," said Mountjoy. "Inform the queen that the quarry's attention has been caught."

His metaphor drew a brief smile from Thomasin as she hurried after her sister. At least it would give her another chance to search for the missing letter.

TWENTY-THREE

The morning was fresh; the air smelled clean. Queen Catherine had gone ahead early to the chapel, leaving her ladies to break their fast before they joined her.

Sir Richard was looking awkward as Thomasin turned the corner. He was waiting with Sir Matthew and Barnaby outside the council room, where the Astons' case was being tried. With all the preliminaries over, the first formal hearing of the case was scheduled to begin. There was no sign of Gilbert or Ursula.

"Ah, Thomasin," Sir Richard said, breaking away from the others. "You are well?"

"Well indeed, Father," she replied, hoping that he had not heard of Cecilia's behaviour the night before.

"This case drags on into a second day; all could have been resolved yesterday, if it was not for the Astons. Young Gilbert is so objectionable, but he has studied a little of the law, and fancies himself a lawyer. While his case is very weak, he is still able to launch a response to every argument we put forward, so it is taking far longer than it needs."

"Is there no chance of them winning?"

"Very little, because of their legal status."

"Their illegitimacy?"

"Yes, Thomasin. They would do better to reach some amicable arrangement, whereby Matthew could grant them some small allowance from the total."

"That would be a generous move."

"But it looks unlikely, given the way Aston is going."

"Is there no hope, Father? Can it not be given to Miss Aston? She is the elder of the two."

"That would be most irregular. A woman can't take precedence in inheritance over a man, even then."

"But would it not be even worse for the money to go to Barnaby?"

Thomasin looked back at her cousin, who stood proudly by the door. Her father followed her gaze and sighed.

"It is the law. We can't make it about the people involved. I can't simply advise that it goes to the most pleasant person. He is my nephew. We are family."

"But so is Ellen."

Sir Richard looked pained. "I am aware, and I am all sympathy for her plight. You have told her she is always welcome at Eastwell?"

"Yes, I have, thank you, but she doesn't want to be at Eastwell. She wants to be at Raycroft."

"At Raycroft? With Truegood?"

Thomasin watched while the penny dropped.

"Ah, I had not realised... Does Truegood feel the same?"

"He did. The affection is there, but this situation with Barnaby lingers on, making it seem impossible."

"I see."

"And now the queen has spoken to her of duty and advised her to return to her husband."

Sir Richard nodded. "It is a difficult situation, on all sides."

"Not on his, Father," Thomasin said hotly, indicating Barnaby. "Not on his. I cannot have Ellen sacrificed to that man."

"No, I see. I am afraid my legal hands are tied when it comes to a divorce, but I can only advise him of the best course of action. Perhaps a win today will appease him."

"That was my thinking too, although it is most unfair for the Astons. Well, for Miss Aston, at least. We spoke yesterday, and she seems a most pleasant young woman."

"Can something else be done for her?"

"I don't know, perhaps."

Sir Richard nodded. "That might be the solution. And Cecilia? What of her?"

Thomasin almost jumped in alarm. "What?"

"It came as a surprise that the queen showed her favour; it was most generous of her. We were pleased that she was invited to see the workings of her household."

"Oh, yes, of course."

"She is behaving herself, I hope?"

"She has certainly embraced the role," said Thomasin truthfully, although she felt the sting of omission.

"Right, then I must return. The case will hopefully conclude today. Then there will be nothing to keep us in London, although I am sure your mother will devise something, perhaps with this Cecilia business."

"Yes, perhaps."

Thomasin watched her father walk away. She felt that she had betrayed him, and her mother, when it came to this secret scheme. For once, the queen's orders had to override her loyalty to her family. It sat uncomfortably with Thomasin, but the matter was out of her hands.

"And now Vives," said Queen Catherine, furiously brandishing a letter. "House arrest in Oxford, for writing in sympathy to a friend. It is unbearable, this disrespectful treatment of good men."

King Henry looked back at his wife coolly. She had ambushed him on the way back from the chapel, where he was unprepared for her fury, yet Catherine could not let this matter rest. Thomasin and Ellen waited nervously behind her.

"Bishop Mendoza is elderly in years," the queen continued, "suffering great pain in his legs, despite which, he persists in doing his difficult duty. Guards are still posted at his door, preventing him from leaving his lodgings. Vives is a scholar and a humanist, respected across Europe, who has been so good in the past as to take an interest in the education of our daughter. You yourself expressed thanks to him, a few years before."

"Madam," said Henry, raising his hand ominously, "be reminded that this is not how you speak to your king."

"Is this any way to treat the friends of a queen? Loyal men who have given good service?"

Henry turned slowly, and looked at her with intent, small eyes. Passing courtiers tried to hurry by, but many stopped, captivated by the scene.

"But their service is not to me, now, is it, Madam? In serving your interest, they act against me, the anointed king of this realm. You know what name is given to that? Is that the penalty you wish your friends to incur?"

Catherine did not imagine for a moment that Henry intended to pursue Mendoza or Vives for treason, but the tone of his voice made her proceed with caution. She drew a deep breath. "My Lord, can we not think of the comforts and liberty of two men, deserving of much respect for their learning and service? This has been sufficient to serve as warning; may they now be released?"

"And sent back to the emperor? Whose ships are collected in Flanders and Spain, ready to sail against me? Would you have your England invaded?"

"Of course not, my Lord. I only petition for two men."

"Not a single man can be exempt from justice, not even due to their learning. The case of Luther, justly condemned by your own nephew, the emperor, should have taught you as much."

"Martin Luther was condemned for heresy, in accordance with your own opinion. This is not comparable."

"No, Madam, it is not. This matter comes perilously close to treason."

A shocked silence descended. The word hung between them in the air, noxious and unavoidable.

Catherine spoke softly. "My Lord cannot mean that, I think."

"You presume to tell me what I mean?"

"Of course not." She looked down at her hands, then redoubled her efforts. "Please, will you lift the guard? Do not punish good men for following their conscience. We all have to live with our consciences, as essential for the salvation of our immortal souls."

"I am glad we are in accord," said Henry. "It is precisely for the good of my soul that I pursue this course of action. Any day now Campeggio will arrive, and this papal court can be convened. We all shall answer to a higher authority than your emperor."

He turned and left Catherine standing, walking away towards his lodgings.

The queen looked for a moment as if she would speak, then she pursed her lips and headed towards the abbey, to pray for guidance from that same higher authority.

Behind them, Thomasin heard Mountjoy speaking and paused to listen.

"Follow, go to him, divert him," he was saying to Cecilia, who was at the end of the line. "This is the moment."

Cecilia's ice-blue eyes responded with recognition. "Yes," she replied, "I believe it is."

There was something her sister's expression that filled Thomasin with dread. She took Cecilia by the arm.

"Be careful; the stakes are high. Don't overplay your hand."

Cecilia shrugged the hand away. "I require no maid's advice."

Thomasin blushed hotly at the reply, but her sister was already stalking off in the direction of the king's chambers.

"This will not end well," Thomasin murmured. "Not at all. There is pain brewing here."

Mountjoy looked at her sharply. "You fear the outcome or the scheme?"

Thomasin looked up into his face, with its lines of wisdom and white-grey beard, and decided to trust him. "I fear both. I fear we are being too bold, in meddling between the king and Anne. It may backfire."

"Only if it fails," he replied. "Boldness is sometimes called for in desperate situations. Do you have any reason to suspect that it might?"

Thomasin watched her sister disappear around the corner. "She does not have Anne's range. Her experience in the world, her culture, her subtleties."

"Does she need to? We are not looking to make a new queen; we merely need a pretty face to serve as a diversion."

"You saw her the other night in the hall."

"Yes. She is over-keen, but if she follows instructions, she will do well."

Thomasin sighed. The thought of Cecilia following instructions and acting with caution did not inspire confidence.

"You do not think so?"

"I know my sister, Sir. She has many good qualities, but patience and obedience are not the best among them. She is inclined to let herself get carried away in the moment."

"Perhaps that is what must happen," he said solemnly, "if she is to engage his affection."

Thomasin understood him at once. "But what if there is a child? Surely the king would seek to legitimise it, to marry Cecilia? Wouldn't we be back to the same problem, just replacing Anne with another?"

"Another whom we chose — that is the difference. Cecilia will simply disappear from court, and if he finds her again, she will already have been married to another."

"Do you have anyone in mind?"

"Suffolk is working on it. Do not doubt, or dwell too long on this, and do not voice your concerns to the queen. She must believe in this scheme. It is giving her hope."

"And if it fails?"

"Then we put our hope in the cardinals."

Thomasin found Charles Brandon walking in the gardens with his hounds. The dogs were sober, well-trained, yet filled with the excitement of outdoor smells and sounds as they careered between the bushes. He appeared deep in thought, crossing her line of vision without being aware of her presence, rubbing his long beard, before he paused to pick up a stick and throw it into the middle of the lawn. The dogs raced after it at once, four of them, light in step.

It was a pleasant day, a little chillier than before. The palace chimneys pumped out smoke from many hearths, as a reminder of the many people contained within its walls. Thomasin could not help but wonder what exactly was taking place within the king's chambers, and whether any of his windows looked out across this garden.

"Ah, Mistress Marwood!"

The dogs reached her first, sniffing about her feet, but not jumping up.

"Away, boys, go." They obeyed his command at once.

"Good day, My Lord."

"Good day. You have come to tell me about your sister? How does she fare?"

"Seemingly well, as far as I can see."

"Has she made an impression yet?"

"I believe so, and she is currently with the king in his chamber, so she has a further chance."

"In his chamber? So soon?"

"That is where she was headed. Whether he has admitted her, I cannot say."

Brandon frowned. "She is a little pert, a little forward. She must not yield to him too soon, or else he will not value her."

"I did not think that was the intention, my Lord. We do not want the king to value her, to wish to replace Anne, or the queen, with her. Is she not merely an instrument to rouse Anne's jealousy, to force a further breach?"

He surveyed her for a moment. "You are very shrewd for one so young. Yes, your sister is to be a sacrifice in this matter, although it will suit her well enough, I think, given the rewards it may bring."

"Baron Mountjoy mentioned that you were arranging a possible match for her, afterwards."

"We shall see, we shall see. It is not yet final."

Thomasin nodded. "It was actually my cousin I wished to speak with you about. Ellen Russell?"

He turned and whistled to his dogs. "Yes, and what of her?"

"About her unhappy marriage. She is trapped in a situation with a most odious man, who betrayed her with her own sister, and she longs for her freedom."

"And why do you bring this to me?"

"Her husband is being stubborn in the matter. She repeatedly asks him for a divorce, but he insists that she return to him instead, which is something she cannot bear."

"But it is his right, as her husband."

"Yes, but…"

"Would she consider entering a nunnery?"

"A nunnery?" Thomasin was shocked. "No, she wants to remarry and bear children."

"Can she not find it in her heart to forgive her husband and fulfil her duty?"

"No, Sir, she cannot, and I, for one, cannot blame her. I wonder that so many are opposed to her seeking freedom and advocate her return to misery."

"Who else has spoken in this way, then?"

"Well, the queen said the same to Ellen. It would be a life of misery, and she is but young. She can start again, find love and peace."

"But it is not the way of things. When a woman pledges herself to a man, it is her Christian duty to forgive him, to return to him and cherish him."

"As the queen repeatedly does, but look at the heartache that brings her!"

"You think the queen should withdraw?"

Thomasin floundered, full of emotion. "Yes, no, I don't know! I meant only to speak of my cousin."

"Look," said Brandon, "if her situation is truly untenable, then a life of religious retirement is her best option. If she were to go there for a while, a couple of years, it may then prompt him to seek a divorce himself. Otherwise, it can only happen if it is instigated by the man."

"But he will not do so."

"Then she must retire."

"But why? That is so harsh a punishment, when she has done nothing wrong!"

"If she has left her husband and refused to return to him, then in the eyes of God, she has done wrong, Thomasin, you must understand that. She left him, did she not?"

Thomasin sighed. There was no assistance to be expected from the duke. Ellen's case was looking hopeless.

"The only thing I can suggest is that she thinks this over, reconsiders her position and asks God for guidance."

Thomasin bowed her head and retreated, disappointed. *Why must the world inflict such harsh rules*, she wondered in anger, *so contrary to peace and happiness?*

TWENTY-FOUR

The day was fading. Lately, each evening seemed to steal in a little earlier, with the winter season on the horizon. Thomasin and Nico sat in the flickering light of lanterns, playing cards in the queen's main chamber. The air smelled of woodsmoke and the warming spices in the Venetian's wine glass. Thomasin wasn't drinking; her head was heavy and spinning with recent events.

"An ace!" Nico laughed, as he placed his card with a flourish. "I have been keeping that one back as a surprise."

"A surprise indeed," Thomasin replied, a little weary of the game, laying her nine of spades and seeing him sweep away the trick in victory.

"Thomasin, you seem a little distracted today. Either you are very kindly letting me win, or else your thoughts are elsewhere, I think."

"I am sorry, forgive me, you are right."

"What preys on your mind? Is there anything I can do?"

She thought about the missing letter to Anne Boleyn, vanished into thin air unread, about the chances of Ellen's future happiness, growing fainter and fainter as it seemed, and her own sister, Cecilia, who had been missing these past few hours. No doubt she was caught up in her business with the king.

"It is just so many things, family things."

"Nothing I have done to displease you, I hope?"

"Nothing of the kind," she said, smiling. Nico was always a good companion, thoughtful and sensitive. "It's only difficulties and complications for my family. Things that should be simple never seem to work out as they should."

"I think you have a touch of melancholy tonight. You should drink some of this wine and let me speak to you of love."

"Alas, it is love that makes me question things. Other people's misfortunes in love."

"Ah, that is sad indeed." His eyes grew softer. "A broken heart is the greatest affliction of them all."

She couldn't stop the image of Rafe resurfacing, with his devilish good looks, the thrill of his hand on her skin, but she hurriedly pushed it back down.

"You have experienced that yourself?"

"Of course," he said, shuffling the cards. "We all have, or will, at some point. When I was young, I loved a girl from Verona. Her name was Lidia, and she had eyes like the midnight sky, but her parents had betrothed her to another and would not hear my pleas. I think I cried for a week."

"Is that why you left Venice?"

"Ah, no." He laughed. "I was but sixteen then, and she has married and borne five children since; she would barely know me know, nor greet me in the street. It was a lucky escape, I think. Otherwise, I would never have come here."

Thomasin stared at her cards, trying to decide whether or not this was a gallant thing to say.

"And what of you, Thomasin?" he asked swiftly. "Have you ever been in love?"

The question took her by surprise. Her immediate response was that of confusion: yes, then just as swiftly, no. Of course she had not loved Rafe. It had been infatuation, lust, obsession even, but not that self-sacrificing devotion that she considered to be love. And Will Carey? Perhaps in time they might have reached that place, but their time had run out.

"No," she said swiftly. "I don't think I have."

But then there was Nico, staring back at her with his wide smile. Did she love him? Could she see a future with him? Could he be the one?

"Not at all? No glimmer of it?" His expression was hopeful, leading.

"Not quite," she replied. "I have certainly had … feelings. But I believe love is something eternal, life-long. I would not wish to enter it lightly, nor to walk away from it."

"Admirably spoken. Such a love would be worth having."

"And your Lidia? What happened to your love for her? Did it vanish?"

He looked at her quizzically. "It was not to be. We were too young, but the sixteen-year-old Nico will always love her."

"And what if you had met now, later in life?"

"I don't know. But I am not there, I am here. With you. No other woman could compare."

His words were slick. Almost too slick. Thomasin laid down her cards. "Deal again. I've lost concentration."

"Very well." Nico scooped them up, shuffled them into a pile and smoothed the edges.

Thomasin sighed and looked about the room. It was a quiet evening and they were practically alone, save for Lady Mary in the antechamber. The queen was shut away with Maria Willoughby, Lady Howard was with her husband, and Ellen had announced on the spur of the moment that she needed to make a social visit. Catherine hadn't asked whom she intended to see, but Thomasin guessed her cousin hoped to find Hugh and speak with him. She'd tried to stall her, as there'd been no opportunity yet to tell her cousin of the disastrous conversation she'd had with Brandon, but Nico had arrived at the door, and Ellen had been itching to go.

"Here," said Nico, "your turn to deal."

He pushed the cards towards her, and she picked them up. As soon as she started to hand them out, though, a piece of paper dropped out, different from the rest — lighter, uncoloured. She stared at it in surprise.

"What is that?" asked Nico. "Better read it."

She picked it up and opened the corners. They had been carefully folded over to keep it flat and closed, with each flap brought inwards, turning a square into an octagon. Her name was written upon it, encircled by a heart.

"This is from you?"

"I don't know." He grinned. "Have a look."

There was a verse inside, written in a small, elegant hand. She noticed the handwriting first, with its slight lean, its long loops and tight, controlled use of space. Her eyes skimmed the words. It was addressed, again, to her. But the words seemed to swim before her eyes. Certain phrases jumped out: "the depths of your heart" and "eyes like the hazel boughs in spring" and "eternally joyful smile". She felt herself blushing hotly, failing to recognise his image of her. She'd have to take this away, read it at her own pace later.

"It's a sonnet," he said, as if that was what mattered most. "Like Petrarch wrote to Laura. You see the structure, the rhyming pattern; the lines rhyme in alternating couplets, so you have "rose" and "grows", "cold" and "bold", and so forth, in blocks of four. Do you like it?"

She nodded, wondering who Petrarch and Laura were.

"Are you sure?"

"I will have to read it several times later, to get the real sense of it, but I thank you. I've never had a poem written to me before."

Something inside Thomasin was welling up, a strong emotion suffocating her from within. It was a beautiful idea, thoughtful and skilful, but she felt overwhelmed by it. It demanded too much space alongside all the things that occupied her head: her concerns for Cecilia, the lost letter to Anne Boleyn, Ellen's predicament, even Ursula Aston. The poem seemed to rub up against them, creating friction, as if they might ignite.

"I should go and attend the queen. She'll be emerging soon, I think."

He looked disappointed. "Was it something I said? Was the poem too much?"

"No, not at all. It is charming, only I am mindful of the queen."

"Of course." He rose at once and gave her a neat bow. "I hope we shall meet again soon."

She smiled. "We will."

Taking her hand, he pressed it to his lips. "Perhaps somewhere a little more private."

"Perhaps."

She allowed her smile to give him hope, but also to keep her options open.

Thomasin stood staring at the door after he had left, a hundred thoughts racing through her mind, the letter dangling from her fingers. Appearing from the anteroom, clasping her darning, Lady Mary looked at her quizzically.

"What is the matter with you? Do you not like him?"

"I do, oh, I do. I don't know."

"Then what is it? Is he not perfect, from the little I could hear?"

"Yes, maybe. Perhaps that's it. He's a little too perfect. He's not the stranger to love that I am."

Lady Mary raised her eyebrows. "We are all strangers to love at the beginning, but strangers never become friends unless we give them welcome."

"I suppose not."

"Believe me, if I was thirty years younger, I would not let that one get away."

They were still awaiting the queen's summons, speaking of her situation with the king in hushed tones, when a messenger was admitted to the room. He was a page boy from Henry's inner chamber, fifteen or so, unsure of himself, bursting with the news he had to deliver.

"Mistress Marwood?"

Thomasin's heart thumped. What now? "That's me. What is your message?"

"You are to come at once and remove your sister from the king's presence, if you please, my Lady."

Thomasin looked at Lady Mary with horrified eyes. "Remove her? Did the king send you with this?"

"No, my Lady. It was Lady Carey."

Mary Boleyn? Thomasin got to her feet and grabbed her shawl. "I will come at once."

She followed the boy along the corridors, through the halls and chambers, up and down steps. It was a dark hour, dinner was over, and the castle was being put to sleep. Torches burned on the walls, casting shadows and pools of light on the floor and walls. With every step, Thomasin felt more heavy, more fearful. What had provoked the summons? Mary Boleyn's protection of Anne? Her jealousy? Or had Cecilia made a fool of herself?

They heard the music first. Soft strains of lutes in harmony and the high-pitched notes of a pipe. Laughter followed hard upon them, followed by voices, calling for more wine.

The messenger boy looked at Thomasin anxiously.

"What has she been doing?"

"They have retreated into his inner chambers."

The guards admitted them to a larger, outer room, where various officials sat at dice and cards, drinking and talking. Henry Norris nodded in greeting and, Thomasin was horrified to see, so did William Hatton, the fair-haired favourite of the king who had led Cecilia astray last year and destroyed her wedding. Other faces looked up to see Thomasin's arrival, but it was Mary Boleyn who approached them, frowning deeply.

"For goodness' sake, get your sister out of here," she said between clenched teeth, with no word of warning.

The hostile set of her features disposed Thomasin to play innocent. Although she loathed Cecilia's mission, and found her methods extreme, she was still her sister, and they were united against the Boleyns.

"What can you mean? I don't see her here."

Mary's eyes shone with pure fury. "No. That's because she is in the king's chamber."

"Is she? Surely not, my Lady. My sister can have no business in there."

"Indeed, she does not. She must be called out at once."

"Is your sister not here to do it?"

The reference to Anne made Mary pause. "My sister is from court at present. It would be better if yours was, too."

"I am not her keeper, my Lady, any more than you are to Anne. The king's door is closed. Surely you do not suggest that I burst in there and demand that she leave?"

"You are impertinent, Madam. I suggest no such thing, as you are well aware. Your presence here is sufficient, as is your collusion, which I now require, nay, demand. You must say that your mistress has summoned her on urgent business."

Thomasin was almost starting to enjoy the exchange with her rival, aware that every moment she could draw out, was another moment that Cecilia was spending with the king.

"But the queen has sent no such message. I cannot tell an untruth. All I can do is wait here until my sister emerges."

"But she might be doing anything in there!"

Thomasin shrugged. "She might."

Mary Boleyn looked daggers at her. "I would have thought, given your unwholesome connection with my husband, that you would at the very least perform this small office for me. You owe me that much."

"It is no small office to tell the king an untruth, Madam."

"Do you intend to defy me, then? Imagine when my sister hears of this!"

"You will also have to inform your sister what the king has been doing during her absence from court. I would imagine that will cause a considerable storm."

"You continue to defy me?"

"I am here, am I not? I obeyed your summons."

"And you have a message from your mistress?"

Thomasin sighed, wondering how long she could refuse, now that she was here in the king's rooms. But at that moment, the door to the inner chamber opened and Cecilia appeared, with the shadow of the king behind her, too dark for Thomasin to see clearly. She was fixing her headdress, which had come off during their sport, and her dress was crumpled. The sight of her left little doubt about what might have occurred behind closed doors. As she was leaving, she leaned back into the room, where Henry was whispering to her.

Thomasin came to her senses first, glancing at Mary, who was looking horrified.

"Ah, here she is."

"Take the whore away," Mary Boleyn said with ominous quietness. "Send her back into the country."

Other eyes were watching now, and Thomasin couldn't help but notice the look of amusement on the face of William Hatton, which turned her stomach. Of all the moments to return to court, he had to be present at this one.

Thomasin walked firmly down the length of the chamber, to where Cecilia was still dallying in the doorway. Her sister turned, surprised to see Thomasin there.

"Come, we are leaving."

"Why so?"

"Are you done here?"

King Henry's shadow moved through the dark space in the room behind.

"I am. I have. All that was asked of me and more."

Thomasin took her arm. "Then it is time to go. There are hostile eyes here."

"You mean Hatton? I took pleasure in flaunting the king's favour before him."

"Mary Boleyn. We must leave."

Thomasin led Cecilia away, feeling the weight of the room's gaze upon them. Behind, Henry was calling for his groom, for spices and sweet wine.

"But don't we actually want Mary to see?" asked Cecilia, suffused with a sort of pride. "So that Anne is jealous and they quarrel?"

"Your work is complete."

Mary Boleyn watched them approach, wringing her hands, but Thomasin marched straight past her towards the door. Cecilia dared to drop a curtsey as they passed.

Once the king's doors were closed behind them, Thomasin let out a deep breath.

"Why did you come?" asked Cecilia. "I was not ready to leave. I don't need collecting like a child!"

"It was either I came or Mary Boleyn would have gone in there and dragged you out of the king's bed herself. Would you have preferred that?"

"She would not have dared. She also knows how he likes to take his time."

Thomasin brushed off this reference to Mary's former relations with Henry. "She is furious for her sister. I think she will be rushing in there, right now, to confront the king herself, and then she will send word to Anne. We shall see that woman back at court in the morning, I have no doubt."

"Then we have succeeded, have we not? In what the queen intended?"

"A little too well, I think."

They hurried along the corridor, shivering with the late night cold. The question was burning on Thomasin's lips all the while, and as they turned into the arch that led to the queen's rooms, she could not help but ask, "Did you … was it?"

Cecilia nodded. "It was not as I expected. He was considerate."

Thomasin nodded, a new gulf of experience between them.

"He needed a little encouragement," she added.

"And you?"

Thomasin saw a rare, genuine vulnerability in her sister's cold, blue eyes. "There was a little pain. The Duchess of

Norfolk told me to expect it, as the lot of a maid. But he was satisfied with me, I know it."

Thomasin recalled the conversation she had had with Ellen at Hever, about the avoidance of pregnancy. "And did the duchess speak further advice?" she blustered, shyly.

"Advice? She gave me lots of advice. About how to please him."

"Anything touching upon the getting of a child?"

"Plenty, I assure you. Now we must only wait and see."

Cecilia's words felt like a brittle wall between them.

They had reached Queen Catherine's chamber now, where the guards admitted them. Lady Howard was standing waiting, having been informed by Lady Mary of Thomasin's departure, and the queen's bedroom door stood ajar. She seized upon Cecilia at once, taking her arm and leading her away, quite ignoring Thomasin.

"Is it done? You were intimate? Did he spend himself inside you?"

Thomasin turned away, a feeling of emptiness washing over her. These games, with their emotional high peaks and low valleys, were exhausting and dangerous. She could not foresee what would happen next, not for Cecilia or the queen, nor for Anne and the king. No doubt, though, the Boleyns would be doing their best to repair this damage and return Anne to Henry's favour. Cecilia had given him the very thing that Anne was withholding, but would it play to their advantage, or had she yielded too soon?

In the antechamber, a figure was sitting in the shadows. As Thomasin pushed the door open further, candlelight spilled inside, revealing Ellen's tear-stained face.

"Oh Ellen, what has happened?"

Ellen's eyes were cast down. She sat with her hands in her lap, toying with a ribbon.

Thomasin pulled up a chair before her. "Was it Hugh? Did you find him?"

She nodded and choked back tears.

"What did he say?"

Ellen took a moment to compose herself, but even then, her voice came out in a wobble. "Apparently it is impossible for us to marry. He says these are not his wishes, he would marry me tomorrow if he could, but I am a married woman and that is not likely to change."

"He does not believe you can divorce?"

"He does not. He says if the king can't divorce, then I can't either. And Barnaby is refusing, so I am stuck." The tears flowed freely now. "I am stuck, Thomasin, stuck forever with that awful man. Even the queen says my duty is to return to him, but I can't!"

"I am sorry. I think that Suffolk has influenced him. He said a similar thing to me earlier, but I was called away before I could speak with you."

"I thought he loved me," she said in a desperate voice. "I believed him."

Thomasin moved to take her hand. "I believe he does genuinely care for you. We all saw it at Raycroft. I think he has been influenced, as I said, persuaded that this is not the right course for him. In his heart, I am sure he does still love you, but is doing what he believes to be right."

"But if he loves me and I love him, I don't see why we can't find a way."

"Oh, Ellen, if only things were that simple. When it comes to the law, Barnaby holds all the power. I am sure he is digging his heels in to spite you."

"How can he be so cruel?"

"He is jealous of Hugh, no doubt. And all Suffolk sees is the marriage and your duty, not your happiness. I am so sorry, Ellen. Perhaps it might still all work out."

"Thank you, but I don't see how."

Nor did Thomasin. She smiled brightly, squeezing Ellen's hand in hers, but although she searched, she could find no glimmer of hope to offer her cousin.

TWENTY-FIVE

The change in the air was palpable. The morning brought an autumnal dew that chilled the air and left the late-blooming flowers heavy with moisture, and the castle was filled with a heavy foreboding as the hours of the morning passed.

Anne Boleyn had returned first thing, as the bells of the abbey were ringing for Terce. The little black Boleyn carriage that had brought Thomasin and Ellen from Hever had been sent out to fetch her from Durham Place, no doubt at Mary Boleyn's instigation, and it returned accompanied by Rafe riding alongside. She strode through the courtyard with steely eyes and her lips set in determination, dressed in scarlet and grey. Ellen and Thomasin saw her pass on their way to the gardens, while Cecilia was closeted with the queen and Lady Howard, biding their time for developments. But Anne did not even notice them. She went straight to the king, whose chambers were emptied, courtiers racing like rats to escape as the doors slammed fast behind them. The court retreated, in anticipation of the rumbles of thunder and lightning bound to erupt.

Thomasin traced her finger along leaves heavy with the morning. Ellen seemed a little calmer, standing facing the river, watching the boats crossing back and forth to Lambeth on the other side.

The last of the season's bees buzzed lazily close to the ground, venturing into the hearts of flowers in the hope of treasure.

"Perhaps I should leave court," said Ellen at length, "if Hugh is to stay. Perhaps the best thing is that I live quietly in the country, or in a religious house, as they advise the queen."

Thomasin was horrified. "No, why should you have to give up on life? Barnaby is in the wrong, on two counts: his infidelity and his refusal to release you. You should not have to suffer as a result."

"But I can't be with the man I love."

"You might love again. Anything might happen. Your next love might be a stronger, braver man than Hugh!"

"But I will never be a mother now, never have a family. That's all I really want."

In that moment, Thomasin felt such a rush of hatred for Barnaby that, if he had been standing before her, she would happily have strangled him. "You never know. The sweat might take him, or an illness, or a stray carriage or bolt of lightning, if there is any justice. There is always hope."

Ellen smiled feebly. "Thank you. But I can't live my life based on possibilities. I need something more certain."

"Nothing is certain in this life."

"True. But as you have always told me, we must make our own decisions, be accountable to ourselves, and exercise our free will."

"Yes, and I stand by that. But it doesn't mean punishing yourself. Stay here at court. Hugh will be off again soon, on some trip to the Netherlands, so your paths won't cross. And by the time he returns, you will be stronger, perhaps even with a new love."

Ellen listened. "It could work. So long as Hugh leaves. But then there is the queen. She thinks I should return to Barnaby, too."

"Perhaps she does, because that is what she wishes to do herself: be reunited with her husband. But you know of her kindness; she will not force you to do so. It was her who took pity on you and offered you a place, when Barnaby's guilt was discovered."

"This is true."

"You can always stay with the queen. And with me."

"You won't be here forever, though. I've seen the way Nico looks at you."

The change of subject disarmed Thomasin. Ellen saw the effect upon her at once.

"What? You don't like him?"

"Yes, yes, of course I do." But there was a shadow to her words. "I don't know. It's just, perhaps, I'm not sure. He tries too hard."

"Too hard?"

"Compliments and letters and poetry. I don't know, it feels too much."

"It's only that you are not used to it, I am sure."

"I'm not, you're right. No man has ever treated me that way before. But it feels as if he is making an effort all the time, performing the role of lover, rather than just being himself."

"He's a Venetian. Perhaps that's what they're like."

"Yes, and what if a year or two down the line, when he has secured me, he stops trying so hard? Who will he be, then? I'm not even sure I know the real Nico, or what is behind the charm and polish."

"Then you must talk to him."

The door opposite them opened, and three figures came out into the garden: Sir Richard, Sir Matthew and his son, the odious Barnaby.

"Oh Heavens," exclaimed Ellen. "I thought he had gone."

"Wait, I will head them off."

The trio made their way through the paths that snaked across the garden. Thomasin headed to meet them with mixed emotions, while Ellen waited reluctantly behind.

"Thomasin," said Sir Richard, approaching his daughter. "The queen said we would find you out here. We have come to take our leave. The court case is over, so we no longer have business at court."

"It is over?" Thomasin echoed.

"Oh, yes, it was settled most favourably for Matthew, who is to grant generous annuities for both the Aston siblings. So it is a good result for all."

"I am pleased to hear that," replied Thomasin, smiling at her uncle.

"It seemed the fairest way," Sir Matthew replied, "to give them a solid start in life, as the old man's next of kin."

"So we are leaving now," repeated Sir Richard. "We have already seen Cecilia, who seems in very good spirits this morning, I must say, as she is to remain with the queen a little longer. It seems she has some kind of plan for her."

Thomasin nodded, surprised when Ellen appeared alongside her.

"We will remain at Monk's Place for a few more days, as your mother has errands to run and wishes to see Dr Elyot again, before going into Suffolk."

"You are both welcome to visit us at Monk's Place before they leave," added Sir Matthew, "although I am sure the queen's service occupies your days fully."

Then, unexpectedly, Barnaby spoke up gruffly. "Wife, will you come back with me to Derbyshire? The queen said that she will spare you, if it is your wish."

The fury rose in Thomasin at his blunt, ungentlemanly question, but this was not her battle to fight.

"No, Sir," replied Ellen. "I will not. I am content to remain at court."

The older men said nothing, as if this was the response that they had expected.

"I wish you would reconsider," Barnaby continued. "With this new money in the family, I will be able to afford a larger residence. I intend to buy Larchwick House, you will recall, on the edge of Buxton to the south."

Not even this could tempt Ellen. "I wish you joy of it," she added with pursed lips. "And I bid you good day."

Barnaby was about to protest, but Sir Matthew placed a warning hand on his arm. "She has spoken. Be content."

"Farewell, Daughter," said Sir Richard, wrapping Thomasin in his arm in an uncharacteristically warm gesture. "Stay out of draughts and avoid wet foods. I'll send word when we reach Eastwell."

"Farewell, Father, may you have a safe and speedy journey. No more carriage accidents."

And she thought again of Lady Boleyn's letter, baffled at its complete disappearance.

"Most definitely not." Sir Richard shuddered. "Oh, the Aston girl was asking after you. I think she wished to see you before they return to Prittlewell."

"Ursula?"

"Yes, she seems like the nicer of the pair. They were at breakfast, but I think they are lingering a little while the paperwork is copied."

"I will seek her out, thank you. Give my love to Mother."

"Oh, and Cardinal Campeggio has arrived in Dartford. He has written requesting wine, as there is nothing decent to drink in the town, he says."

"Then he will be here within days, surely," Thomasin nodded. "The queen will be pleased to hear it."

"As will the king," said Sir Richard. "Both of them believe him to be on their side, but he can't please one without disappointing the other. It remains to be seen what the outcome will be."

"The queen had better dispatch him some claret," said Matthew, smiling. "That will help him make up his mind."

Ursula Aston was coming from St Stephen's Chapel when Thomasin spied her in the distance. They met halfway along the corridor to the great hall and the legal chambers, in air thick with smoke and disputation.

"I am pleased to see you. I wished to thank you for your kindness."

"It was my pleasure; after all, we are cousins, and I know what it is to be a stranger at court."

"You have heard about our case? Your uncle was most generous."

"Yes, he is a good man. I am so pleased he has made provision for you. Perhaps it will allow you a little more freedom."

Ursula nodded. "We can make some repairs to the inn and extend the stables. And Mother's last years will be comfortable. But I wanted to thank you most for your advice. It has been turning over in my mind ever since, and has helped me see things differently."

"Oh?"

"I have decided I will consider any proposals that come along. I need not go too far from home; Mother could even live with us, if it were to happen." She blushed. "But I get ahead of myself. I think your words just helped me remove the block. I was dismissing it outright, without proper consideration."

"That is good," said Thomasin. "But be certain that any suitor is genuine, that he does not come after you now for the money."

"I have considered this." Ursula nodded. "We intend to keep our new income quiet, and besides, Gilbert would sniff out any man who did not have my best intentions at heart. He is not too bad, in that sense. He does want the best for me."

"I am glad to hear it. When do you depart?"

"This afternoon. Gilbert is collecting the copies of the documents, and then we will leave."

"Be sure to write to me, and let me know how you fare, and all about those suitors."

Ursula blushed. "I promise I will. Perhaps in time, I might even send you a wedding invitation."

"I sincerely hope that you will. It is not so far from Suffolk, after all. We are practically neighbours."

Thomasin watched her walk away. The sun slanted gently across the stones, but despite the warmth, she had a sudden sense of foreboding about the place, a dissatisfaction she could not shake. Unanswered questions and trials lay ahead. The approach of Cardinal Campeggio meant that soon, the royal marriage would come under official scrutiny, with all the pain and grief that entailed.

Ellen's broken heart filled her with a sense of frustration over the cruelty of men and their laws, along with the speed with which the king had been happy to fall into Cecilia's arms while Anne was away. Were people always destined to suffer? To inflict cruelty upon each other when their wishes clashed?

With a sigh, she turned and headed back up to the queen's apartments.

TWENTY-SIX

Lady Howard was holding court with all the other women clustered around her, hanging on her every word. Cecilia stood beside her in a new gown of russet and cream, chin held high and emitting a sort of self-satisfied glow. Even Queen Catherine, seated beside her, waited with excitement to hear what had been achieved. Charles Brandon and Mary Tudor sat at the table, drinking wine with Baron Mountjoy. Thomasin was taken aback by the scene, having left the rooms so quiet. Now, there was a thrill in the air, a bubble of success. She joined the group, noticing that Ellen stood on the far side, her head bowed low.

"At first he refused to admit her," Lady Howard was saying. "He said that she had chosen to leave court and could not just come back as and when she wished. He said that she was his subject too, and must wait upon his pleasure, that she had no right to barge into his apartments."

Thomasin realised she was speaking of Anne Boleyn and the king.

"And what did she reply?" asked Maria Willoughby.

"She was furious. As we had hoped."

A murmur of excitement ran round the room. Lady Howard took her time, enjoying her audience.

"She could hardly speak, spitting out her fury like a cat. I was entranced by her. The king can only have been disgusted."

"Did he send her away?" asked Catherine.

"No, not yet. I think he was held in the same captivation as the rest of us."

"So what did she say?"

"She said that she had every right, as his betrothed, to demand answers from him, given the news that had reached her ears. He replied that she had no right to question the king's choices. His private business was his own, and if she continued to deny him his freedom with her, then what did she expect?"

"Then they have not lain together," said Catherine, nodding her head in confirmation. "She is holding him at arm's length in hopes of a marriage."

"How furious she must be about Cecilia," added Lady Mary, with a sort of glee. "This has played out so well, right into her fears and insecurities. The arrogance of her! Does she really think she is the only woman at court? Pray, go on."

"Well," continued Lady Howard, "she refused to leave, although he kept requesting it. She demanded that he never see the Lady concerned again." She shot a satisfied glance at Cecilia. "She hurled all manner of insulting terms at the king, calling him weak and less than a man for submitting to temptation, saying he had undermined their love and that he was not worthy of her. I thought that he was about to explode at her sharpness."

The room was agog. Surely this must spell the end for Anne Boleyn?

"But he did not?" asked Maria.

"He merely stood and observed her, like a wild animal set loose, and she went on, lashing him with her tongue, until he rose to his feet. He looked most kingly and held up his hand to stop her, saying that she would do well to remember who she was, and who he was, and that only God might dictate to a king. And then he left!"

"He left the chamber?" echoed Lady Mary.

"Yes, he walked straight out and left her alone, and has now ridden out hunting."

"So where is she?"

"She retired to her family's rooms, where my husband told me all of this."

"Well," said Mountjoy, separating himself from the group, "it seems that your plan has been most successful. With a wedge driven between the king and his paramour, he will be more open to suggestion from those who wish her harm. I shall have a word with Wolsey."

"Thank you, Baron," said Catherine. "We also await the arrival of Campeggio, and his news from Rome, and we hope to count upon his support in the forthcoming trial."

"Indeed, my Lady." He bowed and departed.

The room sighed in collective relief. The plan had provoked the desired conflict between the king and Anne Boleyn. All that remained to be seen was whether it would drive him back into the arms of the queen.

Brandon rose to his feet. "Now we must tie these ends up and conduct a marriage, to reward our happy servant. Come," he said to Cecilia, "let us speak of the arrangements and make it as speedy as possible, as you have deserved."

A marriage? Thomasin wondered at the words.

A huge smile spread across Cecilia's face. "I can't wait to be mistress of Raycroft."

Thomasin's stomach lurched as the words struck her ears. Hugh Truegood? Cecilia was to marry Hugh. This was what had lain behind Brandon's efforts to detach him from Ellen; he was to be the reward for the loss of Cecilia's virtue.

"Raycroft?" she stammered, looking wildly to Ellen, but her cousin had frozen, her eyes closed. "Must it be so?"

"A most suitable match," boomed Brandon. "Two young people of the right age and sort, a match that greatly pleases the queen."

"Don't look alarmed," added Cecilia. "It is all very new, very sudden, and Father doesn't even know yet, but he will be delighted, I am sure."

"But…" stuttered Thomasin, looking from her to Ellen and back again.

Her sister didn't read her desperate cues, or else ignored them, taking Brandon's extended hand as he led her to the table.

Then Lady Howard's voice rang out, as clear as a bell. "One more thing."

The group all turned and looked back to her again. She was standing, looking proud and fierce, holding up something in her hand. A piece of paper, folded and addressed.

There was no doubt. Thomasin recognised Lady Boleyn's missing letter at once. Her insides turned cold. Lady Howard was staring straight at her.

"Here we have a letter addressed to Anne Boleyn," the fiery little woman announced, turning to address the room. "Someone in the queen's household has been corresponding with that woman!"

A gasp ran round the room. Queen Catherine herself stood up, frowning. "Give that to me." She took the letter and turned it over in her jewelled hands. Thomasin noticed with relief that the seal was unbroken, so the contents had not been read. "What could this mean? How did you come by it, Duchess?"

"I found it, hidden under the cushion of a chair, where someone had thought no one would look. Goodness knows what intrigues it might contain. Perhaps the writer even warned Anne of our plan."

The thought of this hung in the air. Thomasin could hear them wondering, turning a simple matter into a conspiracy. Her palms turned clammy.

The queen examined the letter. "Let us be calm and proceed with caution. It may be nothing of the kind. I do not know the hand. Who would have brought such a thing here, into my chamber?"

"Should we open it?" asked Maria. "See what it says? Then we may have our answer."

"No," said Catherine at once. "There is a sanctity about a sealed letter. It would be wrong to do so."

"More wrong than Anne's attempts to usurp your crown and marital bed?" Lady Howard asked.

"It's mine," burst out Ellen, suddenly. "I was charged to deliver it."

Thomasin could not have her cousin take the blame for her. "No," she said, drawing all eyes to her. "This is not Ellen's fault; she seeks to protect me. It's my letter. I was charged to deliver it to Anne and, lacking the opportunity, I tucked it under the cushion in the antechamber."

"You?" Catherine's face was a picture of bewilderment.

"You?" echoed Lady Howard. "I never trusted you! No doubt you have been planning with the Boleyns all this time, sharing the queen's secrets!"

Thomasin was aghast. Ignoring the duchess, she turned instead to Catherine. "There is nothing sinister in this matter, my Lady, I give you my word. On our way to London from the country, my family suffered an accident in our carriage, which required a smith. It was pouring with rain and we were forced to shelter at the nearest house, which happened to be Hever. We were most grateful for the hospitality of Lady Boleyn, who was the only family member present. Upon our departure in the morning, she bid me deliver this letter to her daughter, a task which I did not invite and which made me feel uncomfortable, but which I felt obliged to fulfil after her kindness."

The whole room was staring at Thomasin.

"My cousin speaks the truth," said Ellen. "I was also present on the journey and stayed at Hever, and I saw Lady Boleyn hand her the letter."

Catherine was eyeing the pair dubiously.

"My Lady, you have no cause to doubt my loyalty," urged Thomasin. "I have ever been your true servant, such as you yourself believed this summer when you made me the gift of a ring, upon the discovery of the Venetian plot. The presence of this letter here is more confirmation that I value your Ladyship more highly than I ever have the Boleyns. Had I been in their service, I would simply have delivered it upon my arrival here. It was out of concern for my Lady's feelings that I held it back, unwilling to cause you pain or do a service to those who cause you harm."

"So she says," burst out Lady Howard with spite. "The letter might contain anything at all. Until it is opened, we do not know its secrets."

"It is simply a letter from a mother to a daughter. But I lost it several days ago. You must have been holding onto it all this time, Duchess. I wonder why you did not simply speak up, for the matter could have simply been resolved."

"Like you," Lady Howard snapped back at once, "I have no desire to cause the queen pain."

"And yet you have caused this drama." Thomasin's hands were shaking, but she stood her ground against the duchess.

"What impertinence!" Lady Howard cried. "How she stands there so brazenly after being the go-between with that awful woman. And her very own sister, having just made the sacrifice she has."

"A sacrifice that brings her more than adequate rewards," Ellen chimed in.

Seated at the side with Charles Brandon, Cecilia made no move to comment or intervene.

"Stop," called Catherine, raising her hand. "Mistress Marwood, you claim that this is a letter entrusted to you by Lady Boleyn, for her daughter Anne."

"Yes, my Lady."

"Then you must discharge your duty and deliver it."

"Pardon, my Lady?"

The queen handed Thomasin the letter. "It is your duty to deliver this into Mistress Boleyn's hands. Go and do so now."

"Deliver the letter?" exclaimed Lady Howard. "But…"

"Hush!" said Catherine. "We will have no more mischief in my chambers. Maria, make ready to accompany me to chapel."

"Yes, my Lady."

"Don't stand there staring," Catherine said sharply to Thomasin. "You have your instructions. Off you go."

It was with trepidation that Thomasin made her way down the corridors in the direction of the Boleyn chambers. It sounded merely a simple matter, to place the letter in Anne's hands, mutter a few words of explanation and withdraw, but her steps were heavy, and a weight hung about her heart. The Duchess of Norfolk's dreadful attempts to discredit her may have harmed her good relations with the queen, hard upon the terrible news that Cecilia was to marry Hugh. Thomasin could not imagine how Ellen must be feeling. Surely if Cecilia had any decency, and Thomasin could explain the situation to her, she would not go through with the match? For no matter how self-centred and vain her elder sister was, she was not heartless. Surely she would not wish to become the wife of a man who still loved another?

"Thomasin?"

She turned to see Nico, coming along the corridor. He was as golden and glowing as ever, if not a little dishevelled, as if he was in a hurry. In one sense, he was a welcome distraction; in another, he was a delay to the inevitable action she must take.

"Where are you headed?" he asked, brandishing a sheaf of papers.

"To the Boleyns. I must deliver a letter there."

Nico winced. "By all accounts it is a battlefield in there at the moment."

"Oh no, I had feared as much. But I must do what the queen insists."

"Good luck, sweetheart," he said, leaning in to plant a kiss upon her cheek. It took Thomasin a little by surprise, but it was not unpleasant. "I am glad to have come upon you like this," he continued. "As you can see from all these papers, Cromwell is keeping me busy making copies of his records. He has announced his intention to go to his house at Chelsea later today, and I am to accompany him. It may be for a week or more, so I shall not return to court for a little while. I shall be thinking of you, though."

Thomasin felt sorry to lose a friend, even temporarily. "I hope your work is speedily concluded."

He stepped closer. "Will you miss me, Thomasin?"

"Of course."

"I mean, really miss me? Will you long to have me beside you?"

Thomasin was unsure whether she would go that far. "I shall miss seeing you, of course."

"Perhaps, when I return, we might find the occasion to spend a little private time together, if you would like to."

He bent and tried to kiss her lips. She drew back a little at the speed of the gesture.

"You are a little hesitant. I understand. It is to be expected in a maid."

His openness made her blush. He was handsome, elegant, devoted. What was it, then, that made her feelings lag behind his? Was it simply the speed at which he was racing? His comment about her being a maid made her uncomfortable. Was he hoping that their relationship would develop along more physical lines upon his return? How many other women had he known?

She stepped back. "I must deliver my letter."

"Certainly." He seemed a little hurt. "Now is not the time or place. I hope I shall see you upon my return."

Thomasin watched him walk away, with a mixture of feelings she did not quite understand.

The voices reached Thomasin before she arrived at the Boleyns' door. They were all raised in unison so that none of their words could be heard.

She hesitated, torn between the desire to listen and the need to escape. But she could not wait to be rid of the troublesome letter, so it was better done sooner rather than later.

The voices came to an abrupt halt when Thomasin knocked. The door was thrown open by the tall, imposing figure of the Duke of Norfolk. At close quarters, he was even more intimidating than his stern looks appeared at a distance: the height, the breadth, the full beard.

Behind him, she could see Anne and her father, and Mary Boleyn and Rafe, standing awkwardly, interrupted in the middle of a family debate. Anne herself was red-faced, her cheeks streaked with tears, her black eyes burning with fury.

"Yes?" demanded Thomas Howard abruptly, as if she was bringing firewood.

Thomasin summoned her courage. "I bring a letter for Lady Anne."

Coming forward, Mary Boleyn glared at her. "You!" She turned back to address the room. "It was her sister that did it, and this one, brazen as anything, enticed away my Will!"

Thomasin was horrified.

"Is that what you do, you Marwood sisters?" demanded Mary. "Chase after married men?"

Too late she realised the irony of her words. Her affair with the king had not been forgotten.

"My Lady," said Thomasin pointedly, but with dignity, "my mistress is the wife of the king. I cannot comment upon what choices married men make. I am here to deliver a letter." She turned towards Anne and held out the folded paper. "It is from your mother."

"My mother?" Anne stalked towards her and plucked it from her hand. "What can she be doing, sending it to you?"

"We were at Hever, on the way to London. Your mother was kind enough to give us hospitality during a storm while our carriage was mended. I had wished to deliver it sooner, but it was misplaced. It has not been opened, I swear. You can see yourself from the seal."

Anne flipped it over, examined the seal and snapped it in half. Thomasin sensed Rafe's eyes upon her. At least he knew the truth of her words.

"Are we to tolerate this?" asked Mary, but her father intervened.

"Hold your tongue. Anne, what does it say?"

The room fell silent, waiting as Anne read.

"She is well," Anne explained, "save for her headaches. She writes of our estates, of the repairs to the church roof, of the revenue raised from the sheep, a new cook she has hired from Appledore." She paused.

"What is it?" asked Thomas Boleyn, impatiently.

"It is advice, from mother to daughter, nothing of significance." But she lifted her eyes to Thomasin's. "What did you say to Mother?"

"Me? Nothing. What do you mean?"

"You must have said something to her, influenced her somehow."

"I did no such thing. I was polite to my hostess, as her generosity deserved."

"Listen to this." Anne turned back to the room, quoting aloud from the letter. "'When you are queen, be sure to take this young woman, Thomasin Marwood, into your household as a favour to your mother. She is a good girl, and her looks remind me of you.'"

Thomasin was astonished. "I had no idea she had written such a thing." Had she known, she would have destroyed the letter rather than deliver it.

"It would fall to you to choose your household," urged Mary. "And if she is in it, I certainly will not be."

"This is not a matter of my choosing, I assure you!" Thomasin confirmed. The thought of serving Anne grated upon her, not only because of her loyalty to Catherine, but also due to the combative, volatile nature of the Boleyns and her distrust of Anne.

"It is merely Mother's fancy," said Anne. "She will have forgotten it already."

"Of course she will," added her father, turning to Thomasin. "You have discharged your duty. We give you thanks for your pains."

Thomasin bowed her head at his acknowledgement, but Thomas Howard was already closing the door. The last thing she saw was Rafe's face, as the Boleyns were enfolded into their privacy again. She lingered outside the door for a moment, waiting to hear whether the argument would start up again, but there was silence.

She had barely turned away, when Thomasin heard the door open again behind her. She was surprised to see that Rafe had slipped out after her.

"I just have a moment," he said, fixing those dark tapering eyes upon her face. "Thomasin, it is good to see you. That letter comes as a surprise."

"It does. I had no idea that was what she had written."

"It matters not. Like they said, she will have forgotten." He glanced back to the chamber. "Hell has broken loose in here, due to your sister, I think."

Thomasin shrugged. "I am not responsible for her behaviour. I do not condone what she did."

"But maybe the outcome?"

"I do not wish to meddle in anyone else's matters of the heart."

"How about your own?" He stepped closer. "Thomasin, I have missed you. Can we not be close again?"

The attraction between them was undeniable. For a moment, the desire flickered up again. It would be easy as anything to lean in to his kiss, and let those passionate feelings overcome her again. She pulled away.

"I must get back. The queen expects me."

"Is it because of that Italian?"

"He is Venetian."

"A foreigner. How do you know you can trust him?"

"Please stop. I must return."

"I am still here, Thomasin. I have not forgotten what we shared. Have you?"

She had not. Of course, she had not. But so many sensible reasons stood between her and desire. Why was it not possible to combine the behaviour of Nico with the passion of Rafe?

"It is good to see you, but you must not think of me that way," she said. "I must return."

"You have no feelings for me?"

She could not affirm that.

"Then you do?" he asked, clutching at her silence. "You do, I know it!"

"I must return. Let me go, Rafe."

Her footsteps echoed down the corridor, just as the voices of the Boleyns started to rise again in discord.

At the approach to Queen Catherine's chambers, a familiar figure stood waiting. Thomasin's father was looking anxious and out of breath, still in his travelling clothes.

"What is this news?" He came pacing towards her, wringing his hands. "I was at the stables, about to depart, when a summons came from the queen. Something about Cecilia's marriage? Do you know of this?"

"Unfortunately, I have just learned of it myself today. The queen has approved a marriage between Cecilia and Sir Hugh. Suffolk has brokered it."

"Sir Hugh Truegood? Of Raycroft? I had no idea. I thought Ellen…"

"Indeed. The only reason for our recent invitation to Raycroft was the affection shared between Hugh and Ellen, but he has been quite talked out of that by Suffolk, because Ellen's divorce seems so uncertain."

"I am all astonishment. Does your mother know of this?"

"Not a thing. Until the last few days, Ellen had hopes of becoming Hugh's wife herself. Now Cecilia swoops in and collects the prize."

"How, in the name of goodness, did this come about?"

Thomasin shrugged, remembering her sister's face as they left the king's chamber. "She has served the queen."

"As have you, but they are not arranging your marriage, are they?"

"No, Father."

He ran his hand through his beard. "It is so sudden, too sudden. Is Cecilia content with this?"

"Like the cat that got the cream. She knows nothing of Ellen."

"I can imagine. But Ellen? She cannot be happy."

"No, she is not. I imagine her heartbroken."

"Truegood can hardly be worth lamenting, if he can be so fickle in his emotions."

"I doubt he has any emotions for Cecilia, but he has been guided by Suffolk, who has taken him under his wing."

"It is a strange business. What do you make of it?"

Thomasin shrugged, new-found cynicism weighing her down. "What does it matter what I think? I have no influence over any of those who have made the match."

Sir Richard put an arm about her shoulders and pulled her close. "If it must go ahead, we have no choice but to accept it. On paper it is a good match for your sister. Ellen will find love again one day, from a man who truly deserves her."

"I hope so."

"As will you, my love, as will you."

Rain fell that night. It dripped down the roofs and streamed along the gutters, to pool among the cobbles. Queen Catherine retired early, and the presence of Lady Howard made the chambers odious to Thomasin.

Cecilia was restless, pacing about the room like a caged animal until Thomasin could bear it no more.

"Come, let us take the air for a little while."

Ellen watched them with mournful eyes, grateful for respite from Hugh's bride-to-be.

Together, they walked through the chill of the corridors, among ancient stones and vaulted ceilings. Torches burned bright on the walls and the odd courtier and servant passed them without comment. Cecilia was unusually quiet, walking quickly and earnestly. Thomasin had to quicken her pace to keep up.

"What bothers you, tonight?"

"What if there is a child?" Cecilia asked suddenly, her face clouded.

"A child?" Thomasin repeated dumbly, drawn out of her own thoughts.

"Yes. Even you must know how it happens."

Thomasin didn't deign to reply.

"But what if I am carrying the king's child?" Cecilia asked again.

"Hugh will take care of it. Pass it off as his own."

"Of course he will," Cecilia dismissed. "But I am a little scared of that. Of being a mother. Bearing a child."

"It is what women do. It's just the way of things."

"But I could have the seed of a child inside me now, starting to grow."

"Yes, you might. When will you know?"

"I suppose I shall have to wait until my flowers come. Two weeks, maybe three."

"Then there is no point in worrying just yet."

They walked on a little further. Thomasin let herself be drawn into her thoughts, until her sister spoke again.

"But women do die in childbed." The concern in her voice was genuine.

"Some do, but more survive, and lots go on to bear many children, like Mother. There is no reason why you should not be the same."

"But some do?"

Thomasin stopped. "You really do fear this?"

Cecilia's pale eyes brimmed with tears. For a moment, her cool outer shell had slipped away. "I do."

Then, suddenly, out of nowhere, Anne Boleyn was coming towards them through the darkness. With a speedy gesture, she tugged at Cecilia's headdress, pulling her backwards. With no witnesses at that time of night, her words were ugly.

"You? You dare show your face here? You little whore, you cheap harlot, did you think you'd creep into the king's bed while I was away? Did you think I'd stand by and let you?"

Cecilia struggled to right herself and turned round to face her attacker, her cheeks flaming. Mary Boleyn stood behind her sister, her face suffused with vengeance.

Thomasin's heart beat fit to burst at the sight of them. She cursed, recommending that they leave the queen's chambers.

"Look at them. The Marwood sisters. Two little country girls, raised on a farm," mocked Anne, "come to play at court. You think he will remember you tomorrow? When you've left, and I'm still here? You were in the right place at the right time and he used you, like any man would, because you threw yourself at him. Mary told me all. Be mindful of who you are,

294

Madam, and who I am to become. When I am queen, you will never darken these corridors again."

Cecilia had composed herself now, recovering from the shock. "He welcomed me with open arms. No doubt it was a relief from your coldness and sharp tongue."

"You mean my dignity," Anne stated. "You fool. Any woman can lie with a man, but you have no idea what it means to keep one."

"The king is not your possession or your lap dog," replied Cecilia. "He has a mind of his own and it was his decision to invite me into his bed. I suggest you chastise him, not me — if you think yourself equal to the king, of course, to speak to him thus. No wonder he was so eager to forget you. Come, sister, the queen shall hear of this." She put her arm through Thomasin's and they swiftly walked away.

"There is no queen here," Anne called after them. "Not yet. Tell your mistress that!"

Thomasin could scarcely breathe, but she was full of admiration for her sister's reply.

"Did I do well?" Cecilia breathed at last, her hands shaking.

Thomasin nodded. "I believe you did. Excellently well, although Anne will never forget this."

Her sister shrugged. "I hope not. Perhaps it will show her that she is not as untouchable as she thinks."

"And now you will marry Hugh?"

"As you see, I cannot remain at court. I know you do not approve."

"It's not that, it's…"

"Ellen. I know. Thomasin, she is married. Married. You must let go of your romantic notion that love will conquer all. It won't. We all have to make our own way in the world, and I can't put my one good chance aside because of her feelings. Surely you can see that?"

"I can see that you deserve to be happy, and so does Ellen. It is a pity that it must be this way."

"We may not always have seen eye to eye, Thomasin, but you are my sister. Ellen had her chance. I'm sorry to be brutal, but there it is. We cannot resolve her situation, nor can Hugh marry a married woman. You have to let this go. And I hope you will give me your blessing."

They had reached the queen's rooms again. As Thomasin opened the door, she saw Ellen, sitting in the glow of a candle, lost in thought. And she was filled with a sudden sense that she had betrayed her cousin.

TWENTY-SEVEN

Thomasin re-read the final words of the letter. Thomas More's words had found their way to her in Sussex — a welcome interruption to the business of Cecilia's marriage. In his neat, scholarly hand, he described the task put to him by Queen Catherine. On a dull afternoon, a few days ago, with clouds building over the city, he had found himself waiting in a quiet, dark street, away from the bustling crowds. The address had brought him to a run-down lodging house, its plasterwork peeling and splashes of mud from the gutters sprayed halfway up the ground floor. The storeys above were overhanging, but the windows were larger, and all were tightly closed against the noxious odours of humanity. But he had time to spare so he entered, and ordered himself a jar of ale, some bread and cheese and sat patiently.

Eventually, a pair of exhausted horses drew to a halt outside. More had risen to his feet at once, and stepped outside to see a small carriage, inside which a large, elderly gentleman in black reclined upon a mountain of cushions, his legs covered with furs and blankets. His servants were making ready for the slow, laborious process of transferring him from his seat, down the step, over the mud and indoors at last. As he pulled himself slowly upright, the new arrival winced in pain and gripped the carriage door with arthritic fingers.

More introduced himself, stating his purpose and allegiance. An old, gnarled hand reached out to grasp his, and a pair of rheumatic eyes watered gently in his direction. It was not his first time in London, the old man explained. His brother Antonio had already ridden ahead, to announce their arrival at court; no doubt they would be reunited soon. And then that awful, ungodly business must begin, he continued, confident of More's approval: the undignified struggle of untangling the King of England's marriage. It was not a task that the cardinal was relishing. In due course, he promised, he would announce his arrival to Queen Catherine and listen to her confession, but for now, as he fumbled forward, all he could do was rest in a darkened room and offer up his grateful prayers.

And so, More concluded in his letter, the long-awaited Cardinal Campeggio had arrived in London. All that remained was for the scholar to wish Thomasin good health, and hope that the wedding was a success, and that he may have the pleasure of her company again, upon her return to court. She folded the paper and tucked it into her travel chest, among her clothes. Then, she slowly rose to her feet and took a deep breath. It was time.

Raycroft Court stood radiant in the October sunshine. The redbrick front shone warmly as Thomasin stepped outside into the morning light and the many mullioned windows gleamed bright. The park had taken on a different mood with the advancement of the season, with leaves still clinging to the trees in shades of red and yellow, while others had shed their coats entirely, giving much work to the busy gardeners. They had been hurrying about for the last two days, sweeping, pruning, and readying everything for the wedding.

It was difficult to believe they had only left this place just over a month ago. How utterly different everything was now, with this second visit. The grounds where they had ridden together, the graceful pond where Ellen had delighted in feeding the fish, the elegant hallway with its carved wooden staircase: all seemed to belong to another world. Thomasin could almost hear Hugh and Ellen's contented laughter rising and falling along the corridor. Back then, she had been eager to return here soon, to witness what she believed to be an impending wedding. She'd had no idea then that the bride was to be her own sister, instead of her cousin.

She had left Ellen at Westminster. Kissing her cousin's tear-stained cheek, Thomasin had assured her that she must forget Hugh and his fickle emotions.

"Count yourself blessed that you escaped such a match, where he would listen to everything his friends said, and cast aside that which he truly values."

"You are right, of course," replied Ellen, her face composed. "Your words speak to my head, but yet my heart lags behind. Do not write to me. Do not tell me any of the details. I shall pretend it has not happened, then welcome you back to court in two weeks, as if you had just gone out walking in the gardens."

"I shall not speak a word of it, I promise. If my mother hadn't written to the queen requesting my attendance, I would remain here with you."

"I know. You are a good cousin, and the best of friends."

"Keep yourself busy and do not let your mind run on it."

"The only advantage of your absence is that I shall have to do your tasks as well as my own, so I shall have no time to be melancholy. Don't worry about me."

But Ellen had preyed upon Thomasin's mind all through the journey into Kent and Sussex, past the very spot where their carriage had broken, past the chimneys of Hever, just visible above the thinning trees. Briefly, she allowed her thoughts to wander back to Lady Boleyn's letter, to the strange circumstances of its disappearance and rediscovery, to the Duchess of Norfolk's spite, and Lady Boleyn's request. How strange it seemed that Lady Boleyn had taken such a liking to Thomasin in that short space of time. How strange that she had asked Anne to take her into her future household — a move that would go against the wishes of Anne and Thomasin herself. She couldn't help but wonder what the lady had been thinking.

"Ah. Here you are." Sir Richard appeared outside the hall, beside his younger daughter. "I have sought you everywhere."

"I'm sorry, Father. I had to escape from all the activity for a little while."

"Yes, I understand. Your mother is helping Cecilia dress. They are almost ready."

Thomasin couldn't reply. She turned back to the view and watched birds rising up from the trees.

"I know you don't like this match, Thomasin," he continued. "But it is done now. There is no going back. We must move on and see it for the excellent opportunity it is. Cecilia could have hardly done better."

Thomasin turned away.

"Remember both bride and groom go into it willingly."

"Neither has any affection for the other. Cecilia sees a grand house and wealth; Hugh has been told to do this by Suffolk. I am sure they will suit each other very well."

"Is it any worse than her first, that was arranged with Henry Kytson?"

"Infinitely worse, Father, because of the love that existed between Hugh and Ellen."

"Remember, this match was arranged by Suffolk and the queen. Both saw Ellen's marriage as an implacable obstacle, and Cecilia as a more suitable bride. Who are we to argue with them?"

Thomasin could do nothing but bite her tongue. Her experience at court had taught her that the wishes of mere mortals were nothing in comparison with the will of great ones. Perhaps Cecilia had been right, and Thomasin had allowed a romantic vision to cloud her judgement.

"Our feelings matter little. We should be grateful for such a good match for your sister. It may steady her."

Ahead on the path, coming from the chapel, Thomasin spotted Peter Southey, Sir Hugh's steward, who was walking towards the house.

"Ah, I will speak with him," said Sir Richard, "and see whether the arrangements are on track."

Thomasin walked on, along the path, letting her father take Southey out of earshot. Her feet led her towards the little grey chapel, where she had heard Mass a few weeks before. Now, the outside was decorated with the flowers and greenery of the season, such as it was on those autumnal days: the last roses, Michaelmas daisies and marigolds, interspersed with ivy and sweet box.

In the porch, Hugh Truegood was standing alone, dressed in ash-grey and silver. He turned at Thomasin's approach and she read the mix of emotions in his eyes.

"Oh, Hugh," she said at once, unthinking, "it is hard to believe this is happening."

Hugh shrugged. "This match is sealed as fast as my blood now. Even the king desires it."

"The king? Henry gave his approval?"

Hugh shrugged. "Of course. Why would he not?"

And Thomasin realised that Hugh knew nothing of the false mistress plan. He was completely unaware that his bride had shared the king's bed, and perhaps carried his child in her womb.

The truth was on her lips. A few words would perhaps unravel this marriage, as Hugh was an honest, simple man. But it was not within her to do it.

He turned to her with a calm face. "Ellen is a married woman, Thomasin. The law stands against us."

She shrugged. "I had believed you to be in love, that is all."

"What is love, Thomasin?" His chestnut eyes flashed. "How well do I know Ellen, to call it love? We have spent a little time together, we are drawn to each other, but we have not passed more than three days in each other's company. How am I to know that it would have endured beyond the year's end? We had a fancy for each other, as many young people do, but marriage is a matter for family, for dynasties, and the making of heirs. It has nothing to do with love. It is another question altogether."

"You would have loved Ellen, and she you. You know it."

"Oh, what does it matter now?"

As he spoke, a cold wind blew through the trees, making Thomasin shudder.

The Duke and Duchess of Suffolk appeared along the path, decked in gold and jewels.

"Ready, Truegood?" asked Charles Brandon, his eyes moving briefly to Thomasin and back again.

"Ready, my Lord."

"Good, the bride approaches."

Servants were advancing, carrying cushions, a silver basin, books. Thomasin recognised their black and green livery, with the embroidered oak leaf upon the breast. In the distance she saw Southey leading out the bent figure of Lady Truegood, followed by her mother, her father and sister. Without a word,

Thomasin turned and entered the chapel. The sun disappeared behind a cloud.

Cecilia was dressed from head to toe in a pale apricot-coloured silk. It splayed out from her bodice in waves and fell to the ground in folds. The stomacher was embroidered with gold thread and hundreds of tiny pearls in a design of linked chains; no doubt the best that Hugh's extensive suppliers in the Netherlands could find. Her fair hair was pulled back under a gold headdress and caught in a jewelled net that hung down her back. Large diamonds hung at her throat. She glowed as she walked down the aisle on Sir Richard's arm, her golden slippers making no sound on the ancient stones. Thomasin grudgingly admitted that this was the most beautiful her sister had ever been.

Beside Thomasin, her mother was almost shaking with joy. "Such a match," she whispered. "I never dreamed … such beauty … such wealth…"

Thomasin looked across to where Lady Truegood sat, amid a gaggle of elderly female relatives, with Southey behind. The old woman looked clean and alert, with a gentle smile fixed upon her face, although it was difficult to tell if her eyes were watering with age or pleasure. Friar Antony stood waiting at the front, beside two flickering candles, the book open in his hands. To his left, Hugh turned to greet his bride.

Cecilia swept past Thomasin, her long train dragging behind her along the stone floor. The scents of amber and musk lingered in the air. She walked towards her future husband like a warrior, a queen, a saint ascending to Heaven, her usually cold face beaming wide with an unrecognisable smile. This was her victory, her moment of triumph.

But Thomasin felt nothing but numbness. She heard the friar welcome them all, and address the couple. She heard the sermon, the vows they exchanged, the promises made in the sight of God. She stared down at her hands in her lap, the little finger bearing the pearl ring given to her by the queen. What was life's purpose? What was love? She'd always cherished the idea that somehow, things would work out. Do the right thing, be cautious, respectful, devout, and honest, and the rewards would come to you. Love would find a way. But it hadn't worked for Ellen. What if Thomasin had got this wrong? What if all this talk of love was a delusion?

Suddenly people were rising to their feet, clapping and smiling. Hugh had taken Cecilia by the hand and was leading her outside, to where the feast awaited them. Stumbling to her feet, Thomasin followed, out of the stone-clad gloom and into the blinding sunshine that had suddenly appeared. She blinked, rubbing her eyes and seeing only the hazy shapes of the bride and groom heading away from her.

It was done.

TWENTY-EIGHT

It was a beautiful day, the kind Thomasin liked best. Fresh and light, with delicate sunlight dappled across the road and the leaves stirring on the branches. The air smelled of woodsmoke and earth after rain. The sky was a most royal mid-blue, swathed in banks of white cloud. The carriage rumbled forward, through the London streets, bringing her back to court, back to her service with the queen. And yet, Thomasin's heart was heavy as lead in her chest.

She had been away from the palace for two weeks. After Hugh and Cecilia had been married, there was a frenzy of celebrations: dinners, hunting, dancing, even fireworks that split the sky into showers of gold and silver, imported from Brussels. Everything had been of the finest quality: Hugh had chosen excellent wine and food, the musicians had been hired from the Imperial court, the walls had been hung with exquisite tapestries and cloths of silver tissue, and the rooms had been scented with sea coal and herbs. Thomasin had watched the newly married couple for signs of happiness or burgeoning love. She wanted to believe that there might be some merit in this match after all, hoping that Ellen's broken heart was worth it for the sake of Cecilia's happiness.

At the end of a lively dance, she had caught her sister by the arm, her cheeks aglow from the fire.

"Tell me," she had insisted, looking into Cecilia's eyes, "are you content?"

Cecilia had grinned, before whirling away. "Aren't I lucky? Mistress of all this?"

Thomasin had watched the bride dance away, packed her bags and ordered her carriage back to court. If appreciation was there, perhaps in time affection would grow. If Cecilia had all her material wishes granted, what was to stop her from fulfilling the role of the dutiful wife? But Thomasin knew her sister. The doubts niggled away in the back of her mind, but it was out of her hands now. It was between Cecilia and Hugh to make it work.

The street outside was suddenly familiar. Thomasin looked out of the carriage window to see the palace gates come into view, red brick with the royal crest set in the centre, picked out in gold paint. Once they came to a halt in the courtyard, she jumped out onto the cobbles. The place seemed quiet for early afternoon, with a few stable lads leading out horses to be shod, and a maid sweeping away water from the kitchen steps.

Thomasin made her way inside. This route was familiar to her now, with the cold shade of the passageways, their twists and turns, dark corners and sudden vistas. Light streamed down through the glazed windows as she turned away from the passage connecting the service wing to the hall and along a passage with a dark stone floor. A few more turns and there were now rushes underfoot, torches burning, even pictures behind curtains upon the walls. Then, on her right was the staircase. She had climbed this so often, knowing its angles and shallows, counting out its steps. From the top, she walked forward along the panelled gallery, turning left and then right, through a chamber and into the corridor that led to the queen's apartments. Again, all seemed very quiet. It was almost as if she had the palace to herself.

The guards admitted her to Catherine's chambers with looks of surprise. Only a laundress was in the antechamber, gathering up linen. Otherwise, the rooms were empty.

"My Lady went out riding," the woman explained. "They are dining in the orchards to the north of the city."

"Just the queen?"

"King and queen together. They'll be gone until sundown."

Her words took Thomasin by surprise. So Henry and Catherine were out riding in each other's company, like the old days. And if Catherine had consented to go, it must only be because Anne was not present. Perhaps the plot of the false mistress, and the rift it had caused between Henry and Anne, had been a success after all.

Thomasin left the quiet rooms and headed down to the walled garden. This place, with its gentle flowers and discreet arbour, had offered shelter to her on many occasions, and also witnessed the kisses she had exchanged with Nico. She thought that he might be waiting for her there now, having returned from Cromwell's house at Chelsea.

As if Thomasin had summoned him, Nico was sitting there, in a ray of sunshine. His head was bent over some papers he was reading, the light bright in his golden curls. He looked up as she came closer, heading along the gravelled path, then jumped to his feet to greet her.

Approaching, he did not hesitate to lean in and kiss her warmly upon the cheek.

"I had a feeling you would be back. I was thinking of you, and here you are, Thomasin."

His eyes glowed at her.

"I just arrived, not a half hour ago, but I hear the king and queen are out riding."

"Yes, it is quiet as the grave here. My master is handling business in the city and I have been left reading his correspondence. But I am so glad to see you. I have missed you."

Thomasin smiled, wondering whether she should reply and offer the same comment. Had she missed Nico? Her mind had been so full of things up until now, but it was very nice to see him, certainly.

"The marriage has been completed," she said, hearing the formality in her words.

"Completed," he nodded, "yes."

"I was very preoccupied by it before, but now I must try and forget it. I must move on."

"Yes," he smiled, taking her arm. "You must."

They walked, out of habit, round the path and through the archway of late-blooming roses to their favourite arbour seat. Thomasin sat down and Nico was at once beside her, an arm about her shoulders.

"How beautiful you look today. I swear that every time I see you, you are more lovely."

Thomasin smiled. She took a deep breath and allowed the peaceful tones of the garden to surround her.

"It is so good to be back. I did find myself missing this place, thinking of it often, wondering what was happening for the queen."

"And missing me?"

"Of course," she said quickly, as it was expected of her. "And where are the Boleyns? Keeping to their rooms?"

"Oh no," Nico smiled. "The Boleyns have withdrawn for a brief while into Kent. They have gone to Hever."

"To Hever? Really?"

"Soon after you left. They plan to return next week. It is whispered, in some quarters, that Henry sent them away to cool their heels. One of them in particular."

"Well, that is an interesting development, with the approach of Cardinal Campeggio. I wonder if the king still intends to hold his court to enquire into the state of his marriage?"

"It has been rather quiet on that front. Wolsey too has left; he's gone to his palace at Esher in Surrey. It seems he has taken the blame for some private incident between the king and his paramour, I know not what."

Thomasin's secret glowed inside her chest. So Henry had decided that Wolsey was to blame for Cecilia being thrust upon him. How well the plan had turned out for the queen.

"And so we have been very quiet here, all work left for me. Oh, Thomasin, I have missed you!"

He turned and swiftly placed a kiss upon her lips before she had a chance to react.

"You see how much I have missed you?"

Thomasin began to speak, but his lips were on her again, blocking her words with his warm pressure. She returned his kiss, but it seemed to increase his ardour and he leaned further into her, so that she was forced back against the seat.

"You kiss so sweetly," he murmured. "I have thought of this often."

"Have you?" she managed to whisper, between his advances.

He drew back slightly, but still held her in his arms. "Oh, Thomasin, you must know how I feel about you. So many times I have told you, so often you have permitted me to kiss you in this way. You must feel the same way. You must feel my ardour."

He kissed her again, his hand running down onto her thigh.

"My intentions are honourable, you know that, you have my promise, but must we wait? Let us take advantage of the quietness, find an empty chamber, submit to what we both desire."

His words came as a surprise. This was too sudden, too unexpected.

"But Nico, this is too soon. I just got back."

"It is perfect. What better time than this?" His mouth was upon hers again.

She put her hand to his chest to hold him at bay. Temptation lingered just behind her consciousness, but her resolution and reason were stronger.

"Nico, I have often thought that I would yield only to my husband."

"And that shall be me. I am your husband, so why wait? You want an engagement?"

"You have never spoken to me of one before. Never asked me such a thing."

"But I have thought of it often."

He moved towards her again, took her hand and tried to make her rise. "Come, there is a room that would be empty at this hour."

A mixture of emotions flooded her: embarrassment, pressure, and a twinge of anger that she had to defend herself. "No, it is not right at this moment. I want to wait."

"For what? The wedding?"

"Yes, I think it best. What if there was a child? Or if you changed your mind?"

"I would never…"

"But women are more vulnerable. I wish to wait."

His golden eyes glazed over, his mouth close by hers again. "Perhaps you just need to relax, get used to the idea."

Thomasin pushed him away more firmly. "No, it is not that. I wish to wait."

He sat back, frowning. "But all this … I thought…"

"I am sorry if I have misled you, but I want to do things correctly. I want to wait."

The disappointment on his face was painful to see. He struggled to conceal it, but she could see the lines of his mouth and how his brows pinched above his nose. But she knew she was right. She had come close to this with Rafe and learned her lesson. Now she had greater self-control, and when she did yield, it would be on her terms; it would not be sprung upon her like this.

"You can respect that, surely?"

"Of course." Nico leaned back and looked away. "You are a lady. I was carried away by your beauty. My hot Venetian blood, I suppose."

Thomasin stood up. An awkwardness hung between them that she did not wish to prolong. "I hope to see you soon, Nico."

"You are leaving?" His tone was sulky.

"I had better go and put the queen's things in order for her return."

It was a fabricated excuse and he knew it. She felt his eyes upon her back as she hurried out of the garden.

As Thomasin knew, Queen Catherine was not in her chambers; she was out riding in the orchards with her husband. The laundress had gone, and the place smelled heavily of lavender and beeswax. Dust motes swirled in the air.

Thomasin walked to the window and sat looking down at the outer courtyard. It was good to be back. Nico's suggestion had thrown her slightly, but on the whole, she felt composed, certain of herself. This was where she was meant to be: at the heart of things, attending the queen, watching the world unfold. There was no other place she would rather be than this.

Below, a figure in a grey dress was crossing the court path. The woman's head was bent as she read intently from a paper, a letter unfolded in her hands. Although she wore a headdress and coif, her long brown hair tumbled out of the back, and Thomasin recognised Ellen at once. Surely, her cousin was heading this way, coming towards the staircase that would lead her up to these very chambers. If Thomasin waited here, only a few minutes would elapse and they would be reunited. Perhaps they might ignore the topic of marriage, and speak instead of court matters. Yes, she would ask Ellen to fill her in on the details about the king and queen — that would distract them.

Thomasin turned to face the doorway. Sure enough, footsteps approached along the corridor, the guards threw open the door and Ellen entered. At once, Thomasin got to her feet. There was something in her cousin's face — shock, or incredulity. She held the discarded letter in her hand, as if it was an autumn leaf. Something had changed.

"Ellen? What is it?"

The letter fluttered beside Ellen's skirts.

"This. I can't believe it."

"What? What has happened?"

Her cousin stared into her face. "Thomasin, I am free."

"Free? How?"

The image flashed up in her mind of Cecilia walking at Hugh Truegood's side out of the church.

"This letter came. My husband, Barnaby. In Derbyshire."

"Yes, what? What happened?"

"It was a sudden fever. Just three days, according to his housekeeper."

Realisation dawned for Thomasin. "Barnaby is dead?"

Ellen nodded, her eyes filling with tears. "And I am free. Free. Thomasin, can you believe it? Free to marry whomever I choose. And as his wife still, I inherit everything. All the estates, Monk's Place, the money from the Aston case, it is all mine."

"Ellen, my goodness!"

Ellen gave a wry smile. "But it is too late, Thomasin, a week too late."

Thomasin folded her cousin into her arms. Ellen's head drooped against her shoulder like a flower as she dropped the letter and shed her tears. The future lay before them, a bittersweet mix of hope and fear, a new path of opportunity which they must walk with care. And Thomasin could not help but wonder about the nature of fate, with its cruel twists and unexpected blessings. Would either of them find happiness? It seemed so fragile, like a summer rose that turns brown and withers. But surely there was true love out there, waiting for them both?

She kissed the top of Ellen's head.

"Some day soon, you will find love. I truly believe it."

A NOTE TO THE READER

Dear Reader,

Welcome back to the world of the Marwood family. This third book in the series plunges the heroine Thomasin back into the dangerous world of the court and the shifting allegiances of autumn, 1528. Henry and Anne are becoming less and less hopeful of a swift resolution to the King's Great Matter, while Catherine clings to her queenship, believing in her lifelong destiny and the need to save Henry's soul from damnation.

Having established my setting, character and themes in books one and two, I had some difficult decisions to make about which direction I should take *False Mistress* in. These mostly related to the journeys of my fictional characters. While the real historical figures are well mapped out in documented evidence, the paths of my own creations — the Marwoods, Ellen Russell, Rafe Danvers and Nico Amato — are entirely mine to decide. I needed to further unfold their lives, whilst navigating around the known facts.

I felt it was time for a significant milestone in the lives of the Marwood sisters. Someone needed to become engaged or get married or suffer some life-changing event. I didn't want this to be Thomasin yet, as I intend to draw out her romantic possibilities over several more books, so instead my attention turned to Cecilia. Returning from the countryside with renewed vigour, I placed her at the heart of the queen's unfolding plot, in order to flesh out her character more fully and to explore the theme of love and marriage. This also provided me with valuable lessons for Thomasin, watching the inverse relationship between the happiness of her cousin and sister. This book ends with some serious questions about love in the Tudor court, with Thomasin questioning the ideals of romantic love and free will, wondering if they have a place in this world. I also wanted the Marwoods to drive the narrative, rather than simply tagging along as witnesses to actual events. Thomasin is central, with Henry, Catherine, Anne and others as figures that move in and out of her orbit, rather than vice versa.

The idea of the false mistress as a plot to lure Henry away from Anne has no basis in reality. It is entirely the product of my imagination. However, it is known that the pair's relationship was passionate, often stormy, and that there were arguments. I also drew inspiration from suggestions that Anne was desperate enough to use a similar plot herself, when Henry's attention was wandering in 1535. With the impending scrutiny of the papal court, it felt possible that Catherine's allies might take the opportunity of Anne's absence to break her hold over the king. As the author of one book about Henry's mistresses, and another about Tudor sexual practices, I also have serious doubts that Henry remained celibate for the entire period 1527-32, before he and Anne consummated their marriage. Sex was considered essential for health at the time, a bodily function as necessary as eating and sleeping, and manuals of the time voice concerns about male abstinence. I found it easy to imagine a scenario where Henry could be physically tempted to stray, but not necessarily emotionally. Hence the brevity of the false mistress plot, and the rapidity of Cecilia's removal from court afterwards.

Fans of Anne Boleyn won't necessarily enjoy her portrayal in *False Mistress*. I apologise for that. I am not at all anti-Anne, although a reader might be forgiven for assuming that from this book. I am very much a fan of hers, and her biographer. My plan is to draw out her character development over many books, gradually increasing Thomasin's understanding and appreciation of a complex figure. At this stage of the story, Thomasin is very supportive of her mistress, Catherine of Aragon, in whose household she serves. Thus, witnessing the queen's private sorrow, Thomasin's sympathies are firmly against Anne, and I have deliberately played up certain controversial aspects of her character to explain Thomasin's responses. I wanted Anne to have the opportunity to vent her anger at Cecilia, but also to demonstrate awareness of the fragility of her own position. In later books, as Catherine recedes, Thomasin will arrive at a fuller understanding of the complexities of Anne's character, coming to see her as vulnerable and well rounded, even to love her. Lady Boleyn's letter contains the first foreshadowing of their future closeness.

I am currently planning the fourth book in the Marwood Series, which will take place over the Christmas season of 1528-9 at Greenwich. Reviews do matter to writers and I would appreciate a review on **Amazon** or **Goodreads**. Often, we're writing in isolation, working in something of a vacuum, living most intensely in our heads, sending manuscripts into the ether. It's lovely to receive feedback and contact from readers, to know our work is being enjoyed and to see the ways we can improve when planning our next part of the story. You can contact me **on Twitter** (@PrufrocksPeach; I am a T. S. Eliot fan) via **my author page on Facebook** (Amy Licence Author), or **via my website**.

Kind regards,

Amy Licence

www.amylicence.weebly.com

Sapere Books is an exciting new publisher of brilliant fiction and popular history.

To find out more about our latest releases and our monthly bargain books visit our website:
saperebooks.com

Printed in Great Britain
by Amazon

38200707R00175